D1610469

27 OCT 2014

MILADY CHARLOTTE

Based on fact, this is the dramatic story of Charlotte Walpole, who left her comfortable Norfolk home to act at Drury Lane, married Sir Edward Atkyns, and attempted to rescue Marie Antoinette from the guillotine. It is also the story of Homer, the passionate, impulsive girl from the Cornish parsonage who joins her distant relation, Charlotte, in London. Involved with them are Richard Danver, in the service of the British government; Jean Pierre de la Vaugon, serving the French government; the lecherous Sir Edward; and Sophie, the young girl for whom the guillotine is waiting.

Books by Jean Plaidy
Published by The House of Ulverscroft:

THE SHADOW OF THE POMEGRANATE
THE SIXTH WIFE
GAY LORD ROBERT

MARY QUEEN OF SCOTLAND:
THE TRIUMPHANT YEAR

THE CAPTIVE QUEEN OF SCOTS
THE MURDER IN THE TOWER
THE PRINCESS OF CELLE
CAROLINE THE QUEEN
THE THIRD GEORGE
VICTORIA IN THE WINGS
THE CAPTIVE OF KENSINGTON PALACE
THE QUEEN AND LORD 'M'
THE QUEEN'S HUSBAND
THE WIDOW OF WINDSOR
WILLIAM'S WIFE
MADAME DU BARRY
GODDESS OF THE GREEN ROOM
THE KING'S ADVENTURER
THE QUEEN OF DIAMONDS
THE WANDERING PRINCE

JEAN PLAIDY

MILADY CHARLOTTE

Complete and Unabridged

ULVERSCROFT
Leicester

First published in Great Britain in 1959
under the pseudonym of
Kathleen Kellow

First Large Print Edition
published 2000
by arrangement with
Robert Hale Limited
London

The moral right of the author has been asserted

British Library CIP Data

Plaidy, Jean, *1906 – 1993*
    Milady Charlotte.—Large print ed.—
Ulverscroft large print series: general fiction
1. Walpole, Charlotte—Fiction
2. Great Britain—History—*1789 – 1820*—Fiction
3. France—History—Revolution—*1789 – 1799*
—Fiction 4. Historical fiction
5. Large type books
I. Title II. Kellow, Kathleen, *1906 – 1993*
823.9'12 [F]

ISBN 0–7089–4186–9

Published by
F. A. Thorpe (Publishing) Ltd.
Anstey, Leicestershire
Set by Words & Graphics Ltd.
Anstey, Leicestershire
Printed and bound in Great Britain by
T. J. International Ltd., Padstow, Cornwall

This book is printed on acid-free paper

1

Even before Homer saw her, Charlotte had been as real to her as her father, her half-sisters, Jennifer and Anne Mary, as real as Tansy the cook and Willie the outside man, as real as the churchyard with its ancient tombstones and the grey mist which swept in from the sea, as the cry of seagulls and the savoury smell of pasties baking in the old cloam oven.

Charlotte, alien to all and everything in that simple country parsonage, exotic, splendid, a figure of romance, had, from the moment Homer had heard of her, sprung to life — not the heroine of a legend, but a flesh-and-blood woman possessed of magnetism, beauty and dignity, all qualities in which Homer felt herself to be lacking. And she longed to be like Charlotte.

Charlotte was an ideal, the spiritual companion of a lonely girl who felt herself to have no real place within those walls which she called home.

★ ★ ★

Homer! Even her name was a reproach. Her father never used it. He would call her 'that child' when she was absent and nothing at all when she was in his presence. Her half-sisters refrained from using it in their father's hearing. Yet there had been Homer Trents in the parsonage for one hundred and fifty years, ever since Cornish Peter Trent had married Jane Homer from Devonshire; but they had been boys and this one was a girl.

Those Homer Trents had all been parsons, and their names were engraved on a plaque in the church. Homer often went in to look at them. She found the church more inviting when it was empty than when her father stood in the pulpit glowering at his congregation, reminding them, as he did at every opportunity, that hellfire would be the destination of most of them.

Alone, Homer would go to the plaque and stare at the list of names. Homer Trent 1625 – 1661; Homer Richard Trent 1661 – 1690 and so on to Homer Lanning Trent 1729 – 1760. That was her grandfather. One day there would be Homer Edgar Trent 1760 to a date as yet unknown. And that would be the end of the Homer Trents because the present one was a girl.

'And I am glad . . . glad!' Homer would

shout, and stand alert listening to the hollow sound of her voice in the empty church.

Glad to have disappointed her father so bitterly? 'Honour thy father' was a commandment.

But, thought Homer, always logical, how could God be angry with her for being glad she was a girl? After all, He had made her so.

How was it that she should be the one Homer Trent who was different — the girl among all those important men? She knew how it had come about although most of it had happened before she was born. There was garrulous Tansy to tell her, and Tansy had told her not once but many times.

★ ★ ★

Tansy had come to the parsonage at the time of the marriage of Homer Edgar Trent.

'Glad to come I was,' said Tansy. 'Not that the parsonage did not seem a gloomy place, particularly at nights when the moon shone and I'd look from me windows out on them old tombstones and fancy I'd see the ghosts of them as lay beneath come out to take a look at the place like.

'Ah, a gloomy place, and the cottage down on the quay was never that. But a place at

3

the parsonage meant plenty to eat, a mug of ale when you craved it, a hot pasty o' nights — and something always baking in the oven. Down at the cottage there might be more laughter, but what's to go with it, eh? What's for supper? Pilchards from the bottom of the barrel so salted you could scarce eat 'em; gruel so watered it looked blue, it did — and in the bad times, nothing but limpets scraped from the rocks.'

Yes, Tansy had been glad to come to the parsonage and she knew the story.

'Parson married the lady. A parson's daughter herself from a parish out beyond Barcelona way. Pale and pretty and frightened — frightened out of her wits, poor dear.'

'What was she frightened of, Tansy?' asked Homer.

'Frightened of duty. Frightened she wouldn't be able to do it. Frightened of Parson. But it wasn't long before she was expecting her first, and there was Parson, proud as you like, taking care of her, different from what you've ever seen him, me dear. He'd talk of the child, calling it by name.'

'By the name of Homer!'

'Making plans, behaving as though the boy was not only born but already preaching in the pulpit.' Tansy drew closer to Homer. '*They* didn't like it.'

4

'You mean the Little People, Tansy?'

Tansy nodded. ''Tis human beings taking on more than they'm entitled to. 'Tis human beings acting like Providence itself.'

'And so . . . '

'The baby was born and it was . . . '

'Jennifer!'

'It were Miss Jennifer, all delicate and pretty with yellow hair, yellower than it is today.'

'And my father was angry. I wonder he didn't kill her.'

'Hush, you wild Homer. He'd not kill. He went about white, thin-lipped and angry, and when the doctor said there should be no more he was like a man stricken. I said to Willie: 'This is the bitterest blow as could come to Parson. A girl — and a delicate wife who'll bear no more'.'

'But she did bear more, Tansy.'

'Ah! To her cost! There must be a boy, you see. There must be a Homer to preach in the church and have his name written there for future generations to marvel at. There must be a Homer Trent for St Miniver's. So what's to do?'

'I'll tell you,' cried Homer. 'She has another baby, and this time it is Anne Mary — still not Homer.'

'And she, poor soul, lies out there buried

5

among the Trents, God rest her.'

'I wonder,' said Homer, her eyes narrowing, 'that he dares to pass her grave at nights.'

'And why should he not? He gave her good Christian burial. He mourned her a whole year after.'

'But if he had been happy with Jennifer, if Anne Mary had never been born, *she* might be here in the kitchen now, Tansy — not under that grey slab of stone.'

'And where would you be, eh, young Homer? That's what I'd like to know.'

'Born to someone else, perhaps — born somewhere far from Miniver's.'

'You! Why, you're your mother's daughter — no other's! Perhaps you've got a bit of him in you too.'

Homer laughed happily, for there was nothing she liked so much as discussing herself.

'And then, Tansy?' she asked.

And Tansy went on: 'Two daughters. A house of mourning. The dead lady's cousin came to look after the children.'

'That was Aunt Agnes!'

'She'd have liked to look after your father, too.'

Homer chuckled. 'But she did not, and when my mother married my father she went away.'

'Her knew her was beaten then.'

'And my mother?'

'A wild creature.'

'I am like her?'

'To your cost, young Homer.'

'She came to work here.'

'Oh yes, she came to work here. Travelling round with the fair, she was, sitting there in a tent telling fortunes with great earrings in her ears; but she wasn't one of the fair people — not her. She was apart. She didn't belong to be there nor here, nor anywhere I know of.'

'What made her come to the house to work?'

' 'Tis hard to say.'

Homer sat at the table, face cupped in her hands, eyes dreamy, trying to look into the past, to probe secrets which had existed before her birth and indeed were the cause of it.

'She came to church one day,' went on Tansy. 'Your father noticed her. Then she came to work in the house.'

Bald statements these. Homer knew that behind them lay worlds of experience as yet beyond her understanding. Why had her father married the strange woman who had left the garish fairground to stroll into his church and listen to his fiery sermons? Why

7

had he, so cold and loveless, taken her into his household and in time married her?

'She was like a witch,' said Tansy. 'There were some as said she was one. The fortunes she told came true. She had the second sight.'

'And was she beautiful?'

'That I can't rightly say. She had that as made you want to look at her and nothing else when she was by. She made the place she was in her place, so that nothing seemed the same when she wasn't there. The year she lived here was like no other. A year she stayed, and it wouldn't have been so long if . . .'

'If she hadn't been going to have a child.'

Tansy nodded.

'*I* was that child!'

'Oh yes, she'd change a place,' went on Tansy. 'She changed us all. Parson was gay like. This time he'd get his Homer. She told him so. She would point to the child within her and laugh. She'd say: 'Don't you fear, Parson Trent. You'll get your Homer'.'

'And he was sure of it because she had proved she could see into the future.'

'There were some, your Aunt Agnes among them, who said a parson had no right marrying a fairground girl. But he cared naught for that. There he'd stand in his pulpit, preaching love, not hate. He were a changed man. She'd changed it all.'

'And the child at last was born.'

Tansy looked at Homer as though she were a baby still. 'A girl! He couldn't believe it. He had been so certain his Tamarisk would give him a son.'

'A girl! Myself! Was he very angry, Tansy?'

'Angry, no. Disappointed, hurt . . . all that. But he believed there'd be a son next time.'

'But there wasn't a next time, Tansy.'

Tansy shook her head. 'She didn't lie long abed. She was up after three days or so — so strong you wouldn't have believed she'd come straight from child-bed. She went about the place, secrets in her face, more like a witch than ever.'

'Then came the christening,' prompted Homer.

'Yes, the christening. I baked a christening cake, and a fine cake it was. And there was yourself in the christening robes Trent babies had worn for years and years. She was there in the church, and when the baby's name was asked she said in a loud voice which everyone could hear — defiant, with laughter in it, as though she had no respect for God's church nor God Himself, 'Homer', she said. And there was silence because we had all thought

9

the name was to be Martha.'

'So I became the first girl Homer. The only one that wasn't a boy.'

'I remember her coming out of the church, you in her arms, walking back to the house, not by way of the path, but wending her way among the tombstones with the wild look in her eyes. I remember her standing there in the hall and placing the baby in the parson's arms. 'There,' she said. 'I told you you would have your Homer. My prophecies always come true.' And she laughed and went upstairs just as though she were a queen — not looking round, mounting them slowly, not looking back — and Parson standing there staring after her, dazed like, the baby in his arms. That night she went away from Miniver's and none here has seen her since.'

★ ★ ★

Homer was different from her sisters. She had always lacked their decorum, their gentility. They were as everyone would expect the parsonage young ladies to be. Their hair was smooth and neat: Jennifer's the colour of primrose petals, Anne Mary's that of August corn after a hot summer; their brows were so fine and light as to be almost invisible.

10

Homer's hair was neither pale yellow nor deep gold; it was nutbrown, except when the sun shone on it; then it was red. It gleamed and sprang back from her brow with great vitality and was too thick to be manageable. Jennifer agreed with Anne Mary that it subtracted from rather than added to her charm. Her eyes were as changeable as her hair — sometimes tawny, sometimes topaz, sometimes green; her brows were thick, her nose short and straight, her mouth wide, her teeth white and strong. While she lived in St Miniver's no one would ever forget her mother and the incongruous marriage between the fairground girl and the parson.

'That one,' said Tansy, 'has too much of her mother in her for comfort.'

'Wait a year or so,' they said in the village, 'and there will be Tamarisk just as we knew her in St Miniver's.'

Homer believed that one day she would leave St Miniver's. She would sit on the cliffs looking out to sea, dreaming that she sailed far away. The sea fascinated her because of its varying moods and colours; she liked to watch its violent fury and cooing charm. The black rocks were like friends because she knew every line of them as she did the cliffs with their golden gorse, ubiquitous valerian and brave sea-pinks. She would listen to the gulls, wheeling, swooping, crying as though they were asking for something which could never be theirs.

The sea had a message for her. The ships which sailed by confirmed it.

St Miniver's is not the world, said the sea, said the ships. And you, Homer Trent, who came unwanted to St Miniver's because God made you a girl who could never have your name on the wall of the church, could find some place, perhaps far from St Miniver's, where there would be a welcome for you.

★ ★ ★

She had grown up knowing herself to be apart. Tansy was her friend more than her half-sisters; Willie the outside man loved her more than her father did.

Often she dreamed that her mother returned to St Miniver's to look for her, to take her away into a world of adventure. She saw her mother as a being infinitely beautiful like the Madonna in the stained glass windows of the church, yet not in blue but in flaming scarlet with great gold circlets in her ears. Homer dreamed that her mother danced across the churchyard in the moonlight and called to her daughter to leave the parsonage and follow her. 'So you came back for me?' Homer would whisper. 'Of course I came back,' would be the answer. 'How could I have left my baby Homer if I had not intended to come back?'

There must be these dreams, for in the night when there was no longer the need to show a defiant face to the world, Homer might have wept if she could not have dreamed her impossible dreams. So she told herself that her mother would come. It was only by believing this that she could forgive her. Her father did not love her; but her mother's desertion was the cruellest wound of all.

Then . . . came Charlotte.

★ ★ ★

Aunt Agnes had come to stay at the parsonage — a large busy woman who showed her efficiency by pointing out the failures of others.

The house was a disgrace, said Aunt Agnes. It needed cleaning from attic to cellar. It was a wonder they were not all sick of some pox. What the place was crying out for was a woman who could look after the parson and keep his servants in order.

What the place needed was, in fact, Aunt Agnes.

She was both triumphantly sly and full of wistful regrets. If Homer Edgar had had any sense he would have married her; then he would have had a wife to look after his family; he would have a son instead of that child Homer who would clearly come to a bad end.

It was a summer's morning, Homer remembered, when she first heard Charlotte's name. It had begun like every other morning, except, of course, that Aunt Agnes was in the house.

The family assembled for prayers — the parson, his three daughters, Aunt Agnes, Tansy, Willie, and Mab and Belle Telfer, the two sisters who worked under Tansy.

Morning prayers were long at the parsonage, particularly on Mondays, which was that day of the week when a parson's duties were less numerous than on others.

Aunt Agnes's responses echoed round the dining-room as though she were eager to impress her piety on the parson. Her watchful eyes were on the girls. She wished to assure the parson what a good wife she would have made, and to stress what he had missed. Homer recognized this and was glad that Aunt Agnes had failed. Of course she was glad. Otherwise how could she have been born?

Homer knew then that whatever happened to her she would always be glad that she was alive.

Prayers over, Tansy with Mab and Belle went to the kitchen, Willie to his outside work, and the family took their places at the table for breakfast.

During meals none of the girls spoke unless spoken to. Occasionally Homer would so far forget herself as to blurt out some inconsequential remark. It was always met with silence. Homer often felt that she could have borne her father's anger more easily than his cold manner of treating her as though she did not exist.

Aunt Agnes talked. It made no difference to her that the parson scarcely answered. Aunt Agnes did not expect answers; she wanted to talk all the time, and always regarded any part others took in the conversation as unnecessary.

She was reading a letter and obviously found its contents startling.

'How Blancy and Robert could allow the girl, I do not know. Would you allow one of your poor motherless mites or even . . . But of course you wouldn't. Robert always believed himself to be so *advanced*. As for Blancy, those girls always ruled her. Mary and Frances are such pleasant girls.

They would never . . . But Charlotte! Why, if she belonged to me, do you know what I would do? I'd go after her and bring her back. I'd marry her off as quickly as I could . . . '

Aunt Agnes smirked while Homer listened, avid for information, keeping very quiet, knowing that a request for it might have silenced Aunt Agnes.

Already Homer was attracted by Charlotte. What had she done? Something amusing? Something exciting? Already Charlotte attracted Homer because she shocked Aunt Agnes.

'Do you know how old Charlotte is?' Aunt Agnes was demanding. 'Nineteen. Old enough to know better; and since she doesn't — old enough for mischief. Blancy writes: 'What do you think, my dear? Charlotte has gone to London to try her fortune . . . ' ' Aunt Agnes paused for effect . . . ' 'on the stage!' Did you hear that? The stage! Robert Walpole's girl. Your own cousin's girl, Mr Trent. His daughter is to be a player . . . in London. Blancy goes on: 'It was no use to remonstrate with her. I tried. I wept and implored. She said she was always meant to be an actress.' The girl has some small fortune of her own and Robert is quite soft, and so is Blancy, to allow it; but it seems Mistress Charlotte is mistress of that household. 'I am going to London,' she says. And not only to London but to Drury Lane she has gone. Vicar, I do not believe you listen to more than half I say.'

Homer's gaze went swiftly to her father.

'You do repeat yourself, Agnes,' he answered wryly, 'so it is only necessary to listen to half you say. But I have understood that Robert has had the extreme folly to allow his youngest daughter to dictate to him, and she has left Norfolk for London.'

'Drury Lane,' Agnes almost screamed. 'For a playhouse. There is only one profession she could have chosen which would have been worse.'

The vicar rose in his chair and began to say grace. Agnes stared at him in angry silence; the girls, their breakfast unfinished, folded their hands and stared at their unemptied plates. This was not unusual. Their father often terminated a meal in this way.

Homer, for once, did not mind leaving half her breakfast. The image of Charlotte had been created and she could think of nothing but the excitement that image aroused in her.

Charlotte in her Norfolk home had felt the need for adventure, and she had decided it should be hers. What a bold and clever person Charlotte must be! She had left home in spite of her parents' objections. They had tried to stop her, but who could stop Charlotte on the road to adventure!

Charlotte had determined to become a player in a place called Drury Lane.

'Drury Lane!' Homer murmured to herself; and from that moment she wanted to be a player; she wanted to be bold and adventurous; she wanted to be like Charlotte.

* * *

Homer had been thirteen when she had first heard of Charlotte, and during the next three years she thought of her continuously.

When Aunt Agnes visited the household, Homer did her best to discover more about Charlotte, but Aunt Agnes grew sullen when Charlotte's name was mentioned, and refused to discuss her. Although this was tiresome it made Homer elated because she was fully aware that had there been bad news of Charlotte, Aunt Agnes would have been ready enough to talk.

Charlotte must be a great success in Drury Lane. One day, thought Homer, I'll run away and find her.

In her dreams, Charlotte was her friend

and they played together at Drury Lane. Homer had no idea what Drury Lane could be like, but her imagination never failed her, and often she would sit, her back resting against the low grey wall which separated the graveyard from the parsonage, and imagine herself and Charlotte acting together on a stage while the audience applauded madly.

Charlotte had taken the place in her dreams which had been occupied by her mother. Charlotte satisfied her. Charlotte had committed no grave sin against her as her mother had.

★ ★ ★

It was the December following that November in which Homer had celebrated her sixteenth birthday — a bright frosty day, with a sharpness in the air. The sea was a brilliant hard blue, and the berries in the hedges were red and plentiful.

With a feeling of exhilaration Homer had watched her father ride off to join the hunt. He would be away for the greater part of the day, and that was a relief.

The elder girls no longer took lessons with her in the schoolroom and she was there alone with Bryant Eeves, her father's curate who had taught them all. Bryant Eeves

19

perturbed her slightly, for he had developed a habit of looking at her when he thought she was not looking his way.

He thought a great deal about Homer — far more than she thought about him. Tansy said he would marry either Jennifer or Anne Mary; it would not matter which, except that it was always better for the eldest to marry first; then he would one day be vicar of St Miniver's Church, and it would keep the living in the family.

'Why,' said Tansy, 'they could name their first son Homer Trent. Homer Trent Eeves — next best thing to Homer Trent.'

So it was accepted in the family that Mr Eeves would marry one of the girls.

Homer liked Mr Eeves. He was so meek. She could lure him from arithmetic, which she hated, to literature and history, which she loved. He often seemed in a bemused state in the schoolroom, Homer noticed. Tansy said: 'You've bewitched that man, young Homer. Maybe it'll be you who is Mrs Eeves of the parsonage, eh? That would not surprise me.'

Homer had leaped to her feet in anger when Tansy had said that; it was an anger which she could not explain. 'Be quiet, Tansy Trelower,' she cried. 'You would shut me up . . . in a prison!'

20

'What's come over you?' demanded Tansy.

'This has come over me,' answered Homer vehemently. 'I will not be shut up in this place. I am going out into the world. I am going to live . . . like Charlotte.'

And ever since she had felt uneasy in the presence of Mr Eeves; yet she had continued to lure him from the lessons he should have set her that they might do what she wanted. And, when she could forget the intense desire of Mr Eeves to please her, she could enjoy those hours in the schoolroom and be glad that her half-sisters did not share them.

She would insist on reading plays, she taking all the principal parts. She was Shylock and Rosalind, Tartuffe and Portia. She forgot she was in the schoolroom with Mr Eeves and imagined she was on a stage with Charlotte.

Mr Eeves had been to London before he came to Cornwall. His family lived in Sussex and there had been occasions when he had taken a coach to the capital to stay with an uncle there. So when Homer had played her parts she would demand to hear about his visits to London.

'Mr Eeves, did you ever go to Drury Lane?'

He had never been to Drury Lane, but he had driven out to Epping and dined at the Baldfaced Stag; he had been to Vauxhall and taken frothed syllabub, scraped beef and burned champagne; he had been to Ranelagh, and he could assure Homer that life in London was full of dangers and quite different from that as lived in St Miniver's.

She took lessons in French but she would lure him from grammatical exercises to discussions about the French Court. She was not interested in the Seven Years' War but in anecdotes concerning Madame de Pompadour and Madame du Barry who had been beloved by the King of France and who were more important to him than anyone else in the country.

'So you see, Mr Eeves,' she declared, her eyes shining, 'how can one go on living for ever in St Miniver's when there are places like Ranelagh, Drury Lane and the Court of France, when there are people like Madame de Pompadour and my cousin Charlotte!'

'But you would not want to be like Madame de Pompadour. She was a very wicked woman.'

'Who is to judge wickedness, Mr Eeves? You say Madame de Pompadour was wicked, but the King of France did not. Aunt Agnes says Charlotte is; I do not.'

'Miss Homer, would you not be content to live here all your life if . . . if you were . . . say . . . married and happy in your marriage?'

Firmly she shook her head. 'No, Mr Eeves. My mother's spirit is inside me. I feel it. I shall never be a good wife in St Miniver's. Perhaps I should have my child as she did, put it into my husband's arms and disappear.'

'I . . . I believe you are not as other people,' he stammered, 'but . . . '

She understood suddenly that quiet Mr Eeves, who had never been reckless in his life, was on the verge of being so. He was asking himself why the parson's youngest daughter should not be the one to share his life.

He was saved from utter indiscretion by a sudden shout from below the schoolroom window.

'Tansy! Miss Jennifer! Miss Anne Mary! Where be you all?' It was Willie, and as she ran to the window, Mr Eeves beside her, Homer heard the shrill gabble of Mab and Belle.

'Down to Dr Eversleigh at once,' Tansy was shrieking. 'You, Mab. And don't stand there gaping. Be off — fast as you can. Tell him Parson have had an accident and he be hurt — bad!'

And so came change. Homer Edgar Trent would never again thunder from the pulpit to the discomfiture of his congregation; he would never again chill the house with his presence. He remained unconscious and died the day they brought him home.

Aunt Agnes was there to take charge, and the funeral ceremonies were prolonged. Gloom was introduced into the parsonage, although Homer felt it to be a false gloom, for no one at heart mourned her father. Poor man, thought Homer, he had left the world to the regret of none.

He lay in his coffin in the darkened room which was hung with crepe; wax candles burned there all through the night, for Aunt Agnes was determined on a proper mourning. It was due to the dead, she said; and only thus could the necessary respect be shown. A mute stood at the door of the room in which was the coffin, and members of his congregation trooped upstairs to pay their last respects. Even the door knocker was swathed in crepe; and although the distance from the house to the church was so small, Aunt Agnes insisted on several black coaches to follow the hearse. The daughters were dressed in heavy black, veils covering their faces that they might hide from onlookers that grief which convention and Aunt Agnes insisted they must feel.

And so Homer Edgar Trent was laid to rest beside the mother of Jennifer and Anne Mary.

Aunt Agnes, who had declared her intention of looking after her orphaned relations, suddenly ceased to feel any enthusiasm for the task. This was when it was discovered that Homer Edgar had left so very little money for his children. Now Aunt Agnes busied herself with settling their future. Mr Eeves took over the duties of the parish while Aunt Agnes made her plans. She called the girls to her in their father's study and talked to them seriously.

'Now, girls, we have to be sensible. Your father's affairs appear to be not quite what we expected. I am a little surprised. There is very little money and we must face the fact. I would have taken you into my household but, as you know, my circumstances are somewhat straitened, and it is quite beyond my powers to do so. I thank God that you are well educated. It is not impossible for girls of your birth, breeding and education to be received into good homes as governesses, companions and so on. You may even find husbands. Mr Eeves will, of course, marry either Jennifer or Anne Mary. If he is going to take your father's place, and it looks as if he is, he at least owes us that.'

'But why?' began Homer impetuously.

'Why? Why indeed! He will live in this house. He will become vicar of this parish. Of course he must marry either Jennifer or Anne Mary. It would be so convenient and so . . . right.'

Homer had ceased to think about the marriage of Mr Eeves. She was thinking of herself as governess or companion in a strange house, and her spirit revolted.

★ ★ ★

Mr Eeves came up with her as she walked on the cliffs. The wind caught her wild hair and her eyes were green on that day.

'Miss Homer,' he said, 'I have to speak to you.'

She turned to him and suddenly she pitied him. Poor Mr Eeves! He had his problems even as she had. She knew that she herself possessed a reckless spirit which would help her to grapple with hers. She might suffer more than he did, but she would live more richly, more fully.

'Miss Homer, I have heard from the Bishop.'

'And it is good news?'

'I am to go to see him. It can mean only one thing. He is sending a man to replace me while I am away. You know what this means?'

'You will be vicar of St Miniver's.'

He nodded. 'After I have seen the Bishop I am going for a short visit to my parents. Then I shall come back to St Miniver's.'

'It is very satisfactory, and it is what we all expected would happen.'

'If I take the living it is only right that I should marry one of the late vicar's daughters. It is expected of me.'

'I am sure, Mr Eeves, that you will always do what is expected of you.'

'I hope I shall — if it be the right thing.'

'It would always be the right thing if you did it.'

'You have a high opinion of me. Homer, dare I hope that you will marry me?'

'That is not what is expected of you.'

'It would be the right thing — for me.'

'No, it would be quite wrong. You must marry Jennifer or Anne Mary. You did intend to marry one of them once.'

'Jennifer,' he admitted.

'And now you have changed your mind?'

'You changed it for me. You, Homer, who

are so bewitching, who excite me, who make me feel that . . . whoever you were I should want to marry you.'

'It cannot be so, Mr Eeves.'

'You do not love me, but you are young. In time you would have an affection for me. Think of it, Miss Homer. If you do not marry me you will have to go away — take some post somewhere — because I do not think it would be wise for you to stay here if you did not marry me. You want adventure. You want to see the world — but not as a lady's maid. That could be most unpleasant for one of your high spirits.'

'Mr Eeves,' said Homer, her eyes brilliant, looking as she did when Tansy said it might have been her mother who stood there, 'when you have seen the Bishop you are going to see your parents. Will you do something for me?'

'Miss Homer, I have been trying to tell you that I would do anything in the world for you.'

'What I plan is best for us both,' she went on eagerly. 'I want you to take a letter from me to someone in London. It is very important that the letter be delivered into the hands of the person to whom it is addressed. Will you do this for me?'

'I will with pleasure.'

'You have never been to a playhouse, Mr Eeves. But if she is not there, they will tell you where to find her.'

'Tell me, Miss Homer, to whom do you refer?'

'To my cousin Charlotte. I shall ask her to let me go to her. I will be her maid, her companion . . . anything she cares to make me.'

'Your cousin . . . but who is this cousin?'

'Charlotte Walpole. She is an actress in Drury Lane. I know she will take me. I know we belong together. I have always known it.'

'Miss Homer, London is not St Miniver's.'

'But you will find her,' cried Homer passionately, 'because she is a famous actress. If you go to the theatre in Drury Lane they will tell you where she is. Mr Eeves . . . ' She took his arm and looked earnestly into his face. ' . . . you *will* do this for me. You *will*!'

He was visibly moved. He would do all in his power to help her, he said.

He was conscious of the mingling feelings within him; his longing for this strange girl was something alien to his whole nature; he knew that the pattern of his life should be neat and orderly, and that so it would be if he married Jennifer.

29

★ ★ ★

Four weeks passed. Aunt Agnes stayed on at the vicarage to act as chaperone to the girls. She hoped to marry one of the elder ones to Mr Grey who officiated until the return of Mr Eeves. Mr Grey, however, had a fiancée waiting for him in Truro, so there would be only one bridegroom available. Aunt Agnes made up her mind to do nothing about the two elder girls until Mr Eeves returned and proposed to one of them. Perhaps the other would stay at the parsonage. Why not? But Homer had a disturbing effect. A post must be found for her.

Aunt Agnes was busily writing to her friends.

'Depend upon it,' she said, 'I shall find a place for you soon, Homer. How fortunate that you have me to help you. Recommendations are so useful.'

One day when she came down to breakfast Aunt Agnes beamed at her delightedly.

'Good fortune at last! My friend Mrs Ardington has heard that Lady Grosley needs a lady's maid. My dear, you will have to be more serious now.'

Homer was not listening. She had no intention of becoming Lady Grosley's lady's maid.

30

A week later there came a letter of instructions from Lady Grosley's housekeeper, and Aunt Agnes said she would call in Anne Pengore, St Miniver's best seamstress, that two new gowns might be made for Homer. She had some dove-grey serge and linen which could be made up into discreet garments, quiet and serviceable.

That very day Mr Eeves came back.

He looked more dignified than he had been when he went away. Naturally, said Tansy, since he was the new master of the vicarage.

Homer could scarcely wait for that moment when he was alone in the study which had been her father's. She knocked and went in.

'Homer!' he said, and at the sight of her all those resolutions to be sensible had deserted him. 'Did you think of what I said while I was away?'

'There was no need to. I had already settled it. Did you find her, Mr Eeves?'

He nodded and took a letter from his pocket.

'It was not so difficult as I imagined it would be,' he said. 'She was playing at the Theatre Royal. I saw her and gave her your letter. This is her answer.'

Homer seized the letter which was sealed

31

with a violet wax. It was a long letter, but Homer read only the first lines which were:

'Dear Cousin,
You must come to me at once ... '

Her eyes skimmed the page. The precious letter would be read and reread, but not now — not here before Mr Eeves's almost reproachful gaze.

It was signed: 'Your cousin who is as eager to meet you as you are to meet her, Charlotte.'

Homer's eyes were like emeralds.

'I knew it! I always knew it!' she cried.

And she believed then that the power which had been her mother's was hers — to adventure into strange worlds, to shape her own life.

2

The coach jolted along the road towards
Exeter where they would spend the night.
Homer could not curb her excitement
although she was aware that she aroused
the interest and amusement of her fellow-
travellers. How could she hide the sparkle
in her eyes? How could she suppress her
eager interest in everything about her? Had
she not lived for nearly seventeen years in
a little town on the Cornish coast, in a
somewhat gloomy household where she had
never felt she was wanted? And now she was
embarking on the great adventure: she was
going to Charlotte.

Everything was so new and startling that
her few regrets were quickly submerged. She
had wept a little to leave Tansy and Willie,
but she had consoled herself. 'Perhaps one
day I shall send the money for you to come
to London to join Charlotte and me!' she had
said. Neither Tansy nor Willie believed this
could be; only Homer, who, because of the
turn of events believed in miracles, thought it
possible. In any case it made parting easier.

Leaving Aunt Agnes was no great wrench,

particularly as she was full of evil prophecies concerning the venture and went about the house declaring that she had always known Homer would come to a bad end. As for Jennifer and Anne Mary, since they had been aware of Mr Eeves's interest in their young half-sister, they could not feel anything but relief to see her go.

Mr Eeves had insisted on taking her to Plymouth where she joined the London coach. It was the first time that Homer had been to Plymouth although she had often gazed in its direction, looking longingly at the Sound and at Rame, the long arm of which, jutting into the sea, hid the town from view.

They had taken the stage wagon and made the journey by way of Gunnislake in order to avoid crossing the Tamar. There were times during that journey when she had thought that he was going to suggest going to London with her to seek his fortune, that he was about to declare his intention of throwing away his new honours all for her sake. But in her heart she knew that when he had put her onto the London coach he would say good-bye to her. Being Mr Eeves, he could do nothing else.

Perhaps, thought Homer, if he had been the man to throw everything up and come to London with me, he would never have had to do so, for perhaps then I would be ready to throw aside all my plans and stay with him!

How ironical life could be!

She made him talk of Charlotte instead of themselves. What was Charlotte like? Was she beautiful? Yes, he thought her beautiful.

And famous?

Yes, he believed that in London she was well known as an actress. Her name was on playbills which were posted outside the theatre.

'And when you told her that I wanted to come to her, when you gave her my letter, what did she say?'

'She was moved. She said: 'But of course'.'

' 'But of course!' ' repeated Homer. 'And did she say it quickly or after a pause? So much depends on that.'

'She said it at once.'

'And she made you promise to put me on the London coach, and she sent the money for my journey. Oh, Charlotte, I knew I was not mistaken in you!'

He had glanced at her then and the joggling stage wagon almost threw her into his arms. That was a moment when he decided he would not let her go alone. But the moment of recklessness had passed; Mr Eeves would never be reckless for more than a moment.

So they had come into Plymouth and she had exchanged the primitive stage wagon for the London coach; and now she was nearing Exeter.

Her fellow travellers were a woman and a man who chattered continuously, so that Homer quickly knew that they were going to London to visit their daughter who had had her first child. There was a merchant who was clearly anxious about the money he carried and somehow managed to remind them all of the dangers to be encountered on the road. There was an elderly lady who was eager that they should all know that she did not usually travel by coach but by post-chaise; and there was the other passenger.

Homer resented the other passenger. This was for two reasons; one because he seemed a more seasoned traveller than the others and would sit back, his arms folded, without the slightest flicker of excitement on his face as though he had spent his life making such journeys; the other reason was because of the sly amusement she saw in his face when his eyes rested upon her. This they did frequently. It was almost as though he were aware that this was the first journey she had made.

Insolent creature! thought Homer; and she disliked him on the spot because she believed he was going to spoil the journey for her.

He was younger than anyone else in the coach except herself, and she guessed him to be in his mid-twenties — a few years younger than Mr Eeves — but by his demeanour one would think he was many years older.

A very high opinion of himself! decided Homer, and her eyes were very green and slightly contemptuous as briefly they met his.

He was dressed in a russet-brown velvet jacket with velvet breeches to match. The ruffles at his sleeves were of fine lace; his cravat was elaborate; and there was silver lace in his hat and silver buckles on his shoes. He would be judged a dandy in St Miniver's. But his face was not that of a dandy. It was square and strong — a rugged face, one might call it; the skin was brown, probably tanned, the nose aquiline. An arrogant nose, in Homer's opinion. The eyes were startlingly blue, contrasting almost incongruously with that brownish skin. The hair was light brown, streaked with blond. She had noticed this when he had taken off his hat and laid it on his knees.

It seemed that every time she looked up, his eyes were upon her, slightly sardonic, waiting for her to betray her ignorance.

She lay back, closing her eyes, pretending to be tired of gazing out of the window.

'In fifteen minutes we shall be in Exeter,' said the elderly lady.

'It is to be hoped we arrive before dark,' added the merchant significantly.

'Ah,' put in the arrogant young man, 'if any gentleman of the road tried his tricks with us, we would give a good account of ourselves.'

'Such talk frightens the ladies,' said the husband, touching his wife's hand.

'*You* are not frightened,' said the young man; and finding that he was looking straight at her, Homer retorted sharply: 'Indeed I am not.'

'I'll warrant,' he went on, 'you're a seasoned traveller.'

'I have never yet felt a single tremor on the road,' murmured Homer.

'I guessed, Miss er . . . .'

'My name is Trent.'

'Miss Trent, I am delighted to make your acquaintance. May I introduce myself? I am Richard Danver.'

Homer inclined her head.

'As we are to be together for some days,'

he went on, 'it is well to get acquainted, do you not think so, Miss Trent?'

'I think,' said Homer primly, 'that if you mean by getting acquainted knowing each other's names, that is at least useful.'

'But not pursuing the acquaintance beyond a knowledge of names?'

Homer glanced out of the window. 'That could prove unnecessary, for at the end of our journey we shall say good-bye and that will be the end of our acquaintance, I doubt not.'

'And yet,' he said, and again she was conscious of that insolent gleam in his eyes, 'it may not be so.'

★ ★ ★

They had eaten a good supper of cold beef and ale, apple pie and cheese in the inn parlour and had retired to their rooms. Strangely enough, Homer could not forget Richard Danver. He had sat next to her at table, and she knew that he had arranged this.

Afterwards, when she had been shown to her room, she had felt so tired that she had lain on her bed fully dressed as she was and, worn out by excitement, for she had scarcely slept for the last few nights, she dozed.

She was awakened by the sound of voices in the yard and immediately recognized one as that of Richard Danver; the other she believed to be the landlord's.

She rose and peered out of the window. She could see him leaning against the stable door, managing to look as though the inn belonged to him. He was speaking in a moderately quiet voice, but her hearing was acute and the wind was in the right direction.

'You know the young lady I mean?'

'Why yes, sir, I do know. 'Twere the very young one, sir.'

'In that odd grey thing and cloak,' went on Richard Danver, 'clearly leaving her remote country village for the first time. Which floor is she on?'

'Her be on the second, sir.'

'Then see that my room is changed to one on the second, will you?'

'Well, sir, if that be your wish . . . '

Homer started back from the window in rage and horror. He meant herself! Who else? Impertinence! And more than impertinence. He was a scoundrel. Why should he want a room on her floor?

She put her hands to her cheeks in horror. They were burning as though she had contracted some fever. This was no fever; it was fury and — a certain fear.

She had heard Aunt Agnes whisper of the dire things which could befall adventurous girls, and she knew now that Aunt Agnes had not been exaggerating. Those glances he had given her on the coach! He was a very wicked man; she was certain of it.

She went to the door and to her dismay found that there was no lock; it merely latched. She pulled the bell-rope and a maid in print gown and mob-cap appeared.

'There is no lock to my door,' complained Homer. 'I shall not sleep in a room which has no lock.'

The maid looked bewildered. 'Well, Miss,' she said, 'there be only one room on this floor with a lock that b'ain't occupied.'

'Show it to me,' commanded Homer; and the girl led her across the passage to a room slightly larger than the one she had left.

'Bring my things here,' she ordered.

'I could ask master,' began the girl.

'Come. We'll delay no more,' said Homer briskly, and going back to her room she picked up her bag and walked with it across the corridor. The maid timidly followed with her cloak.

While she was helping Homer to unpack, the door was flung open and the host, accompanied by Richard Danvers, came into the room.

41

'My dear life!' ejaculated the host.

'It is no use blaming your maid,' said Homer quickly. 'I insisted on changing my room. I refuse to sleep in a room which has no lock and key.'

The host scratched his head.

'If,' went on Homer, looking straight at Richard Danver — contemptuously, she hoped — 'you wish to sleep on this floor, you can take the room which I have vacated.'

His mouth twitched and she was sure he was trying to prevent himself laughing at her.

'But certainly,' he replied. 'I have not the same fear of unlocked doors.'

He bowed, and he and the host went across the landing to the other room. Homer dismissed the maid, and as soon as she had gone, locked the door. She leaned against it, her heart beating wildly. She would not unlock it on any account until morning.

She slept badly. It seemed to her that if the man on the other side of the landing could be kept out of her room, he could not be kept out of her dreams.

* * *

The journey was uneasy. As they crossed lonely heaths and country roads which,

Homer learned, had evil reputations as the happy hunting ground of highwaymen, she was conscious of Richard Danver; and, oddly enough, she found herself believing that they could come to no harm while he was there. When they pulled up at an inn, he would say: 'This young lady insists on a room which can be locked.'

'Do you know,' he said to her one day, 'I believe you are more nervous of some things than others. I have an idea that you would show no more regard for a highwayman than you do for me.'

'I have never encountered a highwayman,' she told him. 'It is difficult to know how one would react until one has had the experience.'

'And you have had experience of rooms which are without locks?'

She regarded him coolly. 'I have heard that it is folly to shut the stable door *after* the horse has been stolen.'

'And you have much that is valuable to protect. Tell me, are you carrying some priceless jewel from Plymouth to London?'

'If I were it would be foolish to admit it to strangers.'

'I was hoping that by this time we should not be considered strangers.'

'As we are merely travellers in the same

coach we could be little more.'

'Unless our acquaintance does not end when we leave the coach.'

'Let us not discuss unlikely contingencies.' He laughed suddenly and turned away.

★ ★ ★

The journey progressed. On rumbled the coach. Through Honiton, Axminster, Bridport and Dorchester; through Blandford and across Salisbury Plain to Stockbridge. They slept at Hartley Row and came through Staines to Brentford and on to Turnham Green.

So many hours spent facing each other! Homer felt she would never be able to forget his face. He was amused by her, she knew. She felt he was perpetually laughing at her. Yet he had been so kind to the elderly lady who had shivered as they passed a gibbet on the road and had hysterics when, just before dusk and the approach to a lonely heath, one of the coach wheels had become stuck in a rut from which it had taken almost an hour to extricate the vehicle.

He was insufferable really — letting her know that he recognized her for a country mouse who was not ripe for the sort of adventure which he would consider amusing.

They came into London at midday and pulled in at the Black Swan in Holborn. Homer alighted, looking about her for Charlotte. Charlotte, who had given her instructions, knew on what coach she would be travelling, so would be there to meet her.

The merchant, greatly relieved to have arrived safely, as was the elderly lady, said a hasty farewell and they went their different ways. The couple were met by their daughter's husband, and it was clear that they had no more interest in their fellow-passengers.

Homer felt somewhat forlorn. Charlotte was a little late, she told herself; but in any case, if it were necessary, she could find her way to Drury Lane.

Seeing her standing there, obviously a visitor from the country, a woman spoke to her.

'Why, lady,' she said, 'you look a stranger to London. Could I help you find what you're looking for?'

The woman had an honest face, Homer decided; she was neatly dressed, and although it was not easy to understand her nasal whine, her smile was friendly.

'You are right,' said Homer. 'I have just left the coach and am expecting to be met.

If I am not I must find my way to Drury Lane . . . '

'It would be a pleasure to point out the way, lady . . . '

'Your best plan,' said a voice close to them, 'would be to return the lady's purse.'

The woman let out a frightened yelp, but Richard Danver was holding her firmly by the shoulder.

The woman began to whine: 'So help me . . . I've got thirteen mouths to feed. I meant no harm . . . '

She dropped the purse and wrenching herself free ran off.

Richard picked up the purse, bowed and handed it to Homer.

'So you saw her take it,' she stammered.

'London,' he replied, with that self-satisfied smile which even at this moment she felt she wanted to slap from his face, 'is a very wicked place for young ladies fresh from the country to be alone in. One must take as much care not to have one's pocket picked as one does to choose a room with a sturdy lock and key.'

'Thank you for saving my purse. Perhaps you can direct me to Drury Lane.'

'I will do more than that. I will take you there. I will deliver you safe and sound into the hands of Miss Charlotte Walpole.'

'How . . . But how did you know?'

He did not answer that question, but with an imperious gesture, like a magician with a wand, he lifted a hand. Immediately a hackney coach pulled up beside them, and before she could protest he had ushered her in and put her bag beside her. Then he instructed the driver and joined her.

She was too startled to speak as they started through the streets, but the noise of the heavy coach rattling along made conversation difficult, and in any case it was disconcerting to see Richard Danver, arms folded, watching her.

At last she said: 'Please tell me how you knew.'

He continued to smile mysteriously. 'There is not much I like about these hackney coaches,' he said, 'but they are convenient, and you may look out through the perforated iron shutters and see what is going on, while out there no one can look in on you. Do you know, I believe that is why they are becoming more popular than the sedan chair.'

'I wish,' retorted Homer vehemently, 'that you would tell me how you knew I was going to Miss Charlotte Walpole.'

'I will. I will. But this is your first visit to London, is it not? Come! You must not look at me at such a moment. Look out at the traders. How they jostle each other! You would never have found your way through these streets. That is a watercress seller. And there you see fine China oranges for sale. Listen to the noise. Is it not deafening? You will enjoy London. I prophesy that, Miss Trent.'

Homer looked out on the gaiety and bustle, the squalor and grandeur which was London; but during that brief period when the coach carried her from the Black Swan to Charlotte's house, in spite of the novelty presented by those colourful streets, she believed that the most vivid memories of these first moments in London would be the closed space of the hackney coach and the aggressive, dominating personality of the man opposite.

They had drawn up before a house; Richard sprang out and took Homer's hand with a gesture which she assured herself was mocking.

'Welcome,' he cried, 'to Old Drury.'

The front door of the house opened and standing there was a young woman who Homer knew was Charlotte. Her smile was warm and affectionate, her eyes large and dark; her brows were heavily marked, and her black curls, caught by a scarlet ribbon, fell over her forehead. She was very beautiful and Homer felt overcome by emotion as she looked at her.

'Why, so you are Homer,' she said. 'How glad I am that you have come.'

'Oh, Charlotte . . . Charlotte!' cried Homer, and she threw herself passionately into Charlotte's arms.

In that moment she had forgotten Richard Danver. She was only conscious of the white portico, of the shadowy luxury of the house beyond the door, of the fragrance and magnetism of Charlotte, who she knew was all she had ever hoped she would be.

Then Charlotte spoke again, and Homer realized that her voice was by no means the least of her attractions. 'Thank you, Richard,' she said, 'for bringing her to me.'

Homer turned from Charlotte to stare at Richard Danver. He was smiling at Charlotte and he was no longer arrogant, no longer insolent, only tender.

★ ★ ★

Charlotte led Homer into the hall, Richard following. It was not a large hall, but very tastefully decorated, and an elegant staircase at the end wound gracefully upwards.

'Come in here, first,' said Charlotte, opening a door on her right. 'My dear, you must be weary. Travelling is so trying; but I trusted Richard to see that you were as comfortable as possible. Jean Pierre and Bettine are here. Come and meet them. Then you shall be shown your room.'

She had put her arm through Homer's and was leading her into a room which, although not large, was luxurious in Homer's eyes. Two windows which reached from ceiling to floor were curtained with white and gold brocade; much of the furniture was gilded, and the room would have been more usual in Paris than in London, though Homer did not know this.

On a sofa sprawled a pretty golden-haired young woman; and a young man, who had been seated near her, rose as Charlotte and Homer entered.

'My cousin, Homer Trent, who has come to stay with me,' said Charlotte. 'This is Miss Bettine Cory who is playing with me, and Monsieur Jean Pierre de la Vaugon who is staying in London on a visit from Paris.'

'It is a great pleasure to see you,' began Homer, but as Bettine put her hands on her shoulders and kissed her cheek, and Jean Pierre took her hand, bowed over it and touched it with his lips, she felt suddenly awkward because Richard Danver had come into the room.

'Richard too!' said Bettine, with a laugh.

'He was so good,' Charlotte told them. 'I did not care that my little cousin should travel alone through the wilds of the West Country, so Richard said he would be travelling that way and would fit his journey in with hers and so look after her for me.'

Bettine set her mouth into lines of mock primness. 'But did they not need a chaperone!'

'Oh no!' laughed Charlotte. 'It was all so decorous, so proper. Homer did not even know he was looking after her until they left the coach.'

'I could wish,' said Jean Pierre, smiling at Homer, 'that the honour could have fallen to me.'

'I'll tell you what it reminds me of,' said Bettine. 'That scene in *The Girl from the Country*. Do you remember, Charlotte?'

'Of course I remember.'

Richard said: 'Charlotte often takes scenes from plays and fits them into her life. It is what is called living dramatically, I suppose.'

'That is the only way to live,' replied Charlotte. 'I see no reason why we should not enjoy ourselves as much in real life as do players on a stage.'

'In a play one person jerks the strings,'

murmured Richard. 'In real life the characters are likely to rebel and perform the most unexpected actions.'

'Meanwhile,' put in Charlotte, 'Homer is getting a poor welcome. We will have some refreshment. Then you shall be shown your room, Homer. Jean Pierre, ring the bell, please.'

Homer watched Jean Pierre as he went to the bell-rope. He was over medium height and would have looked tall but for the presence of Richard Danver; and if, on her first sight of Richard, Homer had thought him a dandy, she no longer did so, for compared with those of Jean Pierre his clothes seemed homespun. Jean Pierre's slim form was clad in elegant jacket and breeches of midnight blue; his waistcoat was a magnificent creation of silver brocade; his stockings were of white silk, and the ruffles of his shirt of silver lace. His manners were as elegant as his clothes, and from the moment Homer had entered the room he had behaved as though she were every bit as interesting as — perhaps even a little more than — the other ladies.

Charlotte took Homer's arm and led her to a chair which seemed, in Homer's view, too elegant for anything but an ornament.

'You must tell us about your journey,' said Charlotte. 'Were there any excitements?'

'It was a most uneventful journey,' Richard answered for her. 'Did you not think so, Miss Trent?'

'Call her Homer,' said Charlotte. 'And Homer, he must be Richard to you. He is one of my dearest friends — so he must be one of yours. Ah, here is Victoire.'

A woman, a year or so older than Charlotte, appeared in the doorway. Homer wondered whether she could really be a servant since she was so well dressed.

'Victoire,' went on Charlotte, 'my cousin has arrived.'

Victoire bobbed a curtsey in Homer's direction, and Homer inclined her head, wondering whether this was how one greeted a servant in this London society which was clearly quite different from anything she had known in the country.

'Brew us some tea,' said Charlotte. 'Cousin, you could drink a dish of tea?'

Homer, feeling Richard Danver's eyes upon her, was about to say there was nothing she would like better; but as she turned to Charlotte she found it impossible to be anything but frank, and she said: 'I have never yet drunk tea. We never had it at the parsonage.'

'Ah,' said Charlotte. 'Then you must try it. You will find it stimulating.'

While they awaited the arrival of the tea, Charlotte bade them all draw their chairs about the table, and they talked of many subjects such as the play in which Charlotte was appearing, about the state of affairs at Versailles and life in St Miniver's.

Tea, Homer found, was not very much to her taste.

'Try a little sugar,' suggested Richard at her side. 'A little sweetness is a great help you will find.'

They were all smiling, waiting for her verdict — Bettine amused, Charlotte with affection shining in her eyes, Jean Pierre tender as though he were very eager for her comfort, and Richard with that almost mocking smile which had irritated her in the coach.

When tea had been drunk the party dispersed. Bettine would see Charlotte later that day at the theatre; Jean Pierre would call very soon; Richard did not say when he would return, and Homer believed it would not be for some time, and that he was glad to have performed his duty and be rid of her.

★ ★ ★

'Now we are alone,' said Charlotte, 'we can talk about ourselves. Let me look at you,

54

Homer . . . really look! I was so touched when I received your letter. It seemed strange that what you had heard of me should have made such a deep impression, and that you should have remembered me for all those years. It must have been at least three years ago when you heard I had come to London.'

'I knew one day we should meet, and that our lives would touch in some way. I know such things. My mother had that gift and I inherited it from her.'

'We shall have so much to say to each other, but first, Homer, let me show you the room I have prepared for you. Come now.'

She led the way up the stairs.

'This is a small house, Homer,' she went on. 'I am not rich. I have only one servant — Victoire — whom you have seen. Actresses do not live in luxury unless . . . This way.'

'Charlotte,' said Homer, startled suddenly, 'I shall be a burden to you.'

Charlotte laughed so that the black curls bobbed on her forehead. 'Neither am I so very poor,' she said, 'and you are going to be my guest for as long as you wish.'

'I must work.'

They had reached a landing and Charlotte turned to smile at her. 'At what do you wish to work?'

'As your companion, as your secretary — perhaps as an actress.'

'You, too, have dreams of becoming an actress. How deep do they go, Homer?'

'How *deep*?'

'Ah, I see, it is a passing fancy. Let me tell you this: All my life I was certain that I would be an actress. I was certain of it. In my parents' Norfolk home I dreamed of greatness. I came to London. I have played in both Drury Lane and Covent Garden. Yet here I am. I shall never be a great actress as . . . say Peg Woffington was great.' She laughed again as though life were a joke and threw open the door of a room where Homer saw a four-poster bed with pink silk curtains, a dressing table with a big mirror, and gilded chairs similar to those which she had seen downstairs.

'This is quite beautiful,' murmured Homer.

'I am glad you like it. I feared you might find it over small.'

Homer had turned to Charlotte and her eyes were brilliant with emotion. 'Everything is exactly what I hoped for — you most of all.'

Charlotte seemed afraid of too much emotion. She said quickly: 'Victoire shall bring hot water, and you will wash and rest perhaps. Then we shall talk. I will leave you now to unpack. Then I will show you the house and we will tell each other our life stories.'

With that she left Homer who, as she unpacked, began to realize how ungainly she must appear in these surroundings.

Victoire came in with her hot water. 'Well, here you are, Mademoiselle,' she said. 'If there is something else you want, please say so.'

'You are not English?'

'I come from France. I joined Mademoiselle Walpole when she was there, to be with her in Paris. But to serve Mademoiselle Walpole in Paris is to wish to serve her in London or in any place where she might be.'

'You are very fond of her.'

Victoire folded her arms across her breast and said: 'To know Mademoiselle Walpole is to love her.'

★ ★ ★

Homer was sitting before the mirror in Charlotte's room and Charlotte was dressing her hair.

'There, you see! Already you look more like a young lady of fashion — if that is how you want to look. Why, when we have had a new dress made for you — a body

57

of silk with a petticoat of satin, shall we say? And what colour? Shall it be green? That would be quite daring — ah then, you will look enchanting. But do not look too like the rest of us, Homer. Preserve your individuality. That is important.'

Charlotte stood up and going to her bed stretched herself upon it.

'Oh yes,' she continued, 'you must have some new clothes, Homer. Tomorrow we will look at materials. You need a good watered tabby for morning wear, and something in paduasoys — have you seen the new material from Padua? — and a dress for gay occasions.'

'But how can I buy these things?'

'Are you not my companion? You have wages.'

'But, Charlotte, I will work for you for nothing.'

'That would be quite unwise. Although we are friends we must be businesslike.'

'But had I not asked to come you would not have engaged a companion.'

'As soon as I received your letter I knew I wanted a companion, and that that companion must be you. Homer, I want to know about the parsonage and your half-sisters and your father and Aunt Agnes who was so shocked because of what I did, but to whom we must be grateful because she brought us together.'

Then Homer told her story as she had lived it, and the prelude to it as Tansy had told it to her. Charlotte listened attentively and at length she said: 'You ran away because you needed to escape, not because you wished to be an actress. I am glad of that.'

Charlotte told her own story after that.

'There were three of us — Mary, Frances and myself. Our father had a large country house in Norfolk and life in it seemed intolerably dull. This began when some travelling players came to Norwich and we were driven in to see them.

'How wonderful it seemed to me — that dark little stage and the curtain which was faded and would not rise and fall when it was required to do so. I did not see that it was a squalid little hall, that the players were second-rate. They played Shakespeare. It was *Romeo and Juliet*; and I thought Juliet the most beautiful creature I had ever seen.

'When we drove back I was in a sort of daze, murmuring snatches of the play to myself; and when the others were asleep, I took a candle and crept into the schoolroom. I opened the Shakespeare and read *Romeo and Juliet* aloud, taking all the parts. I had made my discovery. I was going to be an actress.

'They all laughed at me, of course, and nobody took me seriously. I was undeterred. But so set was I on this career that my parents eventually realized that nothing else would satisfy me.

'I have a little income of my own. I had friends to help me. So to London I came. I lived for a time with a family who were friends of my family, and a part was found for me in the play which was about to be produced at the Theatre Royal. You see, I was fortunate. I had some money and good friends. I was not quite the adventurous girl you imagined me to be, running away from home to make my fortune on the stage.

'I played Jessica in *The Merchant of Venice* and Rosetta in *Love in a Village* and I am now appearing as a soldier in *The Camp*. You must see the play. Would you like to see me act this very day, or would you rather remain here and rest with Victoire in attendance?'

'Could I go to the play like this . . . alone?'

'I could lend you a dress and cloak. I am bigger than you, but Victoire would adjust that in next to no time. And someone murmured to me that he would be delighted to take you, if you were willing.'

Homer flushed. Her thoughts had immediately gone to Richard Danver. It would be stimulating to go with him, particularly in a dress provided by Charlotte.

Charlotte's next words were a little disconcerting. 'I think you have made a conquest of Jean Pierre.'

3

Homer's first week in London was full of so many impressions that she found it difficult to absorb them. She was in a state of perpetual excitement which she could only call happiness; and Charlotte was the sun about which this dazzling world revolved.

This unconventional existence could not have been enjoyed against any but a theatrical background; and life with Charlotte was free and easy and full of fun.

Homer made frequent visits to the theatre in the company of Jean Pierre de la Vaugon, and it seemed that Charlotte was right when she had said that Homer had made a conquest.

His quaint accent, his courtesy and elegance made an appeal to Homer, and she felt he was an admirable escort for her first taste of London life.

She was greatly interested in the theatre, and enjoyed sitting in a four-shilling box looking down on the mixed audience which was unlike any assembly she had ever seen before. It was the greatest fun to watch, not only the play but the audience, to join in the hatred of the villain who might be hissed off the stage if he were lucky, and pelted with orange peel, rotten fruit and bags of soot if he were not. She liked to buy a China orange or an apple from the girls who carried the fruit among the audience between the acts.

And what joy to see the actors and actresses perform behind the footlights, which comprised a row of sixteen candles continuously snuffed by the attendant whose sole duty it was to perform this task. And afterwards to go behind the stage and take refreshment in the Green Room with Charlotte and her friends — those gods and goddesses who had, but a short time before, been performing on the stage!

Jean Pierre was eager to show her other places besides the theatre. He took her to Mrs Salmon's Waxworks near the Temple, and Homer was enthralled by the dummies of the beef-eater in his uniform and the match-seller in gingham gown and muslin apron who stood at the door, an indication of the sights to be seen by those who paid their sixpences. She gazed in wonderment at the figures in the candle-lit room — King George III and his Queen Charlotte, and such characters as dissimilar as Dick Turpin and John Wesley.

One day he took her walking in the Park,

dressed in a new gown which Victoire had made for her. She must, she was told, look her most elegant, for on weekdays only the gentry were allowed to walk in the Park. It was not until after five o'clock on Sundays that it was thrown open to all classes, and then it became no fit place for an elegant young lady.

As they walked by the Serpentine he suggested they sit awhile.

'Mademoiselle Homer,' he said, 'you have the air of bewilderment. Tell me why this is.'

She turned to him. 'It is because my life has changed so suddenly. I cannot believe that three weeks ago I was living in the country, never dreaming that all this existed.'

'And I never dreamed that *you* existed.'

'How could you, since we had never met? But to think that this was here — this wonderful city — and there are people who have no conception of it!'

'Yet, my dear Mademoiselle, this is but a small part of the world. There are other places.'

'There is your home,' she said.

'Ah, Paris. Paris and Versailles . . . equally wonderful, I do assure you.'

'Here,' she said, 'people live what we in the country would have called fantastic

64

lives — you, Charlotte, Bettine and Mr Danver.'

'Not so fantastic. We work as do your friends in the country. Charlotte and Bettine are actresses — hard work, I can tell you. Richard and I are in the diplomatic service of our governments.'

'I did not know this.'

'Did you think our lives were lived solely for the pursuit of pleasure? This is a work-a-day world, my dear Mademoiselle. I am here on a mission for my government. Very soon I shall be returning to France.'

'Oh!' said Homer, blankly.

'Does that mean you will miss me?'

'I shall indeed miss you.'

He laid his hand lightly on hers and she felt a tremor at his touch. 'Alas,' he said, 'very shortly I shall leave London. But perhaps you will come to Paris and we shall certainly meet then.'

'I! Go to Paris!'

'Charlotte would bring you with her if she came, and she comes to Paris when the theatres close for the summer season.'

'She has said nothing of this to me.'

'Perhaps she has not thought of it or had the time. Time passes quickly, does it not? There is so much to do — so little time to talk. Charlotte thinks no more of going to Paris than most people do of going to Bath.'

'And you are surprised that after my country existence I find this life bewildering!'

'I hope, Mademoiselle Homer, you will never lose that air of bewilderment. I find it . . . enchanting.'

He lifted her hand, kissed it again, and she was conscious of that excitement.

'Tomorrow,' he said, 'you and I will go to Vauxhall. I shall insist — whatever Charlotte plans. It shall be our farewell — no, not farewell. That is a sad word. Our *au revoir*.'

★ ★ ★

To Vauxhall they went, and as they wandered among the statues and Homer marvelled at the colonnades, grottoes and rotundas, the gardens, avenues and pavilions, she felt a sudden fear take possession of her. It seemed to her that everything which had happened to her since she had received Charlotte's letter was too wonderful to be really true. She felt as though someone had put a pair of brightly coloured glasses over her eyes so that she saw everything more beautifully coloured than reality could possibly make it.

Nothing could last. Change was coming.

Jean Pierre was going away. He said they would meet again, but would they? Was his assurance that they would do so merely part of this not quite real world into which she had strayed? He was gallant; he was charming; in St Miniver's a man who talked to her and looked at her as he did would be judged a man in love; but this was not St Miniver's.

They might sit beneath the trees when the lamps of Vauxhall were lighted, so that they seemed to be in a universe of constellations, and she might say that she had never seen anything so wonderful — yet her pleasure was becoming tinged with apprehension.

She could not quite understand it. Did she feel thus because Jean Pierre was going back to France? Or was it because she sensed the chill of change, because she felt that all was not quite as it seemed?

★ ★ ★

Homer had been two weeks in London and was determined that she should make herself useful in the house. She insisted on going to the kitchen to help Victoire. She showed her how to make pasties, squab pie and clouted cream. She insisted on sewing for Charlotte — not that this was one of her accomplishments — and she shared the dusting and sweeping with Victoire.

Victoire declared that had she not come she would have had to have help in the house. Charlotte said that there was no doubt that, but for Homer, she would have had to employ a maid.

Now that Jean Pierre had left London, Homer spent a great deal of time in the house, for Charlotte was busy not only playing but rehearsing a new play, and it was pointed out to Homer, who had wanted to explore the city by herself, that it was unwise for a well-dressed young woman to go out alone in the streets of London.

One day when Charlotte was at the theatre and Homer sat in her room mending one of the coats which Charlotte wore in her part in *The Camp*, Victoire came to tell her that a visitor had called.

'It is Mr Danver,' said Victoire.

Homer wished she could think of some excuse to avoid seeing him, but as Victoire had told him she was at home, she could not give him the satisfaction of knowing he affected her so much that she wished to avoid him.

'I will be down shortly,' she told Victoire, and when she was alone she went to her mirror and studied herself. She had not seen him since the day of her arrival and she wondered whether he had deliberately stayed away knowing she was there, for he appeared to be a great friend of Charlotte's.

Charlotte had not mentioned his absence, but that was understandable. Charlotte's life was so full that she did not speak of details as they did in the parsonage. Moreover, there was a trait in Charlotte's character which Homer was discovering. Impulsive as she undoubtedly was, she was also a little vague; the kindest, sweetest person imaginable, yet, although she was Homer's senior by some six or seven years, Homer felt that it was she herself who, when she had settled into her new life and escaped from this feeling of bewilderment, would be the one to look after Charlotte.

She was wearing a dress, the over-skirt of which was made of watered tabby. It was slit from the waist to disclose a silk petticoat, with a green pattern etched on a grey background. Her hair — so unmanageable in the St Miniver's parsonage — was, at Charlotte's suggestion, worn in two plaits which hung over her shoulders. 'By no means fashionable,' Charlotte had said, 'but then really smart women never slavishly follow fashions.'

So, with a faint flush in her cheeks and

the green pattern of her petticoat bringing out the green in her eyes, Homer descended the stairs to meet Richard Danver.

He turned as she entered the room and she had the satisfaction of seeing the startled surprise in his face.

'I see you scarcely recognize the country girl,' she said, with an asperity which seemed to come to her involuntarily when she spoke to him.

'You forget I sat opposite her all those days in the coach, shared meals with her at many an inn, slept in the same inns at night — although I did not see her then, she being safely behind locked doors. Therefore I feel it would be impossible for her to disguise herself from me.'

She felt immediately deflated. That was the effect he had upon her. She said coolly: 'You have chosen the wrong time to call. Charlotte is at the theatre.'

'But I did not call to see Charlotte.'

'Are you telling me you came to see me?'

'I am. Why are you so surprised that I should?'

'I should have thought you could have found something more interesting to do.'

He smiled at her. 'At the moment,' he said, 'I am filling in time between commitments. But I know you long to see London and that,

70

lacking an escort to accompany you through our wicked streets, you are confined to the house.'

'And you are offering your services? It is good of you. But you need not put yourself out. I have plenty to do.'

'Shall I say that you will be doing me a favour by helping me to fill my empty hours? Come, get your cloak.'

She hesitated but he pulled the bell, and before she had time to recover from her astonishment, Victoire had appeared.

'Miss Homer's cloak and bonnet, please, Victoire.'

Victoire hurried away immediately to do his bidding. His arrogance, his way of taking command were so peremptory, Homer decided, that people were in the habit of obeying instantly without question. But not this person! she said to herself grimly.

Victoire returned with the cloak which had been Charlotte's and a hat which they had bought together soon after her arrival. Homer wound the plaits about her head, using the long gilded mirror on the wall through which she saw him watching her with some amusement. He came forward, holding the cloak which he had taken from Victoire. In the mirror her eyes met his; he was smiling as though he found the situation infinitely amusing.

* * *

That jaunt in the company of Richard Danver was quite different from the pleasure trips she had taken with Jean Pierre. She felt even then that every experience she shared with Richard would have that astringent quality. With Charlotte and Jean Pierre she felt as though they were all living in a world of pink and white icing — everything charming, harmless, yet somehow not quite real. At least Richard Danver brought her back to reality.

'What have you seen of London?' he asked.

'A great deal.'

'I know that Monsieur de la Vaugon has been your escort. But what do foreigners know of our London?'

'He took me to Ranelagh, the Park and Vauxhall.'

'So that you now think you know London! Well, today I will show you more of London in a few hours than your Frenchman has shown you in a week. It is meet and fitting that you should see our city through the eyes of one of her citizens. Come along. I have a hackney waiting.'

Then began that drive which she was never to forget. He showed her the houses of the nobility with their beautiful gardens running down to the river; he showed her the gardens of the City in the Strand and Fetter Lane; he showed her Pitt Bridge with its toll gate, and the craft on the river.

She saw men and women exquisitely dressed riding in sedan chairs, bowing and calling to their friends as they passed. He pointed out beaux and fops who were known as *macaronis*. Then they turned east and he took her past the factories of Spitalfields where from early morning until late at night, he told her, men, women and little children toiled at their weaving. He pointed out a chimney sweep, not more than four years old, grimy with soot, an expression of despair and fear on his face as he toiled along beside his master. She saw the beggars — some little more than babies, some blind, some deformed.

Richard watched her as she stared out on this scene, her eyes solemn, her face pale.

'Come,' he said, 'we have had enough of misery. But I wanted you to see it. I fancied you believed that all London was full of charming impulsive actresses like Charlotte, of gay gallants like your French admirer. You had a false picture, and I believe it better to know the truth however unpleasant. Life is not all silks and satins, scarlet ribands and hand-kissing.'

'That,' said Homer, 'is something of which I am fully aware.'

'Then we have had enough. Now let us be gay. First we will eat and wash the taste of what we have seen from our mouths with some good sack or Burgundy.'

She was reminded once more how different he was from Jean Pierre who always prefaced his suggestion with: 'If you wish it, we will do this . . . or that . . . ' As though, she thought indignantly, it were for this man to make the plans and for her to accept his decisions with the utmost meekness. Yet the adventures of the day had both sobered and stimulated her, and she was ready to place herself in his hands.

So, at the Saracen's Head in Snow Hill, Richard ordered a meal which began with salmon and passed on to roast beef; and when she heard of a bean-tansy and declared it reminded her of an old friend, Richard insisted on her trying it and the waiter's telling her how it was made — which was of butter, eggs, bacon, juice of tansy, cloves, salt and pepper.

All this was washed down with Canary sack; and feeling a little dizzy, perhaps from

74

the unaccustomed wine, perhaps from the company, Homer climbed once more into the hackney.

Richard was smiling at her almost benignly.

'Now,' he said, 'refreshed and replete, we will continue on our tour. You have seen fashionable London and work-a-day London, our most elegant and our down-at-heel City. I shall take you now to Tottenham Fair.'

So to Tottenham they went.

This fair was as different from the Liskeard Fair (to which Tansy had once taken her) as London was from St Miniver's. Here it seemed that Richard became a different person from the man she had known. He made her beware of pickpockets who he warned her were to be found in every London street but who abounded in crowds such as this; he steered her quickly past bold-faced women.

They watched a man eat glass and swallow fire; they saw dwarfs and giants, jugglers and tight-rope walkers; they went into one of the booths, where a theatrical entertainment was about to begin, and sat through a performance called *The Mad Lover*.

It was highly diverting and entertaining, and Homer was amazed that this day's adventure could seem so much richer, and more varied than anything she had seen with

Charlotte and Jean Pierre.

After some hours Richard insisted that she must be hungry again, and they sat down at one of the refreshment stalls, fantastically called 'Fair Rosamund's Bower' because it was decorated with trailing leaves; and here they ate spiced beef and oysters, all for the price of three-pence each.

She felt breathless with so many adventures. She told him: 'It has been a very interesting tour.'

Then suddenly he shattered her pleasure. 'I am so glad you enjoyed it,' he said. 'Charlotte told me how lonely you were and begged me to show you the town when I had time.'

'Charlotte asked you!'

He laughed. 'How indignant you are!'

'I am so because I feel I have taken up so much of your time.' Her eyes glinted. He was being deliberately insulting and she had been a fool to let him see how much she had enjoyed the day. She said: 'I do not think you are the sort of man to do something you do not wish to, merely because you are asked.'

His eyes were mocking. 'In ordinary circumstances you would be correct. As you know, I am very fond of . . . Charlotte.'

She bit her lip and turned away, piqued

and angry. She would tell Charlotte in no uncertain terms that never in any circumstances must she ask Richard Danver to do any favours for Homer Trent.

★ ★ ★

It was hard to believe that it was a month since she had said good-bye to Mr Eeves and taken her place in the coach opposite Richard Danver. She was settling into a routine; she had worked as hard and as well as she could; and she no longer felt that she did not earn her keep. Often she went with Charlotte to the theatre and helped her dress between acts; sometimes she took over the prompter's duties and sat in the wings during the entire performance.

She was excited by the theatre; but she had made a great discovery: she did not want to act on that little stage; she wanted to play a heroic role on the stage of life.

Each day she spent with Charlotte, she seemed to love her more — dear, impulsive Charlotte who never seemed able to resist any beggars, who only had to hear a sad story to offer that which she might need herself. It was small wonder that Charlotte had answered as she did when she had received Homer's letter. Charlotte would never say 'no' to anyone in need of help.

Life was full of interest and completely absorbing; it was more wonderful than she had ever thought it could be. There were letters from Jean Pierre whom duty kept in Paris, but he wrote as though they would be meeting soon, if not in London, in his native Paris.

Richard Danver called once or twice, but always when Charlotte was at home, and he seemed to give all his attention to her so that Homer thought: I believe he is in love with Charlotte. Indeed, when he spoke to her, his voice was a degree softer; there were no mocking lights in his eyes when they rested on Charlotte.

Homer told herself that she hoped Charlotte did not love him. Charlotte had too sweet a nature to mate with his arrogance. There were times when she was afraid that Charlotte would tell her that Richard had asked her to marry him.

★ ★ ★

Homer was in the Green Room alone. It was during the last act and very soon Charlotte would be taking her applause. Homer had brought Charlotte's heavy cloak because it had turned cold during the afternoon and she was afraid that Charlotte might be chilled on her way home.

Suddenly she looked up because she was aware that someone had come into the room. Afterwards she told herself that she had shivered before she saw him; and although she might scoff at that idea and remind herself that there could have been a draught from one of the windows, she believed, since she had heard from Tansy of her mother's extraordinary gifts, that she possessed them, and that she had an uncanny notion that she sensed evil in this man.

She started up, angry with herself for blushing and betraying her confusion.

He was tall and about fifteen years older than herself; he was broad, with a somewhat fleshy face and eyes which sparkled as he looked at her as though she were some dainty on a dish and he was a very hungry man.

'Good afternoon,' he said; his voice was cultured, his bow courtly.

'Good afternoon,' responded Homer.

'I hope you are not preparing to depart because I have come.'

She again experienced that feeling of repulsion.

'Tell me,' he went on, 'are you an actress?

79

You are handsome enough to be.'

'I am no actress. I . . . I serve one.'

'Ah,' he said. 'I'll warrant you'd give a great deal to be able to strut on a stage like your mistress, eh?'

'I am content as I am.'

He lifted a finger almost playfully. 'Pretty girls should always seize their opportunities.'

'Then I will seize this to say good-bye to you.'

She turned away to stare out of the window. It was a foolish thing to have done, for it gave him his chance to come swiftly upon her, so that he was standing behind her, cutting off her escape.

It was an odd sensation — one of fear such as she had rarely known before. This was absurd. It was daylight. At any moment someone might come. Very soon the last act would be played out and the stage folk themselves would be crowding in. Therefore why should she experience this numbing fear — she, who prided herself on her fearlessness!

She stood there, holding Charlotte's cloak on her arm, feeling as though she could not move if she tried.

She swung round to face him, and he acted promptly by putting his hands on her shoulders, holding her in a firm and expert grip, pulling her towards him and kissing her on the mouth.

All Homer's fear was replaced by anger. In a second she had brought up the hand which was not holding her cloak and dealt the man a blow across the face, so sharp that he gave a little cry and released her.

Then, not stopping to look back, she ran out of the Green Room, out of the theatre, as fast as she could to the house.

★ ★ ★

She felt ashamed.

If I had been as dignified as Charlotte, she told herself, it would never have happened to me.

She could best forget that unfortunate incident by never referring to it; and if, by some evil chance, she ever met the man again, she would ignore him as though she found him quite beneath her notice.

When she returned to the house she saw that she was still carrying Charlotte's cloak, and she was glad that she had not told Victoire that she had intended taking it, for to have arrived back with it would have involved difficult explanations.

It was half an hour later when a messenger arrived from Charlotte asking Homer if she would care to come to the Green Room where a party was in progress. Fearing she might meet the man again, Homer sent the messenger back to say that she had a headache (something from which she had never suffered) and had decided to go to bed.

She went to her room, still flushed and angry from the encounter. Her dignity was in revolt. That man had believed her to be a servant without pride who thought it was a fine thing to be lightly kissed by a member of the gentry.

And she had slapped his face. She wished she had thought of some cutting remark she might have made, something clever, witty and caustic. How much more dignified that would have been!

Next time — if such a thing should ever happen to her again — she would not be such a simpleton as to allow herself to be caught like that.

I hated him from the moment he came in, she reminded herself. I knew he was evil.

Victoire had heard her remark to the messenger and was solicitously bustling round her. She must go to bed and rest. Victoire would bring her some hot gruel or a posset — infallible remedy for a headache.

There was nothing to do but take what Victoire brought her and go to bed. The posset made her sleep and she did not hear Charlotte return to the house.

★ ★ ★

Charlotte was late down next morning, and Homer had eaten her breakfast and was reading a letter when she appeared.

If Homer had not completely forgotten yesterday's unpleasant incident, when she saw the letter she did so. It was from Jennifer — the first she had received since leaving St Miniver's, and as she read it she felt again the atmosphere of the old parsonage; she could see the ivy-covered tower of the ancient church, the drunken tombstones, the sedate faces of her half-sisters, the knowledgeable one of Tansy and the whimsical one of Willie; she could hear the melancholy cry of the gulls. It all came back to her, so real, that the life of the last month seemed like something from a dream.

'So much has happened since you left us,' she read. 'Everything seems to have changed, and the parsonage is a different place from the one we always knew. Dear

Homer, I hope you are being happy with Charlotte in London and are finding it all so much more exciting than our St Miniver's. I think you were never contented here.

'I must tell you that a week after you left, Mr Eeves proposed to me and I accepted him. We are very happy and are to be married soon. It has all been rather hurried and has caused us a great deal of anxiety. We could not make up our minds what was the best thing to do, Papa's death being so recent. How could we *respectably* marry so soon? And yet how could we and Mr Eeves continue to live at the parsonage unless Mr Eeves was married to one of us? We were at our wits' end, but thankful that Aunt Agnes was with us so that she could chaperone us to some extent.

'However, Mr Eeves took a room, temporarily, in Mrs Tregow's cottage and he will come back to the parsonage after the wedding which must, of course, be *very quiet*.

'Oh dear, I always pictured myself being married in white brocade or satin, and now there must be nothing of that. Mr Eeves is being so kind. Anne Mary is to live with us — also Aunt Agnes. We had feared that it might be necessary for Anne Mary to take some post as governess in a very genteel household. Poor Anne Mary was positively *terrified* at the thought of it, and as I say, Mr Eeves is *so* good.'

Homer let the paper fall from her hands; she was smiling, picturing it all so clearly. Indeed the parsonage would be a different place. Mr Eeves would be a gentle parson and Jennifer was lucky. Homer hoped she would never know how easily she might have missed married bliss with a benign partner like Mr Eeves. She should be very happy — if Aunt Agnes did not prevent it.

She was still smiling when Charlotte came down. She thought how pretty Charlotte looked; her dark curls were falling about her shoulders and she wore a peach-coloured robe trimmed with fur.

'Well,' said Charlotte, 'You look happy this morning.'

'This is a letter from Jennifer.'

'How is life at the parsonage?'

'Quite wonderful. Mr Eeves is going to marry Jennifer.'

'He is the new parson, is he not? Well, it has worked out neatly. Do you think they will be happy?'

'If Aunt Agnes lets them. She is going to live with them.'

'Oh, poor dears! They shouldn't allow it.'

'I should not have allowed it if I had married Mr Eeves.'

'Homer, you are not regretting that you rejected Mr Eeves?'

Homer shook her head emphatically. 'I am sorry for Mr Eeves who must have Aunt Agnes in his house, but I should have been sorrier for him if he had married me. And I know I shall never regret coming to you, Charlotte.' She paused. 'Do you believe we inherit the characteristics of our parents?'

'I do.'

'Then I have inherited something from my strange mother. It is a certain knowledge. And this I believe: My life and yours are bound together. Therefore, whatever happens I shall never regret leaving all that and coming to you. Charlotte, I pray you will never regret my coming either.'

Charlotte was more solemn than Homer had ever seen her before. 'Let us say that wherever one goes the other will go. Was it Ruth who said: 'Where thou goest, there shall I go also . . . '? Never mind who said it. Let us say it now. Homer, this is I think the happiest moment of my life . . . as yet.' She was smiling almost secretively in a way Homer had never seen her smile before.

'Something has happened, Charlotte. Tell me.'

'I am going to be married,' said Charlotte.

'Oh!' Homer could not keep the fear out of her voice.

'But you must not feel the slightest misgiving about that. It will make no difference. Remember, where you go, there shall I go.'

'It is so . . . unexpected.'

'Oh . . . no. We have known each other so long. He is coming here today. I want you to be fond of him, Homer.'

Homer was silent and Charlotte went on: 'How selfish I am . . . thinking of myself. You were unwell last night. How is the headache? Why, Homer, you do look a little pale. All this excitement has been too much for you. You must rest. I insist. I shall be entertaining friends for dinner which will be at two o'clock. Now you must rest awhile to be fresh for our visitors, for this is a great occasion . . . to celebrate our engagement. Victoire . . . Victoire . . . '

Victoire came hurrying in.

'Miss Homer still has her headache and I am going to make her lie down. Warm some milk and she shall rest until dinner-time.'

Oddly enough, the one thing Homer wanted at this moment was to be alone.

She could not understand her emotions. She had often thought that Richard loved Charlotte and that Charlotte was fond of him. Why should it be so upsetting to learn that they were about to be married?

She lay on her bed and when Victoire came in with the milk she pretended to be asleep. Victoire put the milk on the table by the bed and went away.

When she had gone, Homer stared at the ceiling. She was trying to picture Richard Danver as a married man, trying to imagine what it would be like living in the same house with him.

She saw that he would come between her and Charlotte in some way. She had said that where Charlotte went there would she go, but would that be possible if Richard Danver were there too?

Her happy world was changing as she should have known it must. Had Richard meant to tell her this when he had shown her London in its splendour and squalor? Was he saying: This is not only London, this is life!

He disturbed her as she had never been disturbed before.

★ ★ ★

88

It was an hour before dinner and Victoire was standing by her bed.

'And you are well enough to get up, Mademoiselle Homer? I will bring you a hip bath and hot water. And shall I put out your Lyons silk dress? It is a very special occasion. Mademoiselle Charlotte will wish you to look your most charming.'

'Thank you, Victoire.'

'Then you are better?'

'Much better, thank you, Victoire.'

She bathed and put on the silk dress. It suited her because the black over-skirt had a tracing of silver leaves on it, and the petticoat, fichu and cascades of lace at her elbows were emerald green.

She rehearsed what she would say. 'My congratulations, Mr Danver. I hope you will make Charlotte happy.' She must be careful that her voice did not betray the emotion which she could not understand herself. 'My best wishes to you both. May you be as happy as you deserve.' No! That sounded cynical, for he and she were not good friends. 'As happy as Charlotte deserves . . . ' No, too pointed! That would not do. She must curb her emotions. If he were going to share their life in future she would have to be constantly on the alert not to show how he disturbed her. She would say what came to her naturally. At least, she would be telling the truth if she said she wished Charlotte all the happiness in the world.

As she descended the stairs she could hear that some of the guests had already arrived. She could hear Charlotte's laughter. It was very happy laughter.

She thought then that the vagueness which she had sensed in Charlotte's character probably meant that her thoughts had been with the man she loved. She had been expecting the proposal, waiting for it.

Homer opened the door. Charlotte saw her at once and hurried to her.

'My dear Homer, are you better? But you are looking so well now. Do come along.' Charlotte's voice was high-pitched with happiness. Never had she seemed so beautiful. Homer was looking for Richard, but he had not yet come, although there were several people in the room.

'Edward,' called Charlotte, 'this is Homer of whom you have heard so much. Homer, this is Sir Edward Atkyns who will shortly be my husband.'

A man had extricated himself from a group and was coming towards them. His rather fleshy face gave no sign that he had ever seen Homer before.

He took her hand and bowed formally. He

said: 'You and I must be friends. Our dearest Charlotte insists, and now I have seen you, I am sure we shall be.'

Homer was looking into the eyes of the man whose face she had slapped in the Green Room of the Theatre Royal.

4

Homer was bewildered. One question beat perpetually in her brain: What shall I do?

The dainty room with its French-style furniture seemed over-hot, and Charlotte's happy voice rang in her ears, mingling with the suave tones of her betrothed husband.

Never had Homer seen Charlotte look so happy; and to tell would shatter that happiness. Yet was it not better that Charlotte should know what sort of man this was she was planning to marry, than that she should build her happiness on a false and evil foundation?

She was startled by a touch on her elbow, and turning saw Richard Danver smiling at her. He had drawn her aside before she realized he had done so. 'You are looking stormy,' he said.

Homer lifted her eyes to his face and for a moment almost decided to confide in him. His next words, however, sent the angry blood rushing to her face. 'You should curb your jealousy,' he whispered.

'My jealousy!'

'You cannot expect to monopolize Charlotte.

She was bound to marry some time.'

'I think,' she said coldly, 'that you presume too much.'

'My dear Miss Trent, I saw your brows drawn together in disapproval. Disapproval! That expresses little of what I saw in your face. Let me tell you this: You looked like a witch preparing to cast the evil eye on the object of your dislike.'

'Please,' she said impulsively, 'do not tease me. I am not in the mood to endure it. Are you so delighted with Charlotte's choice?'

She fancied he winced a little. He loves her, she thought. I was right. Then could I perhaps ask him what I ought to do . . . but not now.

He hesitated only for a second or so, then he said: 'My dear, Charlotte is not a child. She is an adult person; she is the one to choose her husband — not I, not you.'

She lowered her eyes. In a way he had answered her question.

All through dinner she tried to imagine herself in love — as Charlotte clearly was — and being told that her lover was unworthy. How would she react? By hating her informant? By refusing to believe ill of her lover? She was sure that was how *she* would feel.

What would happen if in front of Charlotte

she accused him? He would deny that he had ever seen her before. He might not say: 'You are a liar, Homer Trent. You are bent on mischief!' But he could imply that; and what if Charlotte believed him? What he would probably say was: 'This is a mistake. I have never set eyes on you before.' And, of course, Charlotte would believe *him*.

Richard was proposing a toast. 'Long life and happiness to the betrothed pair!'

Everyone stood up and drank.

Homer's eyes met Richard's. She could not read what she saw in them, yet she knew that he was no more happy than she was over this betrothal.

★ ★ ★

When all the guests had gone Charlotte glanced delightedly at the empty glasses and the disarranged cushions. 'Well, Homer!' she cried. Then impulsively she held out her arms. Homer hugged her as though she would never let her go.

'You are very, *very* happy?' asked Homer, at length.

'I am,' Charlotte assured her.

'You never mentioned him before.'

Charlotte laughed lightheartedly and Homer knew why she had thought Charlotte a little vague in spite of her kindness; her thoughts had only been half on what was happening about her because she had been thinking continually of her lover.

'I was terrified that something would happen to prevent it,' she said. 'I felt that by not mentioning him I was protecting myself against the evil chance.'

'Why did I not see him before?'

'He has been in the country making arrangements for the wedding.'

'You did not trust him to come back,' said Homer quickly.

'I was afraid. I felt that a man like Edward could not really want to marry an actress.'

'What nonsense! You are worth twenty of him.'

'So prejudiced in my favour! You do not know Edward. He is the kindest, most indulgent man in the world. From the first day he came to the Green Room . . . ' Homer shuddered, but Charlotte did not notice. ' . . . I began to fall in love with him. He had been sitting in one of the boxes, and I had noticed him from the stage. We talked and supped together. And the next day he was in the box again.'

'I see,' said Homer.

'I said to him,' went on Charlotte, ' 'You are devoted to the play, Sir Edward!' and he answered: 'Not the play, Madam, but to you!' ' Charlotte again broke into that high-pitched laughter which denoted happiness. 'Of course, men often come to the theatre; they often chat in the Green Room. They often take their favourite actresses to supper and give them presents. I have always avoided such admirers. I have always told them that I was on the stage to become an actress not the mistress of some fine gentleman. But Edward was different. I knew his intentions were honourable from the first. You see, Edward is not like the young bloods who come to the theatre looking for adventure. He is serious. He wants me to give up the theatre.'

'But, Charlotte, you cannot do that!' Homer felt as though she were being swept along on a swift current to danger and had just sighted a raft. 'Give up your career! That would be impossible. You cannot marry a man who expects you to do that.'

'My dearest Homer, I would give up more than my career for Edward.'

'Charlotte, so you love him very much?'

Charlotte folded her arms across her breast; her eyes were half closed and she nodded slowly. Nothing could have been more eloquent.

I cannot tell her! Homer said to herself. I can never tell her.

Charlotte cried: 'But I shall be late for the theatre. Come, you must help me.'

★ ★ ★

When she had left, Homer went to the kitchen where Victoire was baking. Her face was flushed, her eyes gleaming and she was murmuring to herself.

'Victoire,' said Homer, taking a chair at the table, 'you look as though you have a lover who has promised you a life of bliss.'

'Mademoiselle Charlotte is very happy,' said Victoire, 'and therefore . . . so am I.'

'You think it will be a happy marriage?'

Victoire put her head on one side. 'Anyone who married Mademoiselle Charlotte would be happy. She would arrange that.'

'It takes two people to make a happy marriage.'

'One is enough — providing the other is not too evil.'

'But what if the other is evil?'

'I'll not listen to such talk! Why, Mademoiselle Homer, you are not pleased. You think the marriage will make some change which you do not like.'

'I was not thinking of myself, but of Charlotte.'

'Then you should be happy, for can you doubt that she is?'

'I want her to continue happy.'

'So she shall. This life . . . it is not for Mademoiselle Charlotte. She is not like the other actresses. They are not . . . how shall I say it? . . . they have not the gentility, the purity. Many of them are not good people. They come from . . . the gutters. They think only of the money and the gifts they get from men. Charlotte is different. She comes to be a great actress. She has dreams, as young girls will. But this is not her life. She belongs where she will now be — the mistress of a country estate. Mademoiselle Charlotte will be Milady; and that is well. That is why she is happy and I am happy and you must be happy.'

'But is he good enough to be Charlotte's husband?'

Victoire pursed her lips as though she were blowing imaginary bubbles. 'Who would be good enough for an angel? Perhaps he has his faults. He is a man — no more, no less. But he will take Charlotte from this life. He will set her up in a life which is becoming to her dignity. That is why we must rejoice and say: 'This is a happy event for us all'.'

'I see,' said Homer. 'Thank you, Victoire. You have explained much that I wished to know.'

* * *

Later that day, when Charlotte was still at the theatre, Sir Edward called at the house. He had brought a bouquet with him, and this was not for Charlotte but for Homer.

She received him in the drawing-room with a wildly beating heart and an expression of extreme hauteur. He took her hand and bowed low over it. Then he assumed a look of humility.

'I have come,' he said, 'to make my apologies for what happened in the Green Room. I must tell you that I do not make a habit of behaving in such a way.'

'I am very glad to hear that,' said Homer, 'for Charlotte's sake. That is the only reason why it could be of the slightest interest to me.'

'Naturally,' he went on, still continuing in a humble tone. 'I think I must have been suffering from a temporary madness. You are a very attractive and unusual person.'

'Is it unusual to resent insults? And do you think they should be meekly accepted by those whom you believe to be your inferiors?'

'You have a biting tongue, Miss Homer.'

'I use it for my protection.'

'As you do your hands.' He grimaced and, even disliking him as she was determined to do, she detected something of that charm which had enslaved Charlotte.

'Listen, Miss Homer,' he went on, 'I was wrong. I behaved unpardonably. How can I make you understand? You are a young girl recently come from the country. You are inexperienced in the ways of the world. You do not know of the temptations which beset men. Believe me, we are human, and the best of us fall at times. I love Charlotte devotedly. I am sure you realized that she would be deeply hurt if she knew what had happened.'

Homer's eyes blazed. 'You love Charlotte! Yet you cannot resist kissing — or trying to kiss — every little serving girl you meet!'

'Every little serving girl! You are quite wrong. This was no serving girl. It was you. Surely you know that a man would have to be a saint to resist your charms.'

'I know exactly how I look and that I am no beauty.'

'You have more than beauty, and I am weak and sinful. Please, Homer, do not be a simpleton. You cannot be so cruel as to hurt Charlotte now. What you have to tell her would not prevent our marriage; she is too fond of me for that. I would explain to her and she would understand. But what you could do would be to cast a shadow over our happiness. Homer, don't do it. I ask you, not for myself but for Charlotte.'

She was so uncertain. She felt sure that this man was not to be trusted. Yet he was right when he said that she could not by telling Charlotte what had happened prevent the marriage; she could only spoil Charlotte's happiness. Was Richard Danver right when he said that Charlotte must choose the man she would marry, without any help from him or from her?

'I am unsure about this,' she said. 'I pray you leave me now. I shall do what I decide is best . . . for Charlotte.'

Again that elaborate bow. 'Then I am relieved, for you are a young lady of good sense. Therefore you will forget this regrettable incident, and we shall all continue together as though it has not happened.'

With that he left.

Yet, she thought, however much Charlotte loves him, whatever I should do about this, I know he is evil.

★ ★ ★

A few weeks later Charlotte became Lady Atkyns.

There had been little time for intimate talks; Charlotte was busy with her preparations while Victoire bustled about the house getting ready for the wedding reception which was to be held there; a few days after the ceremony, Charlotte, with her new husband and Victoire, was to leave for the country, and the house in which Homer had experienced her few weeks of life with Charlotte would casually pass into other hands. Homer had believed that life could not go on in the same pretty pattern, but she had not expected such drastic change.

She had learned that Edward was a very rich man and that, although there would be trips to the capital, they would reside chiefly on his large estate at Ketteringham in Norfolk.

Charlotte was delighted — indeed she was ready to be delighted with everything Edward suggested. Homer was filled with apprehension. She would miss London of which she was growing so fond; she would miss the friends who called so frequently at the house. Would life in Ketteringham be a little like life in St Miniver's? Charlotte would be there, of course, but then so would Sir Edward. She wished she could look forward to the future with the same bland contentment which was Charlotte's.

Early in the morning, as soon as Charlotte was up, actors and actresses invaded the house and insisted on decorating the marriage bed. This was Charlotte's bed which Edward would share with her for the next two nights before they all left for the country.

Homer watched them laughing merrily as they tied green and blue ribbons about the posts, and laid sprigs of rosemary, which they had dipped in scented water, about the bed.

Charlotte, dressed in a gown of white and gold brocaded taffeta, looked very beautiful; and in the general gaiety, Homer tried to convince herself that she had been unfair to Sir Edward, that she had taken too seriously his light flirtatious behaviour, that he *must* make one as charming as Charlotte happy. Yet until after the ceremony she was hoping that something would happen to prevent the marriage.

The guests crowded into the house, all eager to drink the health of the bridal pair, and Homer found herself beside Richard Danver.

'It is long since we have seen you,' she said, thinking he looked a little strained.

'I have been to Paris,' he told her.

'And you were determined to come back

in time for the wedding?' He nodded.

'Charlotte looks very happy,' she said.

'Let us hope she will always be as happy as she is this moment.'

'You sound as though you doubt she can be.'

That mocking light came into his eyes. 'My dear Homer, surely only the most romantic young woman would believe a bride could continue to be as happy as she is on her wedding day. And you? Are you hoping that you will always enjoy the same degree of happiness as you do at this moment? Not you, Homer! I do not think you relish the thought of living in the country. Poor Homer! You will go back to that from which you have just escaped. Bad luck!'

'You seem to think that all I am concerned with is my own future and no one else's.'

'We are all concerned with our own future.'

'If Charlotte is happy, I don't care what happens.'

'Why, Homer, you have turned into a saint.'

'Do not mock me,' she said sharply. Then she smiled with pleasure because she saw Jean Pierre de la Vaugon coming towards them.

'Mademoiselle Homer . . . ' he murmured,

taking her hand and kissing it, while Richard Danver looked on with what she believed to be quiet contempt.

'So you came to England for Charlotte's wedding!' said Homer.

'And to see you.'

Even if she did not believe him it was comforting to hear him say so in front of Richard Danver.

'I am glad you came.'

'A wedding is such a joyful occasion,' he replied.

He asked Richard when he had returned from Paris. Homer listened to their voices without hearing what they said. Her emotions were in a tumult.

Richard left her with Jean Pierre, who said earnestly: 'You are troubled?'

She turned her frank gaze upon him. 'Weddings can be alarming,' she said. 'Everyone congratulates, but how can one be sure whether a wedding is a matter for congratulation or condolence?'

'No one can be sure,' he said. 'That is why there must always be at every wedding — Hope. It is the most important guest.'

'Do you know . . . the bridegroom?'

'I have met him on several occasions.'

'Do you think he will make Charlotte a good husband?'

'He must. Charlotte is worthy of the best.'

'That does not mean she will get it.'

'You have something on your mind. You are worried. Could you not tell me?'

She hesitated and he went on: 'You can trust me, you know.'

'It is not easy here . . . ' she began.

'Come with me,' he begged, and he piloted her through the crowd to a back room and through french windows which opened onto the small garden. There was a seat in the garden and he led her to this. She was glad to escape from the hot rooms into the fresh March sunshine.

'We can talk here,' he said. 'Now, I pray you, tell me.'

His arm was along the back of the seat and she drew comfort from it. 'I fear he is not good enough for Charlotte,' she told him. 'Before he knew who I was he tried to kiss me.'

Jean Pierre smiled gravely. 'Deplorable!' he murmured. 'Yet I cannot blame him.'

'Not blame him when that very day he was to become betrothed to Charlotte!'

'You are very charming, Homer.'

'I thought you would listen to me seriously.'

'I beg your pardon. I listen.'

'What should I have done? Should I have told Charlotte?'

He shook his head. 'What good would you have done, Homer? You would not have prevented the marriage, and you would have made her unhappy.'

'That is what he said. It seems that neither you nor he take this matter, of kissing strangers, seriously.'

'But you are a temptress. I believe you swept him off his feet. You must not judge him too harshly.'

'But I do not!' she cried. 'If he can behave so, he will not make Charlotte the sort of husband she should have.'

'But you . . . with your blazing eyes . . . are quite irresistible.' He had put his arm about her shoulders and was drawing her towards him when she heard a step on the stone path. Richard Danver had come into the garden.

'It is chilly out here,' he said, almost sternly. 'If you wished to sit about you should have brought a wrap.'

She rose, guiltily, she believed; and she was angry with herself for feeling this embarrassment.

'Richard is right,' said Jean Pierre. 'It was thoughtless of me to bring you here.'

They went into the house.

Why, Homer asked herself angrily, does he always feel he has to look after me? For Charlotte's sake, I suppose!

The feast which Victoire had prepared for the guests held no charm for her; she felt depressed when the great bowl was passed round the table and the guests dipped into it the sprigs of rosemary which they had taken to church. She could not enjoy the fun and laughter, and although she joined in the dancing she did this listlessly.

It seemed that the celebrations would never end. But at last the guests had departed, and Homer lay in her bed, knowing that in that other bed, with its sprigs of rosemary and its blue and green ribbons, lay Charlotte with her bridegroom.

★ ★ ★

Homer, sitting in the post-chaise with Victoire, was reminded of that other journey when Richard Danver had sat opposite her. This was the more comfortable method of travelling, but she was far from comfortable.

Ahead of them rode Charlotte and Sir Edward.

Eastward they drove, faster than Homer had ever travelled before. Victoire sat bolt upright, smiling complacently. If only she could feel as hopeful for the future as Victoire did!

Clop-clop went the hoofs of the horses; through towns and villages they passed at the incredible speed of nine miles an hour . . . on to the Atkyns manor house in Ketteringham, on to the new life.

5

They came into Ketteringham in the late afternoon. A woman and child had come to the door of the little cottage by the well at the cross-roads, and they both bobbed curtsies as the carriages passed. Homer saw the church set in the Park and she thought what a charming spot that was for it, with the stream running into the two lakes.

But now she could see the Tudor Manor House itself — grand and imposing, its turrets and battlements dominating the scene.

Charlotte's pleasure was apparent as she alighted and stood enraptured. Homer and Victoire were a few paces behind the married pair, and Homer was desperately trying to share the enthusiasm which everyone else seemed to be feeling.

'Welcome home, my dearest,' she heard Edward say; and she saw Charlotte reach for his hand and hold it tenderly. Watching them, thought Homer, one would say: There is a pair of lovers who have not a thought in the world but for each other.

Then Edward lifted Charlotte in his arms and carried her into the house, Charlotte

110

laughing in that utterly joyous way which had been hers since her betrothal.

In the great hall the servants were lined up, waiting to receive them — the housekeeper at the head of one line, the butler at the head of the other. There was no doubt that Sir Edward was a very rich man and lived in the utmost comfort.

'Lady Atkyns, your new mistress,' cried Sir Edward. 'And with us, Miss Homer Trent, cousin and companion of Lady Atkyns, and Victoire, her personal maid.'

The men-servants bowed from the waist and the women curtsied while Charlotte gave them one of her charming smiles, which, Homer noticed, was received with relief by both butler and housekeeper.

'Now Dexter and Mrs Sudden,' said Edward, addressing the butler and house-keeper, 'something with which to refresh ourselves, please. Tea for the ladies . . . unless you would prefer something stronger, my dear?'

Charlotte said that tea would suit her admirably. Did Homer agree? Homer replied that there was nothing she would like better.

Mrs Sudden took Victoire to show her her quarters, and when the servants had disappeared Edward said: 'Come into the library. We will refresh ourselves there.' He had turned to Homer and held out a hand. Homer would have drawn back, but she felt that to do so would have aroused Charlotte's suspicions, so she went forward; and smiling suavely, Edward slipped his arm through hers. Then he led Homer and Charlotte into the library.

Everything about Ketteringham Manor was luxurious; the great library with its panelled walls and blue velvet curtains with gold fringes, was magnificent. The highly polished furniture, the booklined walls, the rich carpets — everything spoke of luxury.

'It will be a great pleasure to show you two the house later,' said Edward. 'I am rather proud of it.'

'Understandably so,' added Charlotte fondly.

'Homer looks disapproving,' said Edward, laying his hand on her shoulder; his hot fingers seemed to burn through her gown so that it was difficult to resist the impulse to throw him angrily off. 'Homer, my dear, do you think it is wrong to be proud of one's home?'

'I am sure Homer does not,' said Charlotte. 'She is a little bewildered, as I am. We did not expect the Manor to be quite so grand, did we, Homer?'

'No,' replied Homer.

'I hope you are going to like it,' said

112

Edward, and he was looking at Homer.

'As long as Charlotte does, my views are of little importance,' said Homer.

'No!' cried Charlotte. 'It is your home, too. Is it not, Edward?'

'Of course it is.' His eyes gleamed as they met hers. 'Homer, I want you to know that it is my wish that you should be happy here. I intend to make you so . . . even as I do Charlotte.'

'I believe Homer has a foolish feeling that she is *de trop*,' said Charlotte.

'Then,' added Edward, 'we must be particularly loving in order to dispel such a foolish feeling.'

Dexter, the butler, then announced that tea was about to be served. It was brought in by a parlourmaid — a buxom girl with dark curls and sleepy dark eyes; she was so plump that her clothes seemed too tight for her, and she had a manner which was different from that of the other servants — faintly furtive, a little secretive.

'Shall I pour out, sir?' she asked, and Homer was in time to see the glance she threw in Sir Edward's direction.

'Ask her ladyship,' replied Edward coolly.

'I think I should like to do it myself,' said Charlotte.

'That will do then, Betsy,' went on Sir

Edward; and the girl dropped a curtsy and went out.

Charlotte said: 'I wanted to do it myself . . . the first time in my new home. I am going to be rather sentimental about it, I'm afraid, because I know I am going to be happy here . . . happier than I have ever been in my life.'

Homer was afraid her hand would tremble as she took the tea from Edward; she did so without looking at him.

The atmosphere of the Manor House was oppressive.

My poor Charlotte! she thought. If you could sense the future as I can you would not feel so lighthearted.

It seemed to her that the entire house mocked her; she found herself remembering the look in the eyes of the serving girl, Betsy; and she thought she understood the meaning of it.

* * *

If happiness and serenity had depended on creature comforts, Ketteringham Manor would have been for Homer all that it was for Charlotte.

Even though it was April, fires were lighted in the bedrooms at night and again in

114

the mornings. Homer remembered waking on wintry mornings in the parsonage; she recalled again her reluctance to wash in the water which Mab or Belle had brought to her and which she knew would be cold before she could use it. She remembered the chill of the dining-room. How different it was in Ketteringham Manor!

Her bedroom was large, and the big windows overlooked the lawns. Her bed was an elaborate affair with velvet hangings; and the valances were fringed with gold. On a carved and gilded table was a beautiful mirror with a frame of mother-of-pearl. There was a small sofa in the room covered in green damask, and chairs to match. Never had Homer slept in — or even seen — such a beautiful room; and yet when she stood alone in it, she longed for the comfort of her little room in Charlotte's house.

Sir Edward had shown them over the house and Charlotte had declared it to be the loveliest in the world; she was ready, she said, to settle down to her new idyllic existence.

Strange, thought Homer, that she should be the one to long for Drury Lane and the colour and gaiety of London. Here were green fields bright with April flowers; and from her window she could see miles of flat green country; she could see the stream which flowed into the two lakes in the Park and then went on its way to join the River Yare. It was beautiful and the house was luxurious; but she could feel nothing but a desire to return to the days before she had known of the existence of Sir Edward Atkyns; she longed for the gay, unconventional days, for the journeys to and from the theatre, and jaunts with Richard Danver and Jean Pierre.

Often she thought of those two, and such thoughts did not make her happier. I feel so alone, she told herself; there is no one whose advice I could ask if I needed it.

What was the meaning of this strange depression, this feeling that tragedy was looming over them, that it was her duty to protect Charlotte? Absurd! She felt it merely because Edward had tried to flirt with her!

She tried to share Charlotte's pleasure in the new life.

In the mornings breakfast was served in the breakfast room and one went down and helped oneself; Homer always contrived to be early in order to avoid Sir Edward.

It was not difficult to fill the days. She often rode out with Charlotte and Edward; and sometimes when Edward went out by himself, for he liked to manage certain estate affairs personally, she and Charlotte would be alone together; and those were the times she liked best.

There were callers at the Manor and calls to be made. Edward, now that he had a wife, wished to live the life of a country squire, which meant that there would be a great deal of entertaining at the Manor House. Charlotte brought all that enthusiasm to the task of being the perfect wife of a country gentleman that she had given to becoming an actress.

During those days Homer began to understand Charlotte as she never had before. Charlotte needed something . . . someone in her life to worship. She must have something to aim for. That was why she had wanted to be an actress; in the same way she now strove to be the perfect wife. Yet how easily she had given up the stage — although at one time she had left her comfortable home for it. Perhaps one day she might have some other enthusiasm, something she longed to do which would make her forget the desire to be the perfect wife to such an imperfect husband.

On the second day after their arrival there was a visitor at the house. Homer was alone when she came; Edward had taken Charlotte for a ride.

Dexter came to the library where Homer was reading and announced that Mrs Frinton had called. 'Shall I show her in, Miss?'

'I dare say she has called to see Sir Edward or Lady Atkyns,' began Homer.

'Oh yes, Miss, but seeing they're not at home . . .'

Dexter seemed half anxious, half amused, as though there was something extraordinary about Mrs Frinton; and Homer was surprised when a tall, handsome and very elegant woman was ushered in.

'My cousin, Lady Atkyns, is out riding with Sir Edward,' said Homer, taking the proffered hand. 'I do not think they will be very long. I do hope you will wait. And in the meantime will you take some refreshment?'

Mrs Frinton said that she would take no refreshment but that she would wait.

'Then do please sit down,' invited Homer.

'Sir Edward is a great friend of mine,' said Mrs Frinton. 'My place is on the borders of the estate. This is really only a neighbourly call to welcome Lady Atkyns.'

'She will be delighted that you called,' murmured Homer politely, 'and so sorry if she misses you.'

'You, too, were an . . . actress?'

'No. I lived with my cousin, though.'

'I see. We were surprised to hear of the

118

marriage. It happened so quickly. I hear Lady Atkyns comes from a Norfolk family.'

'Oh yes. There have been Walpoles in Norfolk for years.'

'I suppose she is very beautiful?'

'Very.'

Mrs Frinton seemed to realize that this was not quite the polite conversation which was expected of her and began to talk of life in the country and how she hoped Homer would come to the next Hunt Ball.

Some fifteen minutes later Sir Edward and Charlotte came in. Homer felt proud of Charlotte, who looked delightful in her riding habit, her cheeks flushed with exercise and her eyes shining with that happiness which Edward's company always gave her.

'Why ... Anthea!' said Edward; and Homer watched him intently as he went forward and took the woman's hand in his. She was aware of a certain tension between them.

'I called on the newly-weds,' said Anthea Frinton lightly.

'So good of you to do so,' murmured Edward. 'Charlotte, my dear, this is Mrs Frinton ... a great friend. I want you two to be fond of each other.'

'I am sure we shall be,' said the unsuspicious Charlotte, glowing under the scrutiny of Anthea Frinton.

'You will drink a glass of wine?' asked Edward.

'I certainly must drink to your future,' replied Mrs Frinton. She turned to Charlotte. 'We were all surprised when we heard of the wedding. Edward was very secretive with his own friends.'

'Ah!' cried Edward. 'I was afraid she wouldn't have me. Look at her! Can you not understand my trepidation? The most beautiful woman in the world . . . famous . . . fêted . . . You can imagine my fears. I would not talk of it until it was a *fait accompli.*'

'I believe,' smiled Mrs Frinton, 'that the odious man is asking for compliments.'

'He is quite absurd!' said Charlotte, lovingly.

And Homer went to the bell rope.

Betsy eventually appeared. Her slumberous dark eyes seemed to ignite as they fell on Mrs Frinton.

'Wine, Betsy,' said Edward.

'Yes, Sir Edward.' Something seemed to flash between them. 'A special occasion,' went on Edward. 'I will myself select something very special. Our first caller — and a very dear friend — comes to drink our health!' He turned and included them all in one of his most charming smiles — Homer, Mrs Frinton and Charlotte. 'You will excuse me, I know.'

He followed Betsy from the room. Homer was sure she saw a smile touch Betsy's lips — a smile of satisfaction, of triumph?

Mrs Frinton turned to Charlotte, and Homer thought she looked like a great cat, purring softly to hide the fierceness of the emotion she was feeling.

★ ★ ★

The next day Sir Ralph and Lady Dunkely called at the Manor. Charlotte and Homer were in the garden and came in to receive them.

Sir Ralph was clearly enchanted by Charlotte's beauty; Lady Dunkely was inclined to be critical. An actress! she was obviously thinking. How could Sir Edward marry an actress when there were so many eligible girls in the county?

She scarcely looked at Homer, immediately placing her as a poor relation.

Sir Edward let loose his charm upon them and the bell-rope was pulled to summon a servant. This time Dexter himself came, and Sir Edward did not make a journey to the cellar to select the wine. Dexter brought it,

121

and glasses were filled and the health of bride and bridegroom drunk.

'So sudden!' complained Lady Dunkely.

And Edward made his speech once more about fearing that the beautiful Charlotte could not really mean she would accept him. Homer asked herself if he learned his gallant speeches off by heart. Was that why he was able to bring them out so neatly at the required moment?

'You were very fortunate,' Sir Ralph told him. 'Your bride is both beautiful and charming.'

'I am perfectly happy,' said Charlotte, smiling at Edward.

'As soon as we have settled in we shall have a ball,' said Edward. 'Charlotte is longing to show you how she is going to entertain us all.'

'Are you going to sing for us, Lady Atkyns?' asked Sir Ralph.

'If you wish it.'

'She has a beautiful voice,' volunteered Homer.

'Yes,' said Lady Dunkely, 'we have heard all about your being on the stage. You were a bold girl!' She lifted her finger playfully. 'You ran away from home to go on the stage. Something dreadful might have happened to you.'

'Well, she did marry me,' put in Edward.

Lady Dunkely laughed. She clearly thought that Charlotte — whom she was ready to accept because, although she was an actress, she was one of the Norfolk Walpoles — had made an excellent match.

'It is to be hoped,' said Sir Ralph, 'that Clare will be home in time for the ball.'

'Clare?' said Edward. 'The last time I saw her she was perched up a tree.'

'Mischievous tomboy!' murmured Lady Dunkely. 'I promise you that the next time you see her she will *not* be up a tree.'

'I should hope not,' said Clare's father. 'If she has not learned how to behave at her finishing school, why have I been paying these wicked bills for two years?'

'Clare took a long time to grow up, Edward,' said Lady Dunkely, 'but now she has, believe me.'

'I shall look forward to meeting Clare,' said Charlotte.

'And she will most certainly look forward to meeting you. She is so fond of Edward.'

They were all fond of Edward, Homer believed; fond of his riches; and they were a little angry, all of them, with Charlotte for marrying him. As for herself, they did not consider her to be of any importance, so they were only mildly polite to her.

It seemed that lots of people had had plans concerning Edward. The Dunkelys possibly for their Clare. Mrs Frinton? Betsy?

How suspicious I am growing! thought Homer.

And when she looked at Edward, so charming to all, so tender to Charlotte, so anxious that she, Homer, should not be made to feel outside the circle of their friendship, she asked herself: Am I being fair to Edward? Am I building up a situation in my mind which does not exist?

★ ★ ★

The days passed quickly. May had come; the evenings were getting longer and Homer was awakened every morning by the birdsong. She liked to walk by herself across the fields and sit on the banks of the stream among the goose grass and the stitchwort.

She was conscious of a growing desire to escape from something. This is how she had felt in the parsonage at St Miniver's. I don't belong here, she told herself, any more than I belonged there. I am living under *his* roof, dependent on him. There are times when I think he remembers this and relishes it.

But she had sworn to stay with Charlotte

124

and she could not desert her, for she was quite certain that one day Charlotte would need her . . . desperately, and she had to be beside her then.

And yet, each day she found the atmosphere more oppressive, each day she felt the tension increasing, the shadow growing, coming nearer.

There was to be a ball at the house — their first since the wedding — and Charlotte was anxious that it should be a success. Invitations had gone out to the whole countryside. Homer pictured the occasion: the spacious ballroom with its great central chandelier and the smaller ones ranged at intervals; the flowers with which the ballroom would be decorated; Edward standing beside Charlotte, introducing her to their guests, and all the critical eyes which would be on Charlotte, the actress whom eligible Sir Edward had married.

'I should feel angry with these people,' Homer told Charlotte, 'if they turned their quizzing glasses on me. But all you do is smile serenely at them as though you have not the slightest objection.'

'Nor have I,' answered Charlotte. 'I feel quite pleased to be stared at. I do not greatly care what they think of me. I know that Edward loves me. That is enough. When

125

you fall in love, Homer, you will understand what I mean.'

'I think,' said Homer, 'I understand now.'

How she loves him! she thought. That is what frightens me. And it was because of this fear that she found such pleasure in solitude out of doors during that lovely springtime.

She returned one late afternoon to find Charlotte waiting for her.

'Miss Craddock is in the sewing-room,' said Charlotte. 'She wants to fit you. Edward and I are going out for a ride. Do go to Miss Craddock now.'

So Homer went to Miss Craddock who was sitting stitching by the window to get the best of the light.

'I am sorry I kept you waiting,' said Homer. She was truly sorry for Miss Craddock, who always looked as though her eyes would one day disappear into her head, so weary would they be of their close work.

Miss Craddock smiled brightly at Homer. It was not often that her clients were as obliging as Lady Atkyns and her cousin.

'It is such a pleasure to work at the Manor now,' she said.

'You are ready for me to try on the gown?' asked Homer.

Miss Craddock rose and Homer slipped

out of her dress and put on the one which was being made for the ball. Charlotte had insisted on her having a new dress. It was such an important occasion, she said; and the things which Homer had acquired in London had been so hastily run up that she wanted her to have something really grand.

'Do not forget,' Charlotte had said, 'we are much richer now.'

Homer had protested. She did not wish to accept gifts from Charlotte's husband, she explained; at which Charlotte was hurt. 'Homer,' she said, 'I do wish you would not feel like that about Edward. It is so . . . unfriendly.'

'My black and emerald will do very well,' Homer insisted. 'Nobody wants to look at me, in any case.'

'What nonsense! You must have a proper ball dress. You are my cousin, are you not? Would you disgrace me?'

And so insistent had Charlotte become that Homer had felt she must give way or explain her aversion towards Edward and the reason for it.

But, she had thought, I can see this situation becoming more and more repugnant.

It was a beautiful dress of silk and lace — the silk cerise colour, the lace cream.

Her soft and rounded shoulders would be exposed, and the silk was drawn in tightly at the waist from which tier upon tier of silk and lace flowed out as though their intention was not so much to call attention to their own magnificence as to that youthful and very feminine waist and bust enclosed in the tightly fitting bodice. She looked dainty and very feminine — a decorative young lady of leisure.

'My!' said Miss Craddock. 'You are going to be the belle of the ball.'

'What! With Lady Atkyns there!'

'Well, you'll be one of the prettiest young ladies, I'll swear.'

Poor Miss Craddock! thought Homer. She must have spent her life saying flattering things to clients.

'What a lot of work in all these frills and flounces,' she said. 'Do your eyes ever ache, Miss Craddock?'

'Oh, you get used to it, Miss. Do you know how many years I've been sewing for ladies?'

'Tell me,' said Homer.

'Forty. Started when I was eleven. Used to come here with my mother. I remember standing and holding the pins and scissors for her. It was Sir Edward's mother we were working for. Making a ball dress for her, see?

She was just married . . . like the present Lady Atkyns. Turn a little to the right, Miss, would you? There! I'm not quite sure of the set of that bodice.'

The next ten minutes were spent in pinning and measuring. Conversation was difficult because Miss Craddock's mouth was full of pins; and while she stood there, Homer's thoughts were not on the dress or on the coming ball; she was thinking of Miss Craddock, coming to the house to make her first gown for Edward's mother. Miss Craddock must know a lot about the family — about Edward.

When she had taken off the ball dress and was back in her everyday gown, she lingered to talk to Miss Craddock, who, sitting in the window seat to make use of the daylight, seemed pleased that Homer should wish to talk to her.

'All those years,' said Homer, 'you have been working here. What was the other Lady Atkyns like . . . Sir Edward's mother?'

Miss Craddock put her head on one side and hesitated, although her busy fingers did not stop. 'Not as beautiful as the present Lady Atkyns, nor as gentle. Although in the beginning she was kind.'

'And she grew less kind?'

'Poor lady, she had so much to put up with.'

'Why was that?'

Miss Craddock hesitated again. She looked at Homer and wondered whether it was wise to tell her of family scandals.

Homer sensed this and said with a laugh: 'I am very discreet, you know.' She thought: This would not be considered good taste. I should not try to uncover family secrets. But Charlotte's happiness is of more importance to me than a matter of taste. And who knows, by knowing a great deal more than I do at present, I may be able to help. It would be foolish — if the best of taste — to let an opportunity like this slip by.

Miss Craddock seemed to assess Homer as a sort of upper servant, not unlike herself. 'Well,' she said at length, 'it was Sir Edward, the present Sir Edward's father. He had his weaknesses . . . ' Miss Craddock paused and then went on, because she found it so difficult to resist a gossip: 'The bottle and the ladies. No one was safe from him when he had drunk too freely. Why, even . . . me!' She tittered. 'Well, one kept out of his way, you understand. The word went round. Poor Lady Atkyns, it soured her.'

'I see,' said Homer. 'I can imagine it would.'

'Very difficult to work for, she was. Nothing satisfied her. She would make you unpick something because of an imagined fault. Ugh! I can tell you it was no fun working at the Manor in those days.'

Homer, glancing out of the window, saw Sir Edward and Charlotte riding towards the stables. She realized then that she must have been with Miss Craddock for about an hour. She looked at the sky and guessed they had returned because it was overcast and rain appeared to be imminent.

'Drat the dark!' murmured Miss Craddock. 'If it gets much worse I'll have to have the candles lighted. And I can't a-bear doing work by candlelight.'

There were shadows in the room now as Homer said: 'The present Lady Atkyns is not a bit like the last one. What about the present Sir Edward, does he take after his father?'

Miss Craddock gave a short laugh. 'Oh, Miss, they are so much alike, you wouldn't know one from t'other.'

'You mean . . . they *look* alike?'

'Yes, they look alike, too, Miss. I'm afraid I'll have to have the candles lighted.'

'I'll ring,' said Homer.

Betsy answered the bell. She said almost insolently: 'Well, what is it?'

'Lights,' said Homer. 'Miss Craddock cannot see to sew.'

'It's not my job to look after the sewing-woman,' grumbled Betsy.

Homer felt angry. 'You will light the candles immediately,' she said sharply.

Betsy flushed and hesitated; then she said: 'All right, Miss, only . . . '

'Please don't argue,' retorted Homer. 'Light them at once.'

The room looked sinister in candlelight, thought Homer. Miss Craddock had now taken her seat by the table, a candle beside her, and Homer went to the window to watch the black clouds scudding by.

'There's such a wind,' she said, 'otherwise it would pour. That girl is insolent,' she added.

'Can you wonder,' replied Miss Craddock. 'I remember a maid they had twenty years ago. Betsy reminds me of her. Pretty girl she was and pleasant, until she started giving herself airs. She had to leave in a hurry. She was married off to one of the farm labourers. That was how it was.'

'I see. And that's what might happen to Betsy . . . you think?'

'I think it's likely, Miss. The trouble is that when they're . . . noticed . . . they give themselves airs. She was rude to Mrs Frinton once. There was a bit of a to-do, I can tell you.'

It was easier to ask indiscreet questions by candlelight.

'And Mrs Frinton is a special friend of Sir Edward's, is she not?'

'*Very* special, Miss,' said Miss Craddock significantly.

They fell silent. Homer had learned so much during that conversation that she felt she had confirmed her worst fears.

★ ★ ★

She left Miss Craddock and was on her way to her room. To reach this from the sewing-room she had to pass through the gallery in which were displayed paintings of the Atkyns family.

The gallery looked ghostly in this light. Through the long windows she could see the darkening angry sky; it cast shadows on the tall pictures and in some strange way seemed to add life to the men and women portrayed there.

She stood before a portrait which she knew to be that of the present Sir Edward's father. Yes, the resemblance was there. This must have been painted when he was at least ten years older than his son was now. There were the marks of debauchery clearly to be seen on his face. Or did she imagine that because of Miss Craddock's insinuations? She could almost imagine that he was leering at her from the frame. And how like the man in the Green Room he was!

She started violently and began to tremble, for there was a movement behind her and a voice said: 'Getting acquainted with the family?'

She swung round. It was very like that moment in the Green Room. There he stood, smiling at her, the same greedy look in his eyes.

'Family portraits are interesting,' she said, trying to force a light note into her voice. 'You are remarkably like your father.'

'You think so, eh? He was considered a gay dog.'

She tried to move away but, as on that other occasion, he was preventing her from doing so.

'As . . . you no doubt are,' she added.

'Well, men will be men, you know.'

'I know nothing about that.'

'Then, my dear and most fierce Homer, it is time you began to learn.'

'Why should I bother to learn that which is not of the slightest interest to me?'

'Because if you took a few lessons you

would find how interesting it could be.'

'I think I am the best judge of that. I must go now. I have things to do.'

'You think you hate me, do you not?' he asked.

'There is no need to think very much about it.'

'Oh, Homer, why are you such an attractive little devil? It makes life so complicated. I should have preferred you to be a plain little mouse. Then you would not have tempted me.'

'I fancy you fall quickly into temptation.'

He shrugged his shoulders. 'Homer, you can be discreet. You have proved that to me.'

'It was much against my will. If I could have prevented Charlotte from marrying you, I would.'

'You are so intense. Never mind. I like it. So fiercely determined to hold aloft the banner of virtue. That is because you do not know what you miss.'

'Sir Edward,' said Homer, 'understand now and for ever. I am not Betsy. I am not Mrs Frinton. So do not imagine that I am prepared to deceive Charlotte with you. You should be careful. I might tell Charlotte what I know.'

'Charlotte is my wife,' he answered.

'Nothing can alter that. And do not imagine that you will always feel as you do at this moment.'

'What will change me?'

Again she felt his hands on her shoulders. 'I shall, virtuous, angry Homer.'

'Take your hands away.'

'Not until you have kissed me. Come, let us have a truce. I like your fierceness. It makes it more fun to do battle for what one wants. I would not have you fall too easily into my hands. The relationship between us will not be like that. That is why I look forward to it so much.'

While he had been speaking her anger had been rising. She pushed him away with all her might, so that he reeled against the picture of his grandfather. Then she ran as fast as she could out of the darkening gallery.

She reached the bedroom and locked the door, remembering the inn at Exeter and the sardonic lights in the eyes of Richard Danver.

This lock would keep her safe at night — unless, of course, he had duplicate keys to the doors.

She shivered at the thought.

How can I stay in this house . . . with him? she asked herself. Yet how can I leave Charlotte?

6

Next morning Homer was up early. She was the first down to breakfast and then went to the stables to ask one of the grooms to saddle a horse for her. She wanted to get away from the house to be alone with her thoughts; she wanted to find some solution to her problem.

But even as she reached the stables she thought: It would be one of *his* horses that I should ride. Everything in this place belongs to him. Is that why he thinks that we all do . . . even I?

She did not take the horse; instead she wandered along by the stream to the lakes; she sat on a stile and stared broodingly at the green fields studded with cowslips, daisies and buttercups. She was reminded of the fields about the parsonage, and she thought: I never then had such a pressing problem to face. Then I knew I must get away some time; now I know I must get away soon.

She wanted to stay outside all the morning, for the heavy rain of the previous night had freshened the countryside so that it was even more beautiful than before.

When she returned to the Manor and went up to her room, Charlotte came to her.

'It was such a lovely morning after the rain,' she explained. 'I was up early and went walking.'

'What a creature you are for early morning walks! I have some news, Homer.'

'Good news?'

'The best possible. I am not sure yet . . . but almost. I do not want to say anything to Edward until I am absolutely sure, because it would be such a disappointment if I were wrong.'

'I understand,' said Homer.

'Is that all you have to say? But is it not marvellous . . . if it is so, of course!'

'You should wait until you are sure before you begin to rejoice too much.'

'So cautious! That's not like you, Homer.'

'What I mean is . . . if it is so, it is wonderful, and I am happy for you. But, Charlotte, I do not want you to be disappointed.'

Charlotte put an arm about Homer and held her closely against her. 'Sometimes,' she said, 'I think I have too much happiness.'

'Enjoy it,' Homer advised her sombrely, 'while you have it.'

'How gloomy you have become! Homer, I

have been watching you. There is something on your mind.'

'Yes,' said Homer quickly. 'It is this: I . . . I don't think there is really a place for me here.'

'Not a place for you! But that's ridiculous!'

'It was different in London. There I felt I was useful. I helped Victoire and I helped you. Here you are surrounded by servants and there is nothing for me to do.'

'But you can ride; you can read; you can call on people; you can dance at our balls.'

'I do not feel I am earning my keep.'

'But you are with your own people!'

'I am not Edward's 'people'.'

'You are mine, and I am Edward's wife. I can assure you that Edward is delighted to have you here. He often says so.'

'All the same . . . '

Charlotte frowned. 'You are not to talk like that, Homer. If you do you will spoil everything — and all else is quite perfect.'

'Is it?' said Homer wistfully.

'Absolutely. And if *this* is really true . . . What more could I ask? Homer, please don't get ideas about our not wanting you. We both want you; and if you went away I should be so unhappy. Have you forgotten our talk? I thought we were always going to be together.'

'We did say so, but things are different here.'

'Please, Homer, promise me. No more nonsense.'

'No more nonsense,' Homer agreed, for how could she tell Charlotte what was in her mind? How could she shatter such happiness as this? How could she turn glowing Charlotte into a suspicious woman resembling that sour, sad and unhappy one who had also been Lady Atkyns?

* * *

Homer felt safer during the days before the ball. The house was full. Charlotte's sisters, Mary and Frances, with their husbands had come over to Ketteringham to stay for a week, and Charlotte was delighted to have them with her. There were other guests in the house and Homer saw little of Sir Edward.

Charlotte was now sure that she was going to have a child and Sir Edward was delighted; he was very solicitous for Charlotte's health and Homer began to understand why he had married her. He was fond of her in his way — but he was too fond of all women, Homer believed, to be very fond of one. Charlotte had seemed to him an ideal wife, because she was beautiful and accomplished, and she came from one of the best families in Norfolk. He might have found someone of as good a family, but where could he have found a woman as lovely as Charlotte? He had married her that she might give him the heir he wanted and leave him free to philander where he would.

Two days before the ball Homer was in the orchard trying to read in order to stop her mind turning over the eternal question. On that sunny morning the orchards were very pleasant and the apple trees were rosy with blossom, the cherry trees white with it. As she was leaning against a tree she heard someone approaching; such sounds had alarmed her ever since Sir Edward had come upon her in the gallery, and she leaped to her feet ready to hurry away, if it were he.

A figure appeared among the trees and for a moment she thought she must be mistaken, for it was Richard Danver who was coming towards her.

'Good morning, Homer,' he said and bowed ironically. 'Why do you look startled? Did you think I was a ghost?'

'I did not expect to see you.'

'On the other hand I knew I should find you here. Charlotte told me you were in the gardens, and one of the gardeners said he had seen you come to the orchards. So I knew it was only a matter of looking.'

'Charlotte did not tell me you were coming.'

'She did not know, herself, until I arrived. I had been invited to the ball but did not think business would permit. But here I am. Well, Homer, are you glad to see me?'

'Yes . . . yes . . . I think so.'

'You do not sound very sure. But you are always frank. That is good. Anyone else would have said 'Delighted!' however wearisome they found my arrival. I must say you seem to live very comfortably here. How do you like it?'

She hesitated and he looked surprised. 'Are you going to tell me again that you are not sure?' he went on. 'That is strange, because I have always thought you were the sort of person to make up your mind quickly and be very sure about most things in life.'

Then suddenly she blurted out: 'I'm glad you've come.'

It was the sunshine, the scent of blossom and the song of a blackbird that made her feel so happy. Perhaps there was relief in her happiness. She had longed to be with someone whose advice she could ask, whom she could trust. She knew that, however this man might mock her, if it were a question of Charlotte's happiness, he would give her

142

very serious consideration and do all in his power to help.

'Everything is not right, Homer?' he asked.

'Did you ask Charlotte?' she demanded.

'Charlotte told me she was perfectly happy. She seemed quite blissful.'

'There is such a thing as blissful ignorance.'

'And when that state exists it has been said that it is folly to be wise. Homer, what is worrying you?'

She indicated a fallen tree. 'Let us sit there,' she said. 'We should see if anyone were coming.'

'How mysterious you have become!' But he followed her to the tree and they sat down.

'I am afraid for Charlotte,' she began at once. 'I do not think that this marriage is all that she believes it to be.'

'This marriage,' he murmured, staring at the toe of his shoe; 'everyone seems to think it is a very fine match indeed. Charlotte has become Lady Atkyns, the wife of one of the richest men in the county of Norfolk. She lives here in luxury with her indulgent husband.'

'And,' added Homer, 'she is to have a child.'

'I had not heard of this latest addition to her bliss.' His face was turned from Homer and she believed she detected a trace of bitterness in his voice.

'You will hear very soon,' said Homer. 'But I want you to tell me what I ought to do. I am very worried. I am afraid Charlotte's happiness will not endure. He is not the man she believes him to be.'

'Ah!' said Richard.

'I believe he drinks more than is good for him, but that is by no means the worst of it. There is a woman here . . . a neighbour . . . and there is a servant girl.'

Richard nodded.

'If Charlotte discovered,' went on Homer, 'she would be heartbroken. She has set him upon a pedestal. Charlotte must not discover . . . not yet. Perhaps when the child is born she will not care so much. Then at least she will have her baby. I want to keep Charlotte in ignorance of what is happening.'

Richard smiled. 'You must not worry so much, Homer,' he said. 'Charlotte made this marriage. If she has acted unwisely she will have to know eventually. You can do nothing about it.'

'But that is not all. Charlotte and I once said that we would never be separated, and now . . . I want to leave here. In fact, I do not think I can stay.'

'You . . . Homer!' he began, and she saw

the horror in his face.

'I must tell you this: I saw him once in the Green Room when I had taken a cloak there for Charlotte. It was before I had been introduced to him. He tried to kiss me and I slapped his face.'

Richard smiled faintly.

She went on: 'It is nothing to smile about. It was far from amusing. Then Charlotte brought him home and told me he was the man she was going to marry. I said nothing to her. I wonder now whether I ought to have told her. I did not know what to do. I am afraid I am very ignorant. However, I kept silent, and so they were married. And now . . . '

'He has begun to persecute you . . . in this house?'

'There was one occasion. He suggested that we ought to be 'friends'. He seemed to be confident that eventually we should be. I told him I hated him and he merely laughed at me. Richard, I am afraid of him. I am afraid to stay in this house.'

'The . . . *swine*!' said Richard, with quick intensity.

'You see,' she went on, relief flooding her voice, because it was wonderful to confide in someone, and most of all in him, for he had always seemed so certain of his powers to deal with any matter, 'you see, Richard, I cannot stay here, and yet . . . how can I go away? I have told Charlotte I want to, and she won't hear of it. And of course it is quite impossible to explain. Tell me what I ought to do.'

He was silent for a long time and she knew that he was very angry.

Then he murmured: 'Poor Charlotte. *Poor* Charlotte!'

'Should I tell her?'

He shook his head. 'She will find out all too soon. I hope with you that it will be after she has her child. I know Charlotte well. She will divert all her devotion to that child. It will save her suffering great anguish. Let us hope that she does not discover what sort of man she has married until she has become a mother.'

It seemed to Homer that he had not yet considered *her* problem. All he could think about was the wrong done to Charlotte.

'We must keep this from Charlotte as long as possible,' he was saying.

'That is what I thought. That is why I cannot explain to her why I must leave here.'

'Yes,' he mused, 'you must leave here. The affairs with other women she might endure. But if she found you and him . . . '

146

Homer leaped to her feet. 'What are you suggesting? That I would be a party to his hateful suggestions?'

He was by her side, towering over her from his great height.

'How angry you quickly become, Homer,' he said. 'You have not changed since our old coaching days. You haven't changed a bit!'

'I feel sorry now,' she retorted, 'that I asked your advice. I see that you have none to give me. You can only think of Charlotte.'

With that she turned from him and walked away.

'Homer,' he called, 'come back. We'll think of something.'

'Thank you,' she cried, over her shoulder, 'I can look after myself.'

Then suddenly she hated the May sunshine; she hated the scent of the pink and white blossom and the tuneful song of the blackbird.

★ ★ ★

In the blaze of the chandeliers the ballroom looked brilliant. Charlotte, radiant in a gown of oyster-coloured satin, stood beside Sir Edward, greeting their guests.

Homer, watching her, wondered how much

147

longer she could continue in her happiness.

As for herself she could find little pleasure in the occasion. Anxious as she was concerning Charlotte, she felt singularly depressed on her own account. Ever since the encounter in the orchard with Richard Danver she had felt thus; she could not forget that he had been almost uninterested in her position and only considered it in its relation to Charlotte.

What had she expected? When she looked back over their acquaintance she was forced to admit that the only time he had shown any interest in her was when Charlotte had asked him to do so. He had guarded her on the coach — at Charlotte's request; he had taken her on a trip through London — again because Charlotte had asked him. Why then should she be so hurt because, when she asked his advice about this matter which concerned Charlotte as well as herself, he should think only of Charlotte?

She was young; she had a beautiful ball dress and this was her first ball. She should be happy.

Yet even the dress, which had appeared magnificent in the solitude of her bedroom, now seemed insignificant in this dazzling company. There was Mrs Frinton, very striking in peacock-blue velvet with sapphires at her throat and ears. The Dunkelys had come, and with them was the daughter of whom she had heard.

So this was Clare. She was about seventeen and certainly very pretty with wide babyish blue eyes and golden hair. She was dressed in pale blue which matched her eyes, and there was a string of pearls about her neck and more pearls wound in her hair. She had a high-pitched voice which was distinctly audible, and she stressed certain words — which struck Homer as absurdly babyish. Homer took a dislike to Clare on the spot.

'Oh, Edward,' she was saying, 'how could you? I shall never forgive you . . . *never!* So *you* are Edward's wife? But you're *beautiful!* All the same, Edward did promise to marry *me!* I know I was only six at the time, but I regarded that promise as binding.'

Sir Ralph and Lady Dunkely looked on at this display with great amusement and admiration. It was obvious that they thought their daughter wonderful.

Edward said: 'She's a scheming woman, Charlotte. We shall have to beware of her.' Homer thought she detected in his voice a note of caress which she had noticed when he had spoken to herself.

Could this child be another? she thought.

Charlotte was calling to her.

'I want you to meet my cousin, Homer Trent,' she told Clare. 'You and she should be friends. You are of an age.'

Homer found herself looking into what she considered a vapid pair of blue eyes. Her own, she guessed, were far from friendly.

'I have just come from my finishing school,' said Clare. 'Have you?'

'No,' said Homer. 'I never went to one. I was taught by my father's curate.'

'How . . . *odd!*' said Clare, and her gaze strayed about the room; it rested invitingly on two young men who came over to her. She allowed them to lead her away.

'I am not sorry,' said Homer to Charlotte, 'that I did not go to a finishing school if that is an example of the finished product.'

Charlotte smiled. 'Stay near me, Homer,' she said. 'I want you to meet all these people too. You look very attractive in that dress.'

'To be truthful,' said Homer, 'I thought I did until I saw the rest of you.'

'And your hair looks lovely.'

'Victoire had great difficulty in doing it. I only hope it remains where it has been put for the rest of the evening.'

'Edward,' said Charlotte, 'do you not think that Homer looks delightful?'

His eyes swept over her and lingered at

her throat. 'Indeed I do,' he murmured. 'Homer, as soon as I have an opportunity of escaping from my duties, you and I will dance together.'

Charlotte smiled at them, so innocently delighted to see what she thought of as Edward's affection for her cousin.

And now here was Richard Danver. He looked taller than ever, thought Homer; he even looked elegant and handsome.

'You look very beautiful, Charlotte,' he said. 'All success to the ball.'

'Thank you, Richard. It was wonderful that you were able to get here. Here's Homer. Doesn't she look adorable? It's her first ball. You must look after her.'

The colour was high in Homer's cheeks. 'I am quite capable of looking after myself, Charlotte,' she said tartly.

'Of course!' cried Charlotte. 'Then look after Richard. He says occasions like this are not much in his line.'

'I am sure he is as capable of looking after himself as I am!'

'We must not forget Charlotte's command,' said Richard lightly.

Homer caught the eye of an elderly man who had been watching her. She smiled and he was at her side.

'I know you,' he said. 'You are Lady

Atkyns's cousin. The musicians are about to play a minuet. I hope I may have the pleasure.'

Homer put her hand into his extended one.

'I shall be delighted,' she said; and without a glance she left Richard.

★ ★ ★

But he was determined that she should not escape him, and she was aware that he watched her continuously.

Somewhat to her surprise she did not lack partners, and temporarily she forgot Charlotte's trouble and her own predicament. She was finding that, contrary to her expectations, she was not unattractive; her vivacity seemed to amuse, and her looks, if not conventionally beautiful, were arresting.

It's this gown, she told herself. Anyone would look attractive in a gown like this.

She enjoyed dancing and the music excited her. Moreover there was the pleasure — and it was a distinct pleasure — of this battle with Richard; evading him, letting him see that she had no lack of partners, that she did not need him to look after her at a ball, as both he and Charlotte seemed to think she did.

She had not danced with Sir Edward; he had so many duty dances to take up his time, as had Charlotte. For a few hours then, she would forget the past and the future, and enjoy herself. But Richard could not be evaded for ever.

There was a lull in the music and she found him at her side, gripping her elbow.

'You have not forgotten, Homer,' he said. 'This you have promised to me.'

'But . . .'

He had steered her away from the man to whom she had been talking.

'Well,' he went on, 'if you did not promise, you should have done so. As I particularly want to talk to you, you should give me some opportunity of doing so.'

'I was just telling Sir James that I would dance this dance with him.'

'Poor Sir James! Let us hope he finds consolation.'

'Well, what is this you wish to say to me?'

'It is too important to speak of while we are dancing. Afterwards we will have supper together. Then we may find our opportunity.'

'I am growing curious.'

'Then for the moment will you also grow lenient. I am afraid I am not a good dancer.'

'I do not think I am either.'

'You seem to have been putting up a good performance.'

'We danced in the parsonage, but of course we did not learn the *new* dances. Charlotte gave me a lesson or so during last week.'

'She must have been a good teacher, or you are a natural dancer.'

The dance separated them and as Homer turned she found herself facing Sir Edward.

'You look enchanting . . . ' he said. She set her lips in a stern line. ' . . . when you smile at Mr Danver,' he added.

She noticed that he was flushed and that his eyes gleamed at her, not quite so greedily as they had in the Green Room and the gallery. He was being cautious in public.

Richard had noticed the change in her expression, and when he touched her hand, the pressure of his fingers was reassuring.

She was glad when the dance was over.

'Let us get some supper now,' said Richard, and he led her to the salon where champagne, crab, lobster, chicken and slices of beef were being served.

'Now,' she said, as they sat at one of the tables, 'what is this you wish to say to me?'

Richard hesitated; he looked about the supper room. 'Well, Homer,' he began, 'I have been thinking about what you told me . . . '

'Oh, there are Homer and Richard!' It was Charlotte's voice.

'Are we spoiling the *tête-à-tête!*' asked Sir Edward.

'Do say so if you'd rather we *didn't* join you.' That was Clare who was in the company of Charlotte, Edward and a young man who had earlier been introduced to Homer as Mr Diprose. 'They were looking so absorbed, were they not?'

Richard had risen and was drawing up chairs for the party.

'This,' said Mr Diprose, looking at Charlotte, 'is the most enjoyable ball I have attended for a long time.'

'So kind of you to say so,' murmured Charlotte.

Clare had drawn her chair closer to Sir Edward, and she was prettily refusing the chicken which he was putting on her plate. Homer listened to her silly voice almost without hearing what she said. 'Oh, but I *couldn't!* Edward, you must think I have a simply *enormous* appetite!'

They began talking of the Hunt Ball which would be held at the Dunkelys'.

'I remember when I used to *creep* out of bed and peep through the banisters at the

155

dancers,' cooed Clare. 'This time I shall be there . . . among them. Won't that be fun! Edward, you *must* promise to dance with me. And you, Mr Diprose.'

Charlotte sat back in her chair looking, Homer detected, slightly tired. We shall have to look after her, she was thinking. We shall have to ask the doctor if it will be wise for her to attend this Hunt Ball.

Richard caught her eye and she knew he was thinking the same. She sensed his impatience with the silly Clare and the sinister Edward.

Clare was happy, continually prattling, determined that the attention of the men should be entirely hers, pouting when Homer or Charlotte spoke and drew attention away from her, even trying to draw Richard into her admiring circle. But without success, Homer noted with grim satisfaction.

She was relieved when supper was over, and the guests began to filter back to the ballroom. Mr Diprose asked Charlotte to dance; Richard laid his hand on Homer's arm; that left Clare for Edward.

They went back to the ballroom and when they had danced for a few minutes, Richard said: 'Let us see if we can find some quiet place in which to talk.'

They went onto the balcony which

156

overlooked the lawns. It was a beautiful night but Richard touched her bare shoulders and said: 'You are overheated. You might catch cold.'

'But it is so lovely out here,' she said. Then she saw that they were not alone. Two figures were seated at the end of the balcony, very close to each other. Evidently they, too, had decided that it was a good idea to get away from the crowd.

Richard drew her back to the ballroom and they danced half-way round the room, but when they reached a door, he quickly drew her through it.

'Where shall we go?' he asked.

'Into one of the smaller rooms. But I expect others have got there first.'

'Let's explore.'

Their feet sank into the carpet and the music became muted.

'It's a wonderful old house,' said Homer. 'The sort of house that was built for hide-and-seek.'

'And occasions such as this one,' added Richard.

'I know a place where we can be quite undisturbed.' She led him along a narrow passage and paused before a door. She opened it and stood for a few seconds on the threshold, for she had seen that, as on the balcony, someone else had had the idea of coming to this place.

There was no light in the room except that of the moon; but it was enough to show her that the two people who were there were Clare and Sir Edward. They were embracing so passionately that Homer did not think they were aware that the door had been opened.

In that moment she heard Richard's quick intake of breath, and she knew that he had also seen. Hastily and quietly she shut the door.

'Come away,' she said. He took her trembling hand. 'Now,' she whispered, 'you have seen. You will understand.'

'I understood before,' he answered; and this time it was he who opened a door. The winter parlour was deserted and he led her into it.

'Sir down, Homer,' he said.

'At such a time!' she cried, her hands clenched. 'And to be so careless. What if it had been Charlotte who had opened the door!'

They were silent for a while and she sensed his anger. At length he said: 'Homer, you must not stay in this house.'

'But how can I go? What can I say to Charlotte? What can I do? I could get a

post of some sort, I suppose. Governess
. . . companion. Oh yes, I could do that.
It is not that which worries me. It is what
I am to say to Charlotte.'

'There is a way, Homer,' he said, 'a way
which would be perfectly natural and which I
think would give Charlotte great pleasure.'

'What do you mean?'

He had come swiftly to her side and laid
his hands on her shoulders. 'You could
marry me.'

She caught her breath. The dim winter
parlour seemed to take on a strange quality
of make-believe. I am not really in the winter
parlour receiving a proposal of marriage, she
thought; I am dreaming I am here.

'Then,' he went on, 'it would be the
most natural thing in the world for you to
leave this place. I venture to think that that
man would not dare pester you if you were
affianced to me.'

'No,' she replied. 'He would not, and I
believe Charlotte would be pleased. But is
there not more to a marriage than warding
off the unwanted attentions of a philanderer
and making a graceful exit from a particular
situation?'

'Oh, Homer,' he said, and his voice held
a deeper note, 'there is indeed a great deal
more.'

'Then,' she began, 'shouldn't we consider this more seriously?'

He drew her to him and kissed her. It was a gentle kiss on the forehead; then he touched her lips with his. She thought how different this was from the passionate embrace between Clare and Edward which she had so recently witnessed.

'Come,' he said, 'let us sit down.' When they had done so he put his arm about her. 'Why, you are shivering, Homer. You must not be afraid.'

'Afraid! I am not afraid! It is a little cold in here after the ballroom.'

'Then let me keep you warm.' He held her closer to him. 'What do you think of my proposition?' His face was resting against her hair and she thought: If anyone looked in they would think we were a pair of lovers.

'Preposterous,' she answered him.

'So you prefer to stay in this house?'

'I want to get away from this house more than anything.'

'But not more than marrying me?'

'More than anything,' she said firmly.

'Ah! Then you do dislike some things more than the thought of marrying me?'

'I think we should be serious.'

'Homer, I am very serious.'

'Do you really want to marry me?'

'Very much.'

'I thought you despised me.'

'Then you are not the intelligent young woman I believed you to be. I can see I shall have to undertake your education when we are married.'

'You talk as though there is no doubt that we shall be.'

'My dear Homer, I am certainly not going to allow you to escape from me.'

'There is something you have forgotten. Should not those about to marry love each other?'

'A romantic passion is not necessary to a happy marriage. My mother and father were singularly devoted; they had a happy home and a happy family; yet my mother did not see my father until the day she became affianced to him. Their parents had decided that a match between them would be highly desirable, and they were right.'

'I see. You think that a marriage between us would be so . . . convenient, that it would be inevitably successful. I do not agree. We never seem to agree. Surely such disagreement does not make for happiness in marriage.'

'Indeed you are wrong. The clash of our temperaments should prove a stimulation for the rest of our lives. Believe me, Homer,

I like your independence, your outspoken ways. They amuse me, and there is nothing I enjoy more than being amused.'

She stood up impatiently. 'Thank you for your offer, Mr Danver. I regret that in the circumstances I cannot accept it.'

He had caught her dress, and she felt one of the lace flounces tear from the skirt. That made her hesitate, and in a moment he had caught her to him. Now she was crushed in his arms; she heard his voice close to her ear, warmer than she had ever heard it before: 'Homer, you little idiot, don't you understand even now how I feel about you?'

She felt waves of emotion surging through her. Was this happiness? It was so intense that it overwhelmed her; never before had she experienced such feelings, and she forgot her problem; she forgot her fear of this house and Sir Edward; she forgot to worry about Charlotte.

Then the door was opened and the spell broken. Someone was looking in on them as they themselves had looked on Edward and Clare.

'Oh!' said a voice; and they heard a note of laughter behind that of assumed surprise.

Richard released her and, flushed and slightly breathless, Homer saw Mrs Frinton standing in the doorway.

'I am sorry,' said Mrs Frinton. 'I am afraid I have disturbed you. Do forgive me.'

'Pray do not leave,' said Richard easily. 'You shall be the first to hear our news. Miss Trent has just promised to marry me.' He had caught Homer's hand and was pressing it firmly as though he were forbidding her to deny this.

Anthea Frinton advanced into the room.

'Congratulations!' she said. 'I am pleased to be the first to hear the news. Will it be so very unexpected?'

'I do not think so,' said Richard. 'Miss Trent and I are friends of long standing. We met frequently in London.'

'Then I will give you my best wishes and leave you. Are you going to make an announcement tonight?'

'We shall tell Charlotte, of course,' replied Richard.

'Of course.' Anthea Frinton left them, closing the door on them with a sly, almost conspiratorial gesture.

When they were alone Homer heard Richard laugh. She wished she could see his face more clearly and read the expression in his eyes.

'But I had not said I would marry you,' she began.

'But you did not deny that you would,' he interrupted. 'Indeed, how could you? It would have been most scandalous if that woman had reported that she had found you in a dark room in the arms of a man who was not your future husband.'

'Please, Richard . . . '

'What, my dear?' he asked tenderly.

'I am afraid all is not well.'

'A moment ago I had your answer,' he told her. 'Let me reassure you once more. Dear Homer, you need have no fear of the future. All will be well with us, I promise you. I promise you, my dear.'

'If only I could be sure . . . '

'How could anyone be sure of anything in this life? You, who have a bold and adventurous spirit, would not have it so. It is the unexpected that gives piquancy to living. You and I found each other's company stimulating — from those first moments in the coach. It will always be like that, Homer. We cannot be disappointed. We are not seeking a fairy-tale world, as poor Charlotte did.'

Now Charlotte had intruded into their privacy, and Homer immediately sensed the change in him. He drew away from her and she saw the outline of his face in the moonlight. It seemed stern.

'That woman was looking for Edward,' he said. 'What if Charlotte were also looking for him? What if she saw . . . what we saw! Homer, she must not know . . . not tonight. We must prevent Charlotte from leaving the ballroom. We should have thought of this before.'

He had taken her arm; his urgency was apparent; and he had ceased to be the lover, for now his thoughts were not with her; she felt jealous of Charlotte. Then she was ashamed, for she too loved Charlotte; and she told herself that the most important thing in the world was to preserve Charlotte's ignorance of the true nature of the man she adored.

★ ★ ★

Charlotte was on the point of leaving the ballroom, and Homer knew that Richard's relief matched her own because they had arrived in time.

'Where *is* everybody?' Charlotte was saying. 'Half the guests seem to have disappeared. I cannot find Edward.'

'They disappeared as we did, Charlotte,' said Richard. 'We have news for you. We wanted you to be the first to know, but the inquisitive Frinton woman burst in on

165

us and we had to tell her.'

Charlotte looked from one to the other and a smile of pleasure touched her face. 'Oh, Richard . . . Homer . . . my dears, what are you telling me?'

'That Homer — after some persuasion — has consented to become my wife.'

Charlotte's eyes were misty. 'You two . . . I'm so happy for you. You see, I've always wanted this.'

'You scheming woman!' cried Richard. 'So that was why you sent me to Plymouth to escort her to London.'

'Not quite then,' responded Charlotte gaily. 'It was when I saw you both together.'

'She realized what a perfect match we were for each other, and that I should know exactly how to turn our dear little Homer into an obedient wife.'

'Then,' said Homer quickly, 'you had better withdraw your proposal, for I do not think you or anyone else can turn me into what I am not.'

Charlotte laughed. 'I shall announce this. It is too wonderful. We must find Edward and tell him. Let's go and look for him. We'll bring him into the ballroom and make the announcement.'

Richard stood before her as though he were barring her way, while Homer said quickly:

'No, please, Charlotte. We do not want an announcement tonight, do we, Richard? It would not be of any great interest to these people. Most of them have never seen me before. I am merely your cousin. And Richard, too, is unknown to most of them. Besides, we would prefer that it should not be made public . . . yet.'

'As you wish,' said Charlotte. It occurred to her then what Homer's marriage would mean to her, and she went on in dismay: 'You will be going away from me.'

'The journey between London and Ketteringham is not so great by post-chaise,' said Richard. 'I promise you that you shall see her frequently. She will become so accustomed to travelling that she will think nothing of it. We will come often, dear Charlotte.'

'I must be content with that. It is only to you that I would let her go, Richard, because we once swore we would never leave each other.'

'This will not be leaving each other, Charlotte,' said Homer earnestly. 'We must meet often. We will come to Ketteringham and you will come to London.'

'Of course. Of course. Our vows stand. We shall never be far from each other. Now tell me, when is the wedding to be?'

'In six weeks' time,' said Richard, and he smiled at Homer's startled glance. 'I would have wished it to be sooner. Unfortunately I leave tomorrow for Paris. I think my mission may take six weeks. Homer, when we are married you will have to get accustomed to a great deal of travelling, I am afraid. Are you a good sailor? But of course you must be. We shall have to cross the Channel frequently.'

Charlotte was looking concerned. 'Richard, how are matters over there? What a disturbing affair that was — I mean that of the diamond necklace. And that odious woman, de la Motte, is now in England.'

'It was a disastrous matter for the Queen and for France,' replied Richard. 'Affairs across the water are in a ferment, I fear.'

'I heard from Jean Pierre,' said Charlotte. 'He, too, seemed uneasy.'

Richard smiled at Homer. 'You see in what you are becoming involved. Politics play a great part in our lives.'

'I think constantly of the Queen,' said Charlotte. 'I hope that Edward and I shall be visiting France before long. It will have to be after my child is born.'

'We are going to take great care of you from now on,' said Homer. 'And you are looking a little tired now. You should be in bed.'

'I must wait until my guests depart.'

'Then you must be very careful not to accept invitations which are going to tax your strength.' That was Richard, and Homer heard again that tender note in his voice.

How vile of me, she thought, to be jealous of Charlotte!

Noticing Richard's expression had become slightly glazed, she turned and saw Edward coming into the room. He was alone and looked sleek and unperturbed. He came over to them.

'News, my dearest,' said Charlotte. 'Richard and Homer have just told me that they are engaged to be married . . . '

'Why,' cried Edward, 'that's excellent news. Richard, you are a fortunate fellow. And Homer . . . ' He put his hands on her shoulders and gazed at her, while she steeled herself not to shake him off. He kissed her cheek in an avuncular way. 'You are a lucky girl. Best of good fortune to you both.'

'As yet it is a secret,' Charlotte warned him.

'Homer's idea,' added Richard. 'For myself I want everyone to know that she has promised to marry me, and that all others — if they value their safety — must not dare so much as to touch her hand.'

Edward flinched slightly, and Homer felt

a sense of security which she had lacked since she had entered this house. Edward understood, and he knew, too, that she had confided her fears in Richard. Edward was being warned and, as he had no wish for his philandering to be discovered, he would in future be discreet in his behaviour.

Clare had appeared beside Charlotte. Her expression was one of feline contentment.

7

When Richard left Norfolk there was time for Homer to think, to review the situation and consider its implications.

She was affianced to him, but theirs would be a marriage of convenience as certainly as that between his parents had been, because, but for her need to escape from Ketteringham Manor, he would not have proposed to her; and their marriage was not based on his love for her, but on his affection for Charlotte.

When they were married they would see Charlotte often; but they would build a life of their own; perhaps they would have children. When she thought of that she experienced a return of that happiness which she had known in the winter parlour.

Charlotte said that she must have some new clothes.

'You must think about your trousseau and I of my baby's layette. We shall keep Miss Craddock fully employed. But I warn you — do not have too many dresses. For when you are married you will very soon be going to Paris; and, believe me, Homer, there is something about Paris dresses which puts ours in the shade.'

'Then Miss Craddock must sew for the baby, not for me.'

'Oh, Homer, how exciting life is!'

She was right; life was exciting; but there was something which Homer had learned and which Charlotte had yet to discover. Life was not composed entirely of pleasure. Charlotte thought she had made the perfect marriage, but that was because she did not really know her husband; Homer knew that her own marriage could not be perfect because it was not based on that which she fully believed should be the basis of all marriages.

She was more convinced than ever that one day she would have to take great care of Charlotte and protect her from brutal reality.

There came letters — one from Richard, one from Jean Pierre. Richard's was brief; he was not a great letter-writer.

'My dear Homer,
'I write from Paris where there is much activity in official circles. My stay here may be shorter than I had at first thought, in which case I shall be seeing you at Ketteringham Manor soon. I see no reason why our marriage should not take place at

172

the earliest possible moment. In fact, the sooner the better. I hope all is well at the Manor. If it should not be, let me know, and as soon as possible I shall be there to take you away. I hope Charlotte is well and happy and that you are the same.

Your future husband,
Richard Danver.'

Not the letter of a lover, decided Homer sadly. Yet there was no mistaking the purpose in it. She knew that no task which came his way would be too much for him. He had determined to remove her from Ketteringham Manor, and no matter what it cost him, he would do it.

Jean Pierre had written:

'My very dear Mademoiselle Homer,

'It was a great regret to me that I could not visit you in your new home. We are very occupied here and I do not think I shall be able to take a holiday for a long time. We have had an important trial here recently. It is this matter of the Queen and a diamond necklace of which you have no doubt heard; and I greatly fear that all did not go as loyal Frenchmen could have wished. There are many lies and scandals in circulation and troubles in the government. But I do not wish to trouble you with our miserable affairs.

'Do you remember, Mademoiselle Homer, when we sat in the Park and we talked together, and I told you how I wished to show you my country? How I wish that a visit could be arranged! Could it not? Perhaps Lady Atkyns and her husband will be visiting Paris, and if they do, you will certainly accompany them. That will be a great pleasure for me.

'I hope you remember me as I remember you. Our little *tête-à-têtes* . . . they gave me so much pleasure, and they have taught me this: wherever I go, whomever I meet, I shall never find one to delight me as did Mademoiselle Homer.

Your affectionate friend,
Jean Pierre de la Vaugon.'

How different were those two letters! The one written by the friend might easily have been the lover's.

Homer thought of Jean Pierre who had given her such passionate looks, and she was disturbed. There were times when she did not understand herself, when she realized that she was an inexperienced girl. Then she remembered her arrival in London and how she had been almost robbed in the first few minutes. She was now as ignorant of love and the relationship between men and women as she had then been of the wicked streets of London.

★ ★ ★

She liked to walk alone in the grounds. She had given up riding since she had reminded herself that to do so she must use Edward's horses.

Six weeks, and I shall leave here! she thought — and that thought gave her courage. She was no longer afraid of Edward. He had received his warning and heeded it. He was pleasant to her in Charlotte's company — indeed his manner had not changed one bit — but he never sought her when she was alone, and she had ceased to be afraid that he would attempt to force himself upon her again.

In her wanderings about the grounds she had discovered a summer-house close to the copse at the end of one of the paddocks, and she had taken a liking to the place because it was so secluded.

One late afternoon, as she wandered by, she heard voices coming from the summer-house, and one of these was Anthea Frinton's. She thrust aside her scruples, because she felt

175

that in the defence of Charlotte's happiness she should have none; and standing among the young conifers in the copse, she strained her ears.

There was a low murmur of another voice, placating, coaxing. She knew that it was Edward's.

'Such a little fool!' Anthea Frinton was saying. 'Surely, Edward, you must see that. And . . . quite indiscreet! The way she hangs about after you is so obvious. It wouldn't deceive anyone . . . except Charlotte!' Anthea Frinton began imitating Clare: ' 'But, Edward, look at me! How pretty *I* am! I am so young . . . so artless!' The girl's little better than an imbecile. If she continues in this way she will spoil her chances of making a good marriage.'

'There's nothing in it, Anthea. How could there be with a child like that! She's only half my age.'

'That might not prove a deterrent.'

'You are absurdly jealous.'

'Take my advice, Edward, and don't let her show you quite such blatant admiration. Mamma and Papa Dunkely won't like it, and there could be trouble in the county. They want to keep their little idiot sweet and pure for a rich husband.'

'My dearest Anthea, you really are jealous

of that child! How can you be . . . when you know how I feel about you . . . when you think of all we have been to each other . . . '

Homer felt disgusted; she made her way through the copse and back to the house.

★ ★ ★

Charlotte had a bad turn and in great concern Edward sent for the doctor.

'I am quite well, Edward,' said Charlotte fondly. 'You fuss me too much.'

'My dear,' replied Edward, 'we cannot fuss you too much, considering your importance to this household.'

Homer, watching them, thought how charmingly he always said what women wanted to hear. In that he was quite different from Richard. She was glad. She found that she was constantly comparing Richard with other men — and being glad.

Dr Sharman arrived and examined Charlotte.

'You are a healthy young woman, Lady Atkyns,' he said. 'There is nothing to fear. Your pregnancy should go along normally, but I do advise you to take care. No late nights . . . no excitements. You understand?'

But Dr Sharman was a little less cheerful

when he was alone with Edward and Homer. He had signed to Homer that he wished her to be present at the interview, and when he said he had a few words to say to Sir Edward, he added: 'I see this young lady is ready to be Lady Atkyns's nurse if need be. Therefore I should like her to hear what I have to say.'

Edward nodded. He was pale and not feigning his concern. 'Dr Sharman,' he said, 'I pray you tell me the truth concerning my wife's health.'

'What I have told Lady Atkyns is true,' replied the doctor. 'She must avoid excitement; but I want to impress this on you both more strongly than I would do in her presence, for I do not want her to fancy something is wrong. Lady Atkyns is healthy; she is strong, as I said. But there could be a danger of her losing the child if there were . . . shall we say . . . too many parties, too many late nights. I merely think that a little more care should be taken in her case than normally. Do not allow her to get over-excited. She must live quietly for the next seven months. Then all will be well.'

'Then that is all?' said Edward, greatly relieved.

'That is all. But I am anxious that she should not feel that there is anything abnormal about this pregnancy. There is not — except that we have had this little warning that she should go carefully.'

'Homer,' said Edward, 'we must see to that.'

'We will,' replied Homer fervently.

★ ★ ★

There was another letter from Richard. Events in Paris had necessitated his lengthening his stay rather than shortening it.

'Go on with your preparations,' he wrote, 'with all speed, for when I return we will be married without delay.'

July had come in very hot, and Charlotte was quite prepared to take life easily. Homer was happy to see that her thoughts were all for the child.

Then Edward decided that he must go away for several nights on estate business.

'My dearest,' he said, 'I do not think it would be wise for you to accompany me. Travelling is something which Dr Sharman meant you to avoid. It will be wretched not to have you with me, but I think it best that you should not come.'

Charlotte was ready to agree, in view of the doctor's warning, that she should stay at the Manor.

'Look after her, Homer,' said Edward.

He laid his hand on her shoulder with a caressing gesture; yet the caress was almost absent-minded. She believed he dared not bother her now that she was affianced to Richard, and a glow of pride in the man she was to marry touched her. Richard was not a man to be trifled with, and Edward was aware of that.

As for herself, she was delighted that Edward was going away. The Manor seemed a different place without him. How enjoyable it would be during those hot summer days to live in this lovely house without Sir Edward, to know that Charlotte was safe from discovering his perfidy, and that the future lay before her, Homer, like an unexplored country which she knew would have something rich to offer.

She and Charlotte watched Sir Edward leave. He took post-chaise, for he said he enjoyed travelling that way rather than in his own carriage. So off he went, the post-boy riding one of the horses and his luggage strapped to the back of the chaise.

Charlotte sighed. 'I should be going with him. Poor Edward! I am afraid he is a little sad to go alone.'

'Nonsense!' said Homer. 'There is the child to think of.'

That was a quiet day. Homer and Charlotte

walked through the grounds and beyond. The hedges were bright with blue harebells, purple scabious and the yellowish stars of agrimony. There was not a breath of wind.

'How warm it is!' said Charlotte. 'Can this weather last?'

'No,' replied Homer. 'It will break in a storm sooner or later. It could not continue as perfect as this.'

They sat by the lake and watched the fish rise to snap at the flies; they listened idly to the drone of bees on the tassels of the lime trees.

A brooding quiet, thought Homer. A peace which could not last.

★ ★ ★

Charlotte seemed a little tired at the end of the day, and Homer suggested that she should retire early. Victoire, who had taken it upon herself to watch over her mistress since she had heard the doctor's verdict, seconded Homer's proposal and went down to the kitchen to prepare one of her special possets.

Homer helped Charlotte to undress and sat beside the bed to talk to her as she had done so often when they were in London.

Charlotte then had talked of the stage, of

parts she had played or longed to play; now she talked of the child.

'I want a boy, Homer. I've set my heart on a boy. That is what Edward wants. I suppose that is why I do too.'

'It is wrong to set your heart on something too strongly,' warned Homer.

Charlotte laughed. 'Homer, you have become a cynic. I shall have to insist on Richard's curing you of that. I tell you I want a boy, and a boy it shall be.'

'And if it is a girl? . . . '

'Then I shall love her just as much as I would a boy. So you see, Madam, you have nothing to fear. How the time flies! Perhaps it is because I am so happy. I find it hard to believe I could have been contented with my lot in London . . . when all this existed.'

'Happiness has nothing to do with places, Charlotte.'

'Now you are a wiseacre. Oh, Homer, how I shall miss you!'

'Yet it is not so long ago that you were unaware of my existence!'

Victoire came in with her posset.

'Now drink this up right away,' she said. 'It will do you the world of good.'

Victoire had left the bedroom door open when she came in, and as she stood by the bed watching Charlotte with the posset, the sound of excited voices came floating up to them.

'Who is that?' asked Charlotte.

'I do not know, Milady,' said Victoire. 'I shall go and discover. You take this . . . while it is hot now.'

'It sounds like Lady Dunkely's voice,' said Homer. 'She must have called to see how you are. I will go and tell her that you retired early on doctor's orders.'

Homer hurried out of the room and down the stairs to the hall. Lady Dunkely was very excited, and Sir Ralph was with her.

'I must see Lady Atkyns,' she was saying. 'Tell her this is of the utmost importance.'

'My dear, calm yourself,' said Sir Ralph. 'It cannot be as bad as you think.'

'Bad!' cried Lady Dunkely. 'It is as bad as it could be. My little girl . . . after all we'd planned . . . after all we'd hoped . . . '

Homer, feeling sick with apprehension, ran down the stairs. 'What is wrong, Lady Dunkely?' she asked.

Lady Dunkely was holding a letter in her hand. She said: 'I want to see Lady Atkyns. This is something she should know.'

'You cannot see her tonight. She has to take special care and has gone to bed. The doctor has ordered this. Tell me what is wrong and I will convey your message to her tomorrow.'

'Tomorrow! Tomorrow will be too late. I want to know where he is . . . where he has taken our little girl. A nice scandal this will be. It will be all over the county.'

'My dear, my dear,' soothed Sir Ralph, 'this is the way to make it known all over the county.'

'She has gone . . . run away . . . our daughter! She has left a note for us. I want Lady Atkyns to read it. She should know. In this note which our daughter has left for us, she writes that she is going away with Sir Edward. They are leaving tonight.'

The next seconds were confused for Homer. She heard Victoire scream, and turning she saw Charlotte lying half-way down the staircase.

* * *

All that night and the next day it was feared that Charlotte would die.

At the end of the day Dr Sharman told Homer that Charlotte had lost her child. He doubted that there could ever be another, even if Charlotte recovered.

Homer, frantic with anxiety, watched by her bedside.

Disillusion had come more quickly than she had thought it would. There was no doubt that Charlotte had heard those revealing words and had, in those few anguished seconds, made her discovery.

'I blame myself,' Homer murmured. 'I should have told her what happened in the Green Room.'

Edward came back after three days, as he had said he would. He had no idea of what had happened and brought presents for Charlotte — a shawl of silver mesh threaded with gold, and a brooch of diamonds.

Homer watched him enter the house, and a bitter smile curved her lips. 'So,' she said, 'you have come.'

'What has happened?' demanded Edward.

She continued to gaze at him, making no attempt to disguise her hatred.

'Charlotte . . . ' began Edward, and she saw that he was frightened.

He started to run up the stairs, but she caught his arm. 'You are not to go to her.'

For the first time since she had known him she saw him angry. 'My wife . . . ' he began.

'Stop!' she cried. 'Charlotte is very ill. No one is to disturb her. Not you . . . least of all, you! She knows about you and Clare Dunkely. It was that which may have killed her.'

He was being punished. His jaw had relaxed and he looked every year of his age; he looked even more; he looked old, tired and frightened.

Homer said: 'You had better come into the library. I will tell you there.'

'I am going to see Charlotte.'

'No,' she cried. 'Charlotte's life is in danger. You brought this about. To see you now would upset her so much that it would kill her. You are not going to finish what you have begun.'

'You are hysterical,' he said.

'Charlotte may be dying.'

His hand was slack on the banister.

'Come into the library,' she said again, almost pleadingly; and he followed her there.

'What happened?' he asked, shutting the door and leaning against it.

'You . . . *you* happened! You came into her life . . . and if she dies you are her murderer.'

'Homer, for God's sake be calm and tell me what has happened.'

Homer sat down at the table and buried her face in her hands. She felt she could not bear to look at him. She said: 'She was in bed resting, and Lady Dunkely came with Sir Ralph. They had brought Clare's letter.'

'Clare's letter? What letter?'

186

'The one she wrote explaining that you and she had gone away together.'

'She wrote . . . *that!*'

'Are you going to pretend she was not with you?'

He shook his head. 'She was with me . . . but it was only for a few days. No one was to know. She was supposed to be visiting an old school friend.'

'I saw the letter she wrote. In it she said that you and she were in love . . . so much that you had decided to go away together.'

'That was quite untrue.'

'Yet you had gone away with her!'

He came to the table and beat on it with his fists. 'I tell you, it was nothing . . . a light affair . . . nothing . . . nothing to upset Charlotte.'

She stood up and faced him, her eyes flashing with hatred. 'Ah, but you see, Charlotte did not know of these love affairs . . . Of Betsy and Mrs Frinton and Heaven knows how many more. She did not know of Clare and the tender love scene on the night of the ball. She did not know that you had tried your wiles on me. I blame myself. I should have warned her after that first time in the Green Room. I am to blame . . . almost as much as you are.' She hesitated and rushed on: 'If Charlotte dies . . . '

'And the child?' he asked.

'There will be no child. At least you have murdered the child, if not Charlotte.'

'Homer, for God's sake, do not talk like that.'

'I will talk as I like. I will talk now as I should have talked before this evil marriage took place.'

His face was puckered in anguish. 'Clare . . . to do that . . . to write to her parents . . . why?'

'I'll tell you why,' cried Homer. 'Because she is more than a vapid little fool; she is a wicked one, too. She wants to ruin Charlotte's life. She wants to marry you herself, I've no doubt. What a pity she did not! You would have been ideally suited. Then you could have deceived each other to your hearts' content.'

'Homer . . . Homer . . . I beg of you be calm. Tell me . . . tell me everything.'

'What more is there to tell? I have told you. You have murdered Charlotte's child. You have ruined Charlotte's life, even if you have not ended it.'

And with that she could no longer bear the intensity of her emotion. She ran out of the library.

* * *

188

Dr Sharman was right when he said that Charlotte was healthy and strong. She did not die, although Homer knew that during the weeks which followed that night of discovery she had no wish to live.

Charlotte sat in her room listless, with Homer at her feet trying to make her take an interest in life.

Charlotte said little. It was not in Charlotte's nature to rage and storm as it was in Homer's; yet Homer felt heartsick to see her so sad, so listless.

She did not see Edward. She had asked that he should not come to her, and he had respected her wishes. Even Homer had to admit that Edward was contrite.

She had learned something of Edward's character during this crisis. He was weak, deceitful, selfish, but he did not wish to be deliberately unkind. He wanted to indulge his appetites, but if possible in secret without causing any inconvenience to those about him. He was shallow, Homer decided; he was a lecher and she despised him; but she did know that he felt a deep sorrow for the unhappiness he had brought to Charlotte.

So Charlotte, who had lost a child and an ideal in one hideous hour, fought a battle with the terrible lethargy which had taken possession of her; and Homer was beside her, helping her to fight it.

Life was not over, Homer pointed out. She would find other things to live for. She must. Did she not remember how once she had longed to be an actress?

'Think of yourself,' implored Homer; 'how, after you had heard the travelling players, you went to the schoolroom and read *Romeo and Juliet*; and you thought that life would have no meaning for you if you did not go on the stage. Did you not, Charlotte?'

Charlotte agreed.

'Then when you married, you ceased to care about the stage. Well, Charlotte, I prophesy this: One day you will cease to care that all this has happened to you, because there will be something in your life . . . some tremendous thing, something of the utmost importance. I swear it.'

Homer, who had been sitting at Charlotte's feet, lifted her face and gazed earnestly at her cousin.

'Your eyes are like great pools of wisdom,' said Charlotte.

'There are certain things which I know, Charlotte; and this is one of them.'

'How earnest you are! You almost make me believe you.'

'And then,' went on Homer, 'you will be glad that you lived through this experience, because all experience is valuable.'

'Where did you learn such wisdom?'

'I was born with it. It was my mother's gift to me. She ran away from me, so she had to leave me something.'

Then Charlotte began to cry gently. It was the first time she had shed tears, and Homer believed this was a good sign.

'Homer, what shall I do when you leave me?' she asked.

'I shall not leave you.'

'But you are to be married.'

'I have changed my mind.'

'Homer . . . no!' Now Charlotte had forgotten her own tragedy and was concerned only with Homer.

'I no longer wish to marry,' said Homer.

'Because of what you have seen of marriage here? Oh, Homer, all men are not alike. Richard is a good man. Marriage with him would be different . . . quite different from . . . '

'I will tell you something, Charlotte. But first I want you to tell me one thing. What are you going to do? Shall you stay here . . . with him?'

'What else can I do, Homer? We are married. My place is with him.'

'But . . . '

Charlotte lifted her head proudly. 'I shall

stay, and that is all. I shall stay because it will be expected of me. But to me he has become as a stranger. I did not know him. There was no Edward as I made him. This man is a stranger to me.'

'You will continue to live with him then?'

'Under his roof,' said Charlotte. 'But I have money of my own. I shall take nothing from him. It will only be for the sake of appearances that I shall stay here.'

'Then, Charlotte, if we take nothing, I shall stay also.'

'And Richard?'

'He only asked me to marry him because he knew I had to get away from here.'

Horror appeared in Charlotte's eyes.

'Oh, Charlotte, you are getting well,' said Homer. 'You can bear to hear these things now.'

★ ★ ★

No one called at the Manor. It was a silent house. Even the servants spoke in whispers. Homer heard that the Dunkelys had gone travelling, taking their daughter with them. They planned to stay in Bath for some months.

It was the beginning of August when Richard arrived at Ketteringham Manor.

Homer had schooled herself as to what she would say to him.

She was first to greet him and she was glad of this. She wanted to tell him herself what had happened, why this house had so greatly changed.

'Why, Homer,' he cried, 'how quiet everything is! Did you get my letter saying I would be here?'

'Yes, Richard,' she said, 'I had your letter.'

He took her hands. 'Well, is this the way to greet the man you are to marry?'

'There is to be no marriage,' she told him.

'What is this?'

'I will tell you what has happened, and then you will see why we need not go on with it.' She told him and saw him turn white with anger as he visualized the anguish of Charlotte.

What a fool I was! she thought. Of course, it is Charlotte whom he loves.

'So you see,' she finished, 'there is no longer any reason why we should marry.'

'So to you it was nothing but a marriage of convenience?'

'I believe it was you who first saw it in that way. You know you suggested marriage because I had to get away. Let us say no more about it. I have seen enough of marriage recently to make me rather wary of it.'

'Homer . . . ' She thought he was going to put his arms about her, but he seemed to change his mind.

'I must stay with Charlotte,' she said. 'I could not leave Charlotte now. She needs me.'

He looked at her and nodded slowly. Then suddenly he became brisk. 'What do you propose to do?'

'Stay with Charlotte wherever she is. She knows everything now. I have told her. We shall take nothing from him, and they will be together only for appearances' sake. But Charlotte is like a wounded creature, Richard. She needs nursing back to happiness. I do not think anyone can do that as well as I can. So my place is with her. You see . . . ?'

'Yes,' he said, 'I do see.'

Then abruptly he left her.

★ ★ ★

Richard's visit was the turning point. Homer felt that he brought the cool wind of reason into a fetid atmosphere.

The Manor was a house of gloom; it was not the place in which tragic lives could be mended.

Richard talked with a chastened Edward, and afterwards told Homer what he had suggested.

He said: 'Come for a walk with me, Homer. I want to get away from the house.'

So they walked through the copse to the summer-house where Homer had once heard Mrs Frinton reproaching Edward for his interest in Clare Dunkely; and when Richard suggested they sit there, Homer believed for a moment that he was going to ask her to waive her decision and go ahead with their marriage.

'Homer,' he said, 'if you all stay in this house you will end up with acute melancholia . . . every one of you.'

'You think the house has anything to do with that!'

'It's the scene of the tragedy. What you all need is to get right away from here.'

'Well?'

'I have persuaded Edward that this is the best thing possible. It is for you to persuade Charlotte.'

'You are suggesting that we should return to London?'

'No. You need a complete change. Different surroundings and gaiety — that is what Charlotte needs. I have to return to Paris and I shall be there for some time, I think. I have suggested to Edward that you leave Norfolk and take up residence in France, either for a short or a long period — whichever is necessary. I am convinced that that is the right thing to do.' He had laid his hand on her arm and she turned to him expectantly. 'Charlotte must not stay here,' he went on. 'She must cast off these melancholy memories. She must rebuild her life. She will do it, and you will help her. First you must persuade her to leave.'

'There we should be among strangers . . . ' she began.

'From what I gather the people here ignore your existence. And strangers? Certainly not! I shall be there. Your friend Jean Pierre will be there. Moreover, Charlotte has paid frequent visits to France and has friends in the capital. I am convinced that it is imperative that Charlotte be brought out of her present mood. She will go into a decline if she remains in this morbid house. Homer, for Charlotte's sake, you must persuade her.'

Homer felt a temporary uplifting of her spirits. She longed to escape from the Manor, which had oppressed her with its impending evil ever since she had set foot in it. To see new places, to be near Richard, to meet again the stimulating Jean Pierre — she longed for all this.

Then she was saddened because she wished Richard's eagerness for them to go to France was because he wanted to have her near him; but she believed that he thought only of Charlotte's good. It was Charlotte whom he loved and she must always be his first consideration. His concern for Charlotte's future had made the fact that his marriage was not to take place a trivial matter.

And in spite of the prospect of change and what it could mean, Homer's heart was heavy.

8

Homer would never forget her first glimpse of Paris. This city with its crowded streets, its muddy gutters, its thousand contrasts, reminded her of London — yet there was a difference; there was about this city an urgency which London had lacked; it had nothing to do with the towers of the Bastille and the Conciergerie, the magnificent façades of the Louvre and Notre Dame, nor was it in the chatter of the people, even though this sounded so much more excited than London talk; it had nothing to do with the cafés in which men and women congregated to drink their wine and gossip, nor with the excited tradesmen who thronged the streets during the day; it was there in the atmosphere of this city, and Homer immediately sensed it. She thought: This is a waiting city . . . a city whose people are alert for some great happening. There was excitement, tension in the very air.

And as she drove through those streets to the house in the Faubourg St Honoré which was to be their home while they were in Paris, she believed Charlotte sensed this too,

198

for she had lost that air of listlessness, and there was a faint colour in her cheeks while her eyes almost sparkled.

'Charlotte,' murmured Homer, 'what is it?'

And Charlotte replied: 'It is good to be in Paris again.'

★ ★ ★

They had brought only Victoire with them, for the large and comfortable house which had been found for them by Jean Pierre was equipped with servants. Victoire was happy to be in her native city, although she shook her head gravely and said that there were many changes since she was last at home.

Jean Pierre was waiting at the house to greet them. He kissed the hands of both Charlotte and Homer.

'How good it is to see you here,' he said to Charlotte; and to Homer: 'Did I not tell you that one day we should meet in Paris? But I do not think you believed me.'

'It seemed too incredible to be true,' admitted Homer.

'Well, now we are here,' said Edward, 'and we propose to stay until we feel the urge to move on, eh, Charlotte?'

Charlotte agreed and Homer noticed that

her voice was a shade softer than it had been for some time when she spoke to Edward.

'You have an excellent cook,' went on Jean Pierre. 'Ah, Mademoiselle Homer, now we are going to show you what good food really is! When you have sampled our French cooking you will realize what you have been missing all your life.'

'Do not praise it too much,' said Homer, 'or I shall expect perfection.'

'Mademoiselle Homer, in France you will find perfection.'

'Is Richard at Versailles?' Charlotte asked.

'Yes, he is there. I doubt not that he will soon be calling upon you.'

'And matters at Versailles?' asked Edward.

Jean Pierre looked over his shoulder. He whispered: 'We do not talk of such things. It is wiser not. Every man and woman may be spying on every other man and woman. Conversation might be repeated and . . . in the circumstances . . . ' He lifted his hands expressively. 'Most of the servant class listen too much and too frequently to the agitators in the Palais Royal and elsewhere. It is necessary to have a care.'

Charlotte caught her breath. 'So . . . things are as bad as that?'

Jean Pierre nodded. 'I pray you let me show you the house. Everything is in order,

I hope. The Comte used this room as his *salon*. I expect you will wish to do the same.'

'Jean Pierre, you are too good,' said Charlotte, 'to take so much trouble to make us comfortable.'

Jean Pierre raised his eyebrows. 'Trouble? What is this trouble? I know only pleasure in finding the best house I can for my friends; and my cousin, he is eager to let his house and go to the country. He finds the air of the country more wholesome at this time. Come, my friends, I will show you the house. I will introduce you to the servants.' He paused. Then he lowered his voice. 'Beware of what you speak. It would be well not to mention politics in their hearing. You are English. You have nothing to do with the conflict which threatens to split France in two. But please to remember. And there is Jeannette ... It is she who will be your cook. I suspect her to be a fervent hater of aristocrats. Nowadays, my friends, those of us who are wise take pains not to offend the susceptibilities of our servants. Be especially careful with Jeannette.'

The house was furnished in a style similar to that of Charlotte's London home, but much more elegant, much more magnificent; and as they went from room to room Homer could not resist hurrying to every window that she might look out on Paris.

She saw the servants who were gathered about the table in the kitchen, helping themselves from a huge dish which contained some savoury stew.

She saw Jeannette, the one of whom they were to beware, a middle-aged woman with dark hair twisted into a knot at the nape of her neck, and bright dark eyes that were veiled, as though they hid some fierce emotion. Anger? Contempt? The contemplation of revenge?

Homer was conscious of a great excitement for the atmosphere of this house was as compelling as that of Ketteringham Manor; in that she had sensed evil; of this she was unsure.

All she knew was that she was glad she had come. That here in Paris Charlotte was going to find the means of overcoming her grief.

* * *

It was a long time before Homer could sleep on her first night in Paris. Impressions of the recent days flashed through her mind. The journey, the crossing of the Channel, the coach ride through the French countryside and her first glimpse of the capital city.

She recalled the people by the wayside,

many of whom seemed thin and pale and poorly clad. She had called the attention of Charlotte and Edward to their state, and Edward had good-naturedly given them money, for which they had been pitiably grateful.

She saw the tall house from the outside, with its many windows like eyes watching, spying; and the elegant rooms with their gilded furniture, the couches and chairs of striped satin with those gilded backs; the rich curtains, the clocks — there seemed to be a clock in every room — all highly decorative, and all of various kinds. At every hour they chimed throughout the house, and it had a queer effect, as though everything in the house was urgently calling attention to the passing of time. But perhaps the others were not so fanciful as she was.

At last she slept to be awakened by Victoire standing at her bedside with coffee and a twist of bread on a tray.

'*Petit déjeuner*, Mademoiselle,' said Victoire. 'Now you are in France you eat as the French eat. I brought it to you because I thought you were so very tired last night and you have slept so late.'

Victoire's gesticulations were more free than they had been in England, her accent more pronounced.

Homer shook the hair out of her eyes and smiled at her.

'Thank you, Victoire. Coming home has done something to you. You look excited.'

'I am in Paris,' said Victoire. 'It is an excitement to be in Paris.'

Victoire poured the *café-au-lait* from the jug into a cup.

'There! Real French *café-au-lait*. There is nothing like it in England, I do assure you.'

'Victoire, you are going to enjoy being here.'

'Being here, yes. But I am not sure that I am going to like all in the house.'

'You want to be in command alone, do you not, as you were in London?'

'There is too much anger in Paris today.' Victoire spread her hands. 'There is talk . . . talk . . . Everyone is excited because there were riots in the Faubourg St Antoine yesterday. I remember riots in Paris when I was a little girl. Well, we are here, in Paris; and that is a good place to be in. I must forget their talk, I suppose. I need not listen. Let them go to their cafés and their outdoor meetings. What is it to me?'

Homer was silent, thinking of Jean Pierre's warnings of the night before.

Victoire implied that if there was trouble

in the *faubourgs* and the gardens of the Palais Royal it had nothing to do with her. But, thought Homer, what if the storm outside were so wild and furious that it resembled a tornado that swept across the land, ravaging everything within its range!

Strange thoughts for her first morning in Paris.

She threw them off, drank the delicious coffee, and agreed that it was the best she had ever tasted; then she told Victoire that she believed she was on the point of falling in love with Paris.

★ ★ ★

Richard had certainly been right when he had suggested this sojourn in Paris. There were many callers at the house, and Charlotte gradually threw off her lethargy and became almost her old self. Not quite, of course — she was a wiser woman; she no longer retained that innocent belief in the idyllic life. But she found great pleasure in reunion with old friends, and she planned her parties and attended theirs.

Richard called once to see how they were settling in, but he had to return to England almost immediately.

'I shall be back within a week, I hope,'

he told Charlotte and Homer. 'Then,' he added to Homer, 'you and I must make an exploration of Paris as once we did of London. Do you remember?'

'Yes,' said Homer, 'I do remember.'

Indeed she remembered every detail of that tour, her pleasure in what she saw, the interest and the stimulation. She remembered also how he had spoiled her pleasure completely when he had told her that he had invited her because Charlotte had begged him to show her the town.

She could still feel that sharp hurt, that jealousy of Charlotte which shamed her. It was during the first days in Paris that Charlotte talked to her of Edward.

Charlotte was in her room and Homer was dressing her hair, a task she liked to perform and one which Charlotte wished her to do because she understood Homer's fierce pride and her determination to make herself of use. Victoire understood this, too, and was ready to stand aside that Homer might take over some of her duties.

Charlotte said: 'Homer, I expect you have noticed that things are changing between Edward and me.'

'Yes,' said Homer. 'I had noticed.'

'I feel I have been harsh,' said Charlotte. 'It is unwise to harbour resentments. Did

206

you ever see a man more contrite than Edward?'

'He seems to have changed since it happened.'

'He is the most generous of men at heart. I feel sometimes that he is desperately trying to make up for all the misery he caused me.'

'You mean that you feel you can live with him again . . . as his wife?'

'I feel that the situation which now exists between us is becoming impossible. Homer, I have to accept Edward as he is, not as I made him out to be. He is my husband. I must remember that.'

'So you will patch up this quarrel.'

'It is the only way of living a normal life, and I think we shall both be happier for it.'

'You find you love him after all.'

'I have an affection for him. What I felt before has gone . . . but still, I understand his temptations. There is something else, Homer. He is drinking far more than is good for him. He has continued to do this since our trouble.'

'If I were you I should hate him,' said Homer fiercely.

'That is because you are younger than I am. I do not hate him. I want to try to make something of our lives. I have felt that, since

I have been in Paris. I do not understand why this should be so.'

'I think I do,' said Homer. 'Can you feel something in the air of this place? An . . . impermanence? Something which makes you feel: Hurry, enjoy what you can, there is not much time left.'

'What odd fancies you get, Homer.'

'There go the clocks,' said Homer. 'They are striking the hour in every room. Another hour has passed. Perhaps you are right, Charlotte. Perhaps we should take what life has given us and try to make it good, not dream impossible dreams.'

★ ★ ★

Jean Pierre's carriage was at the door.

Homer received him, because Charlotte and Edward were out visiting friends.

'But it is you I came to see. I want to take you out in my carriage. Will you come with me?'

'There is nothing I should like better.'

'Then put on your cloak and hat and we will start.'

Homer said: 'I will tell Victoire where I am going. Then, should Edward and Charlotte return before I do, they will know.'

When she was in her hat and cloak she

went in search of Victoire but she could not find her. Jeannette came out of the kitchen quarters.

'She does not appear to be in the house, Mademoiselle,' she said.

'Then would you tell Lady Atkyns, when she returns, that I have gone out with Monsieur de la Vaugon?'

Jeannette nodded. 'I will tell,' she said.

The carriage was a magnificent one; it was adorned with the arms of Jean Pierre's family, which Homer was beginning to discover was very aristocratic.

'I could not find Victoire so I told Jeannette,' she explained, as they bowled through the streets. 'She embarrasses me. It is the way her eyes seem to scorn me.'

'She is a dangerous woman, that Jeannette,' said Jean Pierre. 'I have seen her in the Palais Royal after dark, shouting to the crowd.'

'What does she shout?'

'Revolution. Down with the aristocrats! She is not the only one.'

'Why does she serve us when she feels as she does?'

'She wishes to eat the food supplied by the aristocrats. She likes the comforts that come from them. It is only in the cafés and the Palais Royal that she hates them so violently.'

'What a pity there must be all this hatred.'

'A pity! you say, Mademoiselle Homer.' He laughed bitterly. 'It is a mild way of describing what it is. There are times when one feels that we are living on a precipice. But I am to show you Paris . . . our gay city, our laughing city. Do you know where I am going to take you today? To Versailles. I do not think you have seen the château yet.'

'No, I have not.'

'I am glad that I shall be the first to show you.'

She looked out through the carriage windows. It was three o'clock and the streets were cleared of the traders and market people who had done their business in the morning. She saw ladies, their hair piled high in most elegant fashion, pomaded and powdered above their delicately tinted faces. They rode in their carriages with their elegant men companions who were bewigged and attired as brilliantly, in their coats of brocade and velvet, as the women. She saw those who were not so wealthy, yet dressed with care and the same Parisian elegance, trying to secure the *cabriolets* which were in great demand, or carefully picking their way on tiptoe through the streets to avoid splashing skirts and stockings with the Paris mud.

They drove past the Palais Royal.

'Some call it the capital of Paris,' Jean Pierre told her, 'for it is like a town in the centre of the city. Here are shops and cafés where anything can be bought. The home of the Orléans family . . . no longer a dignified mansion, but the rendezvous of Parisians of every character. No, we will not stop. The Palais Royal is no place for you these days. See those men standing in groups; they are the agitators. At dusk they are at their most virulent. The Palais Royal changes its character many times during one day. Perhaps . . . some time in the future, we will go strolling there. But not today . . . not today . . . '

Homer would have liked to linger there, to explore this place of which she had heard so much; but she did not ask to do so; she had heard the bitterness in Jean Pierre's voice when he had spoken of the Orléans family; and she knew that this shadow which was hanging over the city was of greater concern to him than to herself or any of her friends.

It was amusing on the road to Versailles which was crowded with people and carriages, and they passed the lumbering *carrabas* carrying its sweating and uncomfortable load.

She caught her breath as the château loomed before her in its beauty and magnificence, and gazed in wonderment at that honey-coloured façade.

'The most magnificent palace in the world,' murmured Jean Pierre. 'Built by the most magnificent of kings. Unfortunately the people of France have taken a great dislike to magnificence.'

'Perhaps,' suggested Homer, 'it is because there is so little magnificence in their own homes.'

'Yet it has always been so,' answered Jean Pierre. Deliberately he threw aside his gloom and smiled at her. 'We shall leave the carriage and I shall take you into the château. If we are lucky we may see the King and Queen.'

'Is that possible?'

'They pass through the Oeil de Bœuf on their way from the state apartments, and members of the nobility congregate there to see them pass, and present petitions.'

They entered the château and Homer was silent as she was taken up the great staircase and through apartments which were sumptuous beyond her imaginings; the elegant furnishings, the great chandeliers, the thick carpets, the frescoes and ornamental ceilings, seemed to her to belong to a world inhabited by gods and goddesses rather than men and women.

They came to that apartment known as the Oeil de Bœuf on account of its window. She was attracted by the frieze above the cornice which was decorated with exquisite sculpture of children at play — their small bodies perfect in every detail, scantily clad so that their perfection might be obvious to all; so beautifully executed were they that they appeared lifelike.

There were several people waiting in the room, and the Swiss Guard at the door gave a quick look at Jean Pierre, bowed immediately and murmured: '*Passez Monsieur, passez dans la Galerie.*' And with an inclination of the head which was a little imperious, Jean Pierre led Homer into the Oeil de Bœuf.

Homer noticed that many glanced at her curiously. She must seem a little odd in her English clothes among these powdered and perfumed people.

Many of them recognized Jean Pierre, she saw, but he made no attempt to introduce her. He took her to the Oeil de Bœuf window and murmured: 'You are known as the English cousin of Lady Atkyns. We must get you presented at Court, for not until then can you attend official functions there.'

'Present *me* at Court! But that's preposterous.'

'I do not think you will always hold that view.'

A silence had fallen among those gathered in the Oeil de Bœuf. Jean Pierre had caught Homer's arm and drew her closer to him.

'We are indeed fortunate,' he whispered. 'Now you will see Louis XVI of France and his Queen, Marie Antoinette.'

The doors were flung open. Homer heard a fanfare of trumpets; she saw several people enter the room in slow procession. Men and women, they were all exquisitely dressed — the men in powdered wigs, the women with their hair piled as high as two feet above their heads, and powdered so white that their delicately tinted complexions made them look like porcelain figures. Never had Homer witnessed such elegance or seen such magnificent gowns.

And then she saw Marie Antoinette herself — the most exquisitely gowned of all. She glittered with diamonds. They were at her throat, on her hands and in her hair, which seemed to be built to an even higher tower than that of the other ladies. She was dressed in a gown of blue and silver; and she was the daintiest creature Homer had ever seen.

With her walked the King, heavy-jowled and plump, his awkwardness accentuated by the dainty charm of his Queen.

There was no time to see more. Jean Pierre was bowing low and, following the example of those about her, Homer dropped the deepest curtsy she had ever made in her life.

The King and Queen of France had passed.

★ ★ ★

Homer could not forget the Queen. So delicately beautiful she had seemed in those exquisite garments, in that magnificent setting. She had caught the impersonal smile, the sheen of those blue eyes. An enchanting creature, thought Homer. A little haughty? Perhaps, but she was the Queen of France. A little defiant? Perhaps, but there was much evil gossip circulating about her. She was kind and generous, Homer was sure of that.

As they drove back to Paris, Jean Pierre said: 'You seem bemused. Did Marie Antoinette cast her spell on you as she does on so many?'

'I thought her charming . . . and the most beautiful creature I have ever seen.'

'She owes a great deal to Rose Bertin, her dressmaker; and, as you know, she possesses one of the finest collections of jewels in Europe.'

'Yet I feel that beneath that elegance and glitter, there is a woman . . . warm-hearted,

215

impulsive and anxious to do good.'

Jean Pierre patted her hand and said: 'Ah, I see you have become enchanted by the Queen of France. She arouses strong feelings — either of hate or devotion.'

Homer was silent for a while; then she said: 'I must thank you for a very interesting experience.'

'I intend to provide you with many interesting experiences, Mademoiselle Homer. Many . . . many. Now I am going to take you into the Bois. There we can leave the carriage and stroll under the trees, or even sit on a bank, for in the Bois one feels one is in the country.'

It was when they had left the carriage and walked under the trees that he told her of his feelings towards her.

'Mademoiselle Homer, I have rarely been so happy as I have been today. Do you know why? It is because you are with me.'

'I have enjoyed it. As I have told you, it has been a wonderful experience.'

'You are different from anyone else I have ever known. I have thought of you continually since I first saw you. Mademoiselle, I think I am in love with you. Tell me, what are your feelings towards me?'

'I enjoy being with you.'

He smiled rapturously. 'More than with anyone else?'

'I am not sure of that. Oh, Monsieur de la Vaugon . . . '

'I pray you, call me Jean Pierre . . . '

'Jean Pierre, I am afraid I am rather foolish. There is so much I do not know. I do not even understand my own emotions.'

'You are so young.'

She shook her head impatiently. 'I feel angry with myself. I am not so very young. I am nearly eighteen. It is old enough to know one's own mind. But I lived so long in the country, where everything seemed simple. Then I went to London and I felt ashamed of my ignorance, not only of manners and customs and such things, but of life. Do you understand me?'

'I think you are adorable. You are so honest. That is one of the qualities I find so endearing. I have wondered often how I shall live without you. But now you are here . . . and that is paradise for me, Homer.'

'Are you asking me to marry you?'

He was silent for a few seconds, then he said: 'It is what I want more than anything, Homer, but . . . '

He hesitated again, and Homer said

quickly: 'It does not matter, because, had you asked me to marry you, I should not have said yes.'

'Not yet,' he replied passionately, 'but one day you would. Do you think I do not understand you, Homer? You are as yet unaware. You have not yet become a woman, but one day . . . one day soon you will, and then . . . and then . . . Oh, I must explain. I am not free to ask you to marry me because I am affianced to my cousin. This match was arranged for us when we were in our cradles. Thus it is in our families.'

'So you are affianced,' she said. 'I thought you were going to tell me that you were married. But why do you look so sad? Marriages of convenience — which I presume this one with your cousin will be — often turn out better than love matches. I have known of people who did not meet until they were affianced, and their marriages turned out very happily.'

She was quoting Richard, and she realized that a faintly bitter note had come into her voice. She was also thinking of Charlotte who had undoubtedly married for love.

He looked wretched, and he went on: 'You do not understand how it is in families such as ours. In all the great families of

France marriages are arranged in this way.' He shrugged his shoulders. 'It is a way of life.'

'And your cousin . . . is she as reluctant as you?'

'Sophie is scarcely out of the schoolroom. Her youth is the reason why we are not already married. Oh Homer, I do not despair. I will arrange something. I will.'

'Please do not,' she said. 'You forget I have not said that I wish to marry you.'

'But you have admitted that you are unsure. Homer, wait . . . wait . . . I beg of you.'

She looked up at the sky. 'It has become overcast. Do you not think we should return to the carriage?'

'Come,' he said. 'I shall hope, Homer. Something in your eyes tells me I may hope.'

'And . . . Sophie?'

He turned to her passionately. 'A short while ago it would have seemed impossible that I could avoid this marriage. Now . . . in Paris . . . nothing seems impossible. There is a feeling of change in the air. Sometimes I think that soon all our old traditions will be as dead as the last thousand years.'

She looked at him with startled eyes. 'But

do you want change, Jean Pierre?'

'There is only one thing I want . . . one thing I care about. I want to marry you, Homer.'

She thought then: how pleasant it was to be wanted, to be loved. This is the first time, she thought, that a man has wanted to marry me because all he cares about is his love for me. She felt a sudden surge of anger against Richard who had disappointed her; and that made her feel more tender towards Jean Pierre.

They drove from the Bois back to the Faubourg St Honoré, and as they turned into the street they saw that a crowd had gathered round a carriage which stood outside the house.

Homer leaned forward in dismay. 'That . . . must be outside our house.'

Jean Pierre called to his driver to stop.

'I think,' he said, 'it would be wiser if we alighted and continued our way on foot. Carriages like this are apt to arouse the annoyance of the crowd.'

Jean Pierre assisted Homer to alight. 'Drive home,' he instructed the coachman.

Homer felt sick with apprehension as she heard the shouts of the crowd. *'À bas la Polignac!'* she heard. *'À bas l'Autrichienne!'*

'What do they mean?' she asked.

220

'The Austrian is, of course, the Queen, and la Polignac is the Duchesse de Polignac, who is one of her greatest friends.'

'But why do they say these things near our house?'

'That we shall discover. I think it would be wise if we slipped through the alley and round to the back of the house. Come, quickly.'

As they were about to turn into the alley, the carriage which had been stationary outside the house suddenly began to move. There was a shout from the crowd, and Homer heard the rattle of stones against the body of the carriage. She saw two very elegant and haughty women seated in the carriage, looking straight ahead of them as though they were quite unaware of the insults of the mob.

She had no time to see more for Jean Pierre was hurrying her through the alley. They entered the house by the back door.

Gaston, one of the menservants, was saying: 'To think I should serve in a house where that woman comes. La Polignac!'

'Well, she has not enjoyed her visit.' That was Jeannette, her voice shaking with laughter. 'Little does she know she has Jeannette to thank for her warm reception; that it was I, Jeannette, the humble cook, who sent young Jacques with the message that she was here.'

Jean Pierre put his fingers to his lips and hurried Homer past the kitchen.

She thought: We are becoming part of this life. If we stay here we shall become as involved as Jeannette and Marie Antoinette.

★ ★ ★

She found Charlotte and Edward in the *salon*, very much shaken by the scene they had witnessed outside their house.

'Oh, there you are, Homer,' cried Charlotte. 'Thank heaven you have come in. What is happening in the streets today? Did you see those people who threw stones at Madame de Polignac's carriage?'

'I was bringing Homer back,' said Jean Pierre. 'I sent my carriage home.'

'That was a wise thing to do,' said Edward.

'And we came in by way of the back door,' added Homer.

'Well,' said Jean Pierre lightly, 'if you entertain such exalted visitors you must expect these disturbances.'

'I knew Gabrielle de Polignac before she became the Queen's friend,' said Charlotte. 'We used to meet every time I came to Paris. Circumstances have changed for Gabrielle.

She has won great favour and she dearly loves the Queen.'

'I imagine,' said Homer, 'that she wishes she had not won such favour, if that is how the people treat her because of it.'

'I do not think she was as disturbed as we are.'

'No doubt she has grown accustomed to hearing insults flung at her,' put in Edward. 'She certainly entered her carriage as though she were unaware of that shouting, screaming mob.'

'Thank God she came to no harm,' said Charlotte. 'I have news for you, Homer. Gabrielle is eager for me to meet the Queen, and she is determined to have me presented at Court.'

Jean Pierre smiled at Homer. 'We have been to Versailles this afternoon. Homer has already seen the Queen.'

'She is like a fairy queen,' said Homer. 'Oh dear, I hope the people do not throw stones at *her* carriage, or shout insults at her.'

'They have been insulting her for many years now,' murmured Jean Pierre.

Homer frowned. It was so difficult to imagine that dainty creature at the mercy of the mob. She felt that there were too many contrasts in this life. She thought of the extravagance of the Palace of Versailles and the tattered mob she had seen outside the house.

This was uneasy living, but it was pleasant to see Charlotte excited at the prospect of being presented to the Queen.

9

The time passed with a rapidity which astonished Homer. Each day she awoke wondering what would happen before nightfall; there were the usual gay parties, the visits to Charlotte's friends. If these people who lived so gaily were aware of the tension in the waiting city they gave no sign of it.

'Oh, these Parisians, they are so excitable,' they would say. 'They have always been rude to their kings since they turned on Louis's grandfather, Louis Quinze. Did he not build a road between Versailles and Compiègne to avoid having to pass through Paris?'

Richard visited them only occasionally. Homer thought that he did not come more often because it tortured him to see Charlotte as Edward's wife; perhaps also he felt a little embarrassed in her own presence — not that it was easy to imagine Richard embarrassed — because they had once planned to marry.

She was angry with him for philosophically accepting her refusal. She wondered whether deep within her she hoped that he would in his somewhat buccaneering way seek to force her to keep her word; had he really wanted her, she was convinced, he would have done so. She believed him to be a man who would not hesitate to enforce his will — but it was not his will that they should marry.

Then he came at the end of October to tell them that he was called back to England, and he thought he would probably be there for a few months.

Before he left he asked Homer to spend a few hours with him. 'A little jaunt,' he said, 'something to remember when we cannot meet.'

She had come under the influence of Paris during her weeks there. It was apparent in her dress.

He commented on this. 'Mind you,' he said, 'nothing could disguise the essential Homer. Now I am going to take you to the Pavillon Mazarin where you can drink a glass of punch just as though you were in London.'

A *cabriolet* had come to the door of the house for them and he said, as they drove through the November mist: 'I am glad the winter is with us. On winter nights men and women prefer the warmth of the hearth to the gardens of the Palais Royal. If anything is going to happen it will not be until the spring or summer. Then I shall be back.'

'You want to be here . . . should anything happen?'

He looked at her quizzically. 'Do you not remember Charlotte commanded me to look after you?'

'So you still think I am incapable of looking after myself?'

'Who shall say who is capable of that task in Paris in this year 1788?'

They had reached the Pavillon Mazarin and were warmly welcomed by Regny, who had once been known as a lemonade-seller and now called himself a seller of good English punch.

'Welcome! Welcome to milord and milady,' he said. 'You will drink some hot punch. Oh, here is your punch, milord . . . milady . . . even as you drink it in England, eh?'

Over his glass Richard smiled at her. 'You see how popular is everything that comes from our country. All smart Parisians are now drinking *le thé* and you see the fashionable beaux in their coats with triple capes. They are the last word in fashion, my dear. Why? Because they are elegant? Hardly that. No. Because they come from England.'

'I am sure,' said Homer, 'that you did not bring me here to discuss the fashions.'

'You are right. Homer, I am uneasy. It is

due to me that you are here. Remember, it was my suggestion that you should come to Paris.'

'It was a good suggestion. Do you see how Charlotte has changed since she came here?'

'She is happy now, is she not?'

'I do not think she can be quite as happy as she once was. But she is finding so much in life to interest her. Although she has not yet been formally presented — it seems this is a most involved ceremony and takes weeks to arrange — her friend Madame de Polignac has taken her to the Petit Trianon and introduced her, without formality, to the Queen. Richard, I think Charlotte adores the Queen.'

'Dear Charlotte! She is an idealist. First the stage. Then Edward. Now the Queen.' He frowned. 'I do not think that any one of these enthusiasms could bring her anything but frustration, unhappiness.'

'You are wishing you had not brought her to Paris.'

'She had to leave that gloomy Manor House. And what could have provided a more startling contrast?'

'It roused her from her lethargy, Richard. We had to do that.'

'Take care of her, Homer.'

'You think I can do that?'

'Few better. You are the opposite of Charlotte. Astringent where she is sweet. Stubborn where she is yielding. With a natural cynicism to set against her idealism.'

'In fact,' she said bitterly, 'in your opinion I am everything that Charlotte is not.'

'You are too honest not to see it yourself.'

'Yes,' she said, 'I do see it.'

'If there should be trouble, it would be necessary for you to leave Paris at once. You might have to persuade Charlotte to do that. Edward has arranged to take a house in Lille but Charlotte, on account of her devotion to the Queen, might not wish to go so far from Versailles. You must persuade her, Homer. If there were trouble the most dangerously placed person in France would be the Queen.'

'I would do my best.'

'You would succeed, Homer.'

'You must not have too high an opinion of my powers.'

'How else could I sleep in peace while I am in England?' She fancied there was a tender note in his voice and she found herself suddenly very happy.

But he was staring at the punch in his glass.

He said: 'You have seen a great deal of

your friend Jean Pierre lately?'

'He is much occupied in his department.'

'There is good in all things. That will keep him out of mischief.'

'Mischief?'

'I was thinking of little Sophie. She adores him, you know. She will make him such a good wife.'

'She is a friend of yours?'

'I met her at her parents' house — an enchanting creature. It is a pity she is so young. But in a year or so she will be ready for marriage, and then our Jean Pierre will be a happy husband.'

She felt herself flushing a little, and he went on slyly: 'Don't tell me that our gallant has not mentioned his Sophie to you.'

'He has told me of his engagement.'

'Ah!' Richard drained his glass. 'Come,' he said, 'we will go back now. I have to say my farewells and be off within the next few hours. Our little talk has done me much good. I shall go to England with an easier mind.'

* * *

Strange days. She saw little of Jean Pierre, and when he did visit the house he seemed harassed; but since it had been announced

230

that the affairs of the country necessitated the summoning of the Estates General he had had little time for private engagements.

There was a quietness in the streets and the weather turned bitterly cold.

Homer knew that Sir Edward was slipping back into his old habits; he was drinking very heavily and she believed he had formed an attachment with a young married woman who often visited the house.

She believed too that Charlotte was aware of this and that she did not greatly care. Charlotte was enchanted by the friends she was meeting at the intimate parties at the Petit Trianon. She was waiting for the time when she would be presented at Court and thus be enabled to join the Queen's party on any occasion.

Moreover, she was determined that, once she herself had been presented, she would present Homer.

She talked a great deal of the Queen who undoubtedly fascinated her.

Marie Antoinette, it seemed, was equally charmed by the lovely young English actress; and Homer heard that the Queen's regard for Lady Atkyns almost rivalled that which she felt for Madame de Polignac and the Princesse de Lamballe.

There were evenings when Homer would

go to Charlotte's room and comb her hair. She would hear of small supper parties which had been held in the intimate rooms of the Petit Trianon or in the Queen's very private apartments at Versailles. Charlotte would tell Homer how the Queen had been dressed, what she had said.

'Charlotte,' said Homer anxiously, 'it would seem that you love the Queen.'

'All love her who know her.'

'Yet there would seem to be many in France who feel anything but love for her.'

Charlotte's eyes glowed. 'I think that is one of the reasons why she affects me so strongly. She is so beautiful, so dainty, so charming, so lighthearted; and there is danger all about her. Do you not see, it makes her ... so appealing? I must tell you this. When we went into her private apartment a few days ago I saw a sheet of paper on the floor. I picked it up absently. I glanced at it in dismay, for written on it was something horrible, obscene ... about her. It explained what they would do to her if she fell into their hands. I tried to hide it, but she had seen it and she held out her hand for it. I begged to be allowed not to show it, but she insisted. And when she read it, it was I who wept. *She* laughed and burned it in the flame of a candle. 'Why, my dear friend,' she said to me, 'you should not let this upset you. With me . . . such missiles have become a commonplace.' Then she behaved as though she had forgotten it. Homer, I can explain this to you and to no other. I have a longing to protect her from all those people. That is the effect she has on me. I make silly scenes in my mind. They are about to attack her, they come to her with knives and clubs. And I stand before her and take the blows intended for her.'

Homer laughed and put her arms round Charlotte. 'You are a dreamer. You are an idealist, who endow those you love with qualities they do not possess. You must always have some cause in your life in order to be happy. You will be the greatest actress. You will be the perfect wife. And now you will save the Queen should the mob attempt that which they have long threatened.'

'You think me absurd?'

'I think you the dearest person in the world and I love you . . . ' She paused and added defiantly, for her mind had involuntarily conjured up an image of Richard ' . . . better than anyone else in the world.'

So Charlotte went to Court and dreamed her dreams; Edward paid his secret visits to his new friend; and Homer waited for news of Richard and Jean Pierre — those two who were rarely out of her thoughts.

If I loved Jean Pierre, she thought, I must be continually jealous of Sophie; and if I loved Richard, I must be jealous of Charlotte.

How fortunate that I love neither of them!

★ ★ ★

The new year had come and they were midway through January.

Charlotte was giving a supper party one evening and Homer, eager as ever to play a useful part in the house, had taken on the duties of secretary and companion to Charlotte, and in this capacity made the arrangements for social engagements such as this one.

It was early afternoon, and Charlotte had driven out to visit a friend; Sir Edward had gone out soon after, on one of his secret engagements; and Homer, checking her list of what must be done, decided to make some last-minute arrangements for the supper.

She went down to the kitchens. She did not like visiting them as they always seemed to her to be dominated by Jeannette. There was invariably an atmosphere of hostility there and, because she could not break through it, Homer found herself becoming haughty — in a way which was quite alien to her true nature.

There was no one in the kitchens when she entered. She looked at the great oven and the spits in readiness for tonight's meal, and presumed then that everyone was resting for an hour before the final preparations began.

Then a door opened and Jeannette appeared in her cloak and bonnet; she was carrying a great parcel.

She looked at Homer and was so startled that she tripped forward and the parcel fell from her hands, its contents being scattered all over the floor.

Homer stared down at the pieces of bread, and bones with meat adhering to them.

'What . . . ?' she began.

Jeannette stared at her defiantly.

'I was stealing them,' she said, 'that's what.'

'But why should you do that, Jeannette? Do you not have enough to eat in this house?'

Jeannette tossed her dark head; her hands were on her hips in an attitude of belligerence. Thus she looks, thought Homer, when she harangues the crowd in the Palais Royal. 'In *this* house there is plenty . . . In this house! But we do not all live in this house.'

'Then you were taking those scraps to your

friends. Why, Jeannette, there is nothing to be angry about in that. Do you think I do not understand that if one has friends who need food one would take it to them?'

'You would call it stealing. And so it is.'

'Oh,' said Homer earnestly, 'who is to say which of us would resist that temptation if we had friends in need?'

Jeannette was staring at her as though she did not understand.

'Come,' said Homer, 'let us pick up these things. We will pack them up more securely and then you can take them to your friends.'

She bent and began picking up the food. Then she went to a cupboard and brought out the remains of a chicken which she put into the parcel.

Jeannette hesitated; then she shrugged her shoulders, picked up the parcel and walked out.

Homer was glad this incident had occurred, because she felt that a bridgehead had been made and that it might be possible for her to cross it.

She was not going to waste this opportunity, so she went frequently to the kitchens. Now and then she would say: 'This will be needed no more. It will do for your parcel, Jeannette.'

And Jeannette who, she knew, had been suspicious of her intentions, gradually began to sense her sympathy and understanding and realized that she was not luring her into a trap which would result in her being dismissed from the house as a thief.

Jeannette said one day: 'Mademoiselle is not one of *them*. At heart she is one of us.'

'Us . . . them? What is the difference?'

'All this difference,' said Jeannette fiercely. 'They have plenty and we have nothing. For years it has been so . . . but the time is coming when that shall be changed.'

It was some weeks before Jeannette really brought herself to trust Homer. Then, one day, when Homer had put a succulent piece of venison into her parcel, she said: 'He has grown plump, my little one, since you began to put these dainties into his parcel.'

'Your little one?'

'I said friends, did I? It is for one only that I steal. Would I risk losing my place here for . . . friends? Not I. But for little Armand . . . Ah, Mademoiselle, I would risk not only my place in this rich house but my life.'

'So you have a son, Jeannette?'

Jeannette's voice momentarily lost all its aggressiveness. 'Four years old this June. It is difficult to keep a son when one has to work. But how else could I feed him, Mademoiselle? He is with a woman and I do not trust her. That is why every day I go to see him in the Rue du Poirer. There I watch him eat what I have brought; I tell her then that if anything should happen to him it will be the worse for her.'

'She would not dare let anything happen to him, Jeannette. I am sure of that.'

They exchanged a laugh together; and after that Homer often put little things into the daily parcel which she thought a child would like.

* * *

It was early spring before Charlotte was presented at Court.

Such a great occasion demanded a good deal of preparation. Madame de Polignac arranged that Rose Bertin herself should make the dress, and Rose, secure in the Queen's patronage, deigned to do so.

The dress was as magnificent as those which Homer had seen in the Château of Versailles, and Edward called in Court jewellers to supply Charlotte with diamonds and sapphire ornaments.

Madame de Polignac was to present her formally to the Queen, and Charlotte practised her curtsy every day.

Edward was delighted at Charlotte's pleasure, because, thought Homer, such is his nature that the more pleasure Charlotte enjoys the more freely can he indulge his friendship with his mistresses.

As for Homer she found herself constantly amazed by the contrasts about her. Did neither Edward nor Charlotte realize that with the coming of spring the hatred in the streets was rising?

Charlotte was absorbed by Court life; Edward with his mistresses; but Homer each day would exchange a few words with Jeannette, and she could not turn her back on that other kind of life which was lived by so many people in this seething city.

There came the day for Charlotte's presentation. The hairdresser had arrived at the house with his pounds of powder and pomade in order to exercise his skill on Charlotte's hair.

Jean Pierre had said he would arrive in good time to take Homer to Versailles, where she would watch the ceremony with those of the nobility who had not been presented but were entitled to view the spectacle from a point of vantage in the *galerie*.

Homer had not seen Charlotte so gay since those days before she had discovered

Edward's true nature; and watching her Homer could not repress a shiver, for it seemed to her that once again Charlotte was building her happiness on a flimsy foundation. Perhaps she herself understood more of what was happening in this city than Charlotte could. Charlotte was 'Milady', and as such out of touch with the other side. Homer here, as in England, was considered to be the poor relation. She was glad of that now since it was for this reason that she had been able to understand the meaning of those oppressive shadows which hung over France, and to have some sympathy for those who created them.

In the bustle of preparations Homer had not been to the kitchen on the previous day, but before changing from her plain morning dress to that splendid one in which she was to go to Versailles, she decided she would go and help Jeannette with her daily parcel.

To her surprise Jeannette was not in the kitchen.

Gaston said: 'She is in the bedroom. She had a fall yesterday and strained herself. She was sick and unable to get up this morning.'

Homer went with speed to that room on the lower ground floor in which the women servants slept.

She found Jeannette on her straw pallet, feverish and a little delirious.

'Jeannette,' said Homer, kneeling by the pallet, 'what has happened? You are ill.'

'Mademoiselle . . . Armand . . . '

'He will be cared for until you can see him again. We must think of you, Jeannette. I shall call the doctor to see you.'

'My ankle . . . ' began Jeannette.

Homer looked at it. 'It is swollen. You have strained something.'

'But Mademoiselle, it will not let me walk . . . I did not see Armand yesterday . . . I did not tell you all. If I do not take the money for him and the food, old Pigalle will turn him into the streets. I shall lose my Armand. Mademoiselle, I am frantic . . . What shall I do?'

'You must rest,' said Homer. 'You have a fever. You must be calm and rest. I shall go to see Armand. I will see that all is well with him. Will that satisfy you?'

'But Mademoiselle . . . I did not see him yesterday, and today . . . '

'I shall go today. Does that content you? I shall go now . . . without delay.'

'Mademoiselle, you are good. You are not one of them, Mademoiselle. You are one of us.'

'There is no difference, I tell you. Now

rest happily. First I shall send someone for the doctor.'

'No . . . no . . . '

'Very well, first I shall go to Armand. Then you will rest perhaps.'

'I trust you, Mademoiselle. It is strange that it should be you I trust.'

★ ★ ★

Homer came up from the lower floor to find Victoire agitatedly looking for her.

'Mademoiselle Homer, there is your hair to be done. You will never be ready in time.'

'In time . . . ' said Homer blankly. Then she remembered Charlotte's presentation.

'Oh Victoire, I cannot go.'

'Not go! With Milady almost ready, and your dress there, and Monsieur de la Vaugon coming for you in his carriage!'

'Jeannette is ill. Victoire, you must send someone for the doctor. And I have something I must do quickly for her. I have promised. If I am in time, later I will go to see Charlotte presented. As for clothes . . . never mind.'

'You have gone crazy, Mademoiselle.'

'Please, Victoire, send for the doctor. Send Gaston.'

Homer sped upstairs and, taking a shawl,

wrapped that about herself and ran out of the house, Victoire calling after her that she must have gone mad.

★ ★ ★

She did not feel the cold March wind on her cheeks, nor did she notice the snowflakes which fluttered onto her shawl and were melted by the warmth of her body. She had to find her way to the Rue du Poirer.

She had never been in that district of Paris before, and if her mind had not been on her mission she would have wept at what she saw. Children, barefooted and barelegged, sat about on door-steps, their eyes enormous in their thin and dirty faces.

She saw some of the notorious *marcheuses* of the Pont-au-Bled district, with the marks of disease on their faces, sunk so low that now they were glad to earn a few sous by running errands for those who followed the profession which had once been theirs — and who would doubtless come to the same sorry end. She saw the cafés crowded with those who had a *sou* or two to spare for a hot drink; she saw a baker's shop with barricades at the windows and the words 'Give us bread' scrawled on a wall.

She asked a woman the way to the Rue

du Poirer. The woman laughed at her and said: 'And what would you be doing there, my pretty one? No need for you to go to such a place. You come along with me.'

Homer turned and ran, not knowing where she ran.

But at last a group of children showed her the way and she found the house — dirty, evil-smelling — and she mounted the stairs to the room in which Armand sat, a small solemn pale-faced child with legs like sticks and an expectant look on his face which turned to disappointment when she entered.

Homer had had the forethought to bring money with her, and when the slut who was in charge refused to let her take Armand without payment she produced it.

It seemed to her hours before she was able to finish with the haggling business and walk with Armand out into the cold street.

When she told him that she had come to take him to his mother his little face lit up with a pleasure which made Homer want to weep. He was shivering; she was not sure whether it was with anticipation or the cold weather. In any case, he was so poorly clad that she feared he would take cold if he were not immediately protected.

Then, she thought grimly, this hideous

adventure of mine would all have been for nothing.

She picked him up in her arms — he was so thin that he was pitiably light — and she held the shawl round them both while she looked about her for a *cabriolet*. But there was none in this district and she trudged on with her burden as quickly as she could.

She asked the way of a *café-au-lait* woman who stood on the corner of a street, her urn on her back; and at last she reached the district of the Faubourg St Honoré and when she was almost home she heard her name called.

A carriage was coming towards her, and with relief she saw that it was Jean Pierre's.

'Homer! What are you doing? I have come to take you to Versailles.'

He had opened the door of the carriage and stepped out. In his vivid blue satin coat and powdered wig he looked so incongruous after her recent surroundings that Homer almost burst into hysterical laughter.

'Take us back to the house, please . . . as quickly as you can.'

'Victoire said you had gone mad.'

'There was little time to explain.'

'What have you there?'

'A child. Take him. Oh . . . no . . . not in that satin coat.'

He took the child from her, and Armand gazed at him as though he did not quite believe he was real.

'Who is this child?'

'I will explain as we go along.'

'Well?' he said, when they were seated in the carriage and he had handed Armand to her.

'Armand is Jeannette's son. She is not well enough to go to him, so Armand must come to Jeannette.'

'Jeannette! But what has this to do with you?'

She was suddenly as fierce as one of the revolutionaries in the Palais Royal. 'This!' she said. 'That the troubles of one of us should be the troubles of us all.'

He was silent for a while, then he said: 'Do you realize that you have spoilt Charlotte's presentation?'

'She has not gone?'

'Oh yes, she has gone. But you were to have been there.'

'As a spectator. I should have liked to see it. But I had this to do.'

They reached the house. 'It is too late for us to go to Versailles now, for you could not go dressed as you are.'

'I could not go in any case. I have more important things to do. Armand, I am going

246

to take you to your mother at once . . . You understand me?'

He nodded.

She took his hand and led him down to the servants' bedroom. Jean Pierre followed her.

Jeannette turned her eyes to the door. She saw the child, his hand in Homer's. Then he ran to her and threw himself into her outstretched arms.

Homer and Jean Pierre then saw something which they had never thought to see: fiery Jeannette, with the tears coursing down her cheeks as she stroked the hair of her son.

★ ★ ★

Homer imperiously took charge.

The doctor had called, she discovered. There was nothing wrong with Jeannette but a sprained ankle which would right itself in a few days, and an immense anxiety which had been the cause of fever.

That anxiety had been removed, and a few days' rest would set the ankle to rights.

Homer ordered that hot soup be brought to the bedroom. The little boy, seated on the bed beside his mother, was given a bowl of this, and Jeannette took one also.

Homer felt a lump in her throat to see the mother's joy in watching those mouthfuls of hot soup being swallowed by her child.

She thought of the hideous room which must have been this boy's home; she pictured him, waiting every day for his mother who came and gave him the only love he knew, together with the good things stolen from the kitchen of the rich house.

When the soup was finished, she called for a bath of hot water to be brought to the bedroom.

'We are going to wash you, Armand,' she said, 'because, if you are going to live in a house like this, you must be very much cleaner than you are.'

'To live in a house like this?' asked Jeannette.

'Of course,' said Homer. 'Why not? Is there not room? Armand will be useful in the kitchen. Will you not, Armand?'

Armand nodded, hunching his shoulders as he laughed.

'You will be with your mother, and that is where a little boy like you should be.'

'But Milady has promised this?' asked Jeannette.

'I have promised,' said Homer.

Jean Pierre looked at her with astonishment tinged with amusement.

'You will be a very domineering woman,' he said. 'You will have your way.'

'As far as this is concerned, why not? Do you think I cannot persuade Charlotte to let Armand stay? If you do, you do not know me and you do not know Charlotte.'

She bathed the boy and sent Gaston out to buy some clothes which the little boy could wear. 'These, I fear,' she said, 'should be burned at once. We want Armand in the house, but not his clothes.'

Armand laughed again and Homer realized that though he spoke very little, yet in their short acquaintance he had shown her a whole range of emotions, from despair to complete joy, by his expressions and his laughter.

Homer insisted that Jean Pierre should help her. The beautiful blue satin coat was splashed with water, and the more it was splashed the more Homer laughed. And eventually they were all laughing.

What an extraordinary scene we must present, thought Homer — and perhaps the most extraordinary one was Jean Pierre, at last rid of his satin coat, the fine lawn sleeves of his shirt rolled up as, obeying the instructions of Homer, he helped wash the grime off the little boy from the Rue du Poirer.

When Armand was dressed in his new clothes he seemed a different boy. He strutted a little, much to the delight of Homer.

'Now, Jeannette,' said Homer, 'all you have to do is rest for a day or so until that ankle is better.'

Jeannette turned her head away; it was difficult for her to show her emotion.

She muttered: 'So . . . he is to stay here . . . always, Mademoiselle.'

'But certainly. He is too young to be parted from his mother.'

'You say so, Mademoiselle, but is that enough?'

'It is enough,' said Homer firmly.

'Oh Mademoiselle . . . it is true. You do not belong to them. You should be one of us.'

Homer knelt suddenly by the bed and said earnestly: 'Jeannette, I have told you. We are all human beings . . . Who are they? Who are we? We are one race. All we have to do is help each other.'

Jeannette shook her head and Homer stood up.

'Now,' she said, 'we will leave you with Armand.'

She and Jean Pierre left the bedroom and went into the *salon*.

Jean Pierre was laughing. 'This will be talked of in the kitchens for months to come.'

'It is nothing. What else could I do?'

He said gently: 'Being Homer, what else? Charlotte's presentation . . . what is that when a woman is crying for her child?'

'Anyone would have done what I did.'

'Ah,' he said. 'If that were but true! We have lived our lives so hemmed in by etiquette that we have not seen that which is crying out to be done. Homer, do you wonder that I am in love with you? You, valiant Homer, who with these small hands and that fierce frown would attempt to hold back a revolution!'

He kissed her swiftly on the cheek. She did not resent this. She knew that today's adventure had brought her closer to Jean Pierre.

* * *

As Homer had anticipated, there was no difficulty whatever in persuading Charlotte to allow Armand to live with his mother.

'Foolish woman,' said Charlotte, when she heard the story. 'Why did she not tell us that she had a child?'

Charlotte had understood about Homer's not attending the presentation.

'How could you when that happened? Of course you did the right thing, Homer. You did what I would expect you to do. Dearest

Homer, you put me to shame. Here am I, thinking of my pleasure, while you are doing deeds of mercy in my house. Yet I do want you to understand. It is not giddy excitement that I seek. The Queen talks to me seriously, Homer. She is disturbed by the sufferings of the people. I have a feeling that I must help her. That sounds ridiculous, does it not? I . . . to help the Queen of France . . . yet . . . '

'These are strange times,' said Homer. 'Of course you are not selfish, Charlotte; I understand your feelings. When I saw her — so dainty, so beautiful, I sensed the danger in which she lives and I too felt that I wanted to protect her. A foolish feeling, you say. But you see I shared it with you.'

'I have talked to her of you,' said Charlotte. 'She is eager for your presentation. We must arrange that.'

'It seems incongruous. Myself . . . presented at Court — and at the Court of France! What would they say in St Miniver's? When it happens I must write and tell them all about it. Oh, Charlotte, I am so glad we came here.'

'And I,' said Charlotte.

Homer saw what her visit to France had given to Charlotte. This devotion she felt towards the Queen, this reverence mingling with the subtle desire to protect — they were exactly what Charlotte had needed to give her a new reason for wanting to go on living.

★ ★ ★

With the coming of the spring the mood of Paris was undergoing a change. As the evenings grew warmer and lighter, the crowds began to assemble in the gardens of the Palais Royal.

In May come the opening of the States General, and a hush of expectancy seemed to fall over the capital.

Charlotte had planned Homer's presentation for June, but during that month the Dauphin died and the Court was plunged into mourning.

★ ★ ★

Homer never forgot that 14th day of July.

All through the previous days the city had been uneasy. Respectable citizens had cowered behind their shutters and listened in fear to the disturbances in the streets. Wild bands of men and women, who came from the haunts of the most vicious, had taken advantage of the situation to parade the streets and loot where they could, not hesitating to attack any who opposed them. Their main targets were the wine shops from which they dragged out the barrels of wine.

The tocsins had been ringing out from the Hotel de Ville to summon all respectable citizens to form a guard to protect their lives and property from the rioters; the citizens had responded, going in their thousands to the Hôtel de Ville to secure arms; and by the end of the day there was a peace — though an uneasy peace — in the streets of the capital.

But those citizens who had been ready to protect their property against the wine-crazed rioters were not the supporters of the Royal family; and on the morning of the fateful 14th, rumour spread through the city that the King's troops were preparing to march on Paris from Versailles.

Edward had ordered that the shutters be put up. 'We should not have stayed so long,' he said. 'We should now be in Lille; and if the people there are of the same mind as they are in Paris, then I think we should return to England.'

Charlotte showed an unaccustomed firmness.

'No, Edward,' she said, 'this is not the time to leave our friends.'

'But of what use can we be to our friends

by remaining here?'

'Who shall say?' asked Charlotte. 'We must be ready for any opportunity to help should it arise.'

Homer left them talking together and went to the kitchen. She sensed the excitement there. They had all been talking at once, but they stopped when she appeared.

'Jeannette,' she said, 'it would be advisable not to go to the market this morning.'

Jeannette shook her head, and there was that gentleness in her voice which was always there now when she addressed Homer. 'No, Mademoiselle, there would be nothing to buy in the markets this morning.' She plucked at Homer's sleeve. 'Stay in the house today, Mademoiselle. Do not on any account go into the streets. In the house you will be safe. It is known that you are English, in this house. The people's quarrel is not with the English, who have ceased to be our enemies now that we have discovered our true enemy . . . at home.'

'How long will this state of affairs exist?' asked Homer.

Jeannette lifted her shoulders. 'Who shall say? But, Mademoiselle, stay behind the shutters . . . until I tell you it is safe to go out.'

'Sir Edward also has asked us not to go

out. Well, we must stay here, I suppose, until this madness is over.'

She thought how wild Jeannette looked — excited, as though some long-anticipated pleasure were about to come to her.

★ ★ ★

Through the closed shutters they could hear the sounds of shouting in the streets. They sat in the *salon* — Charlotte, Edward and Homer — and they knew that the revolution was about to break.

Charlotte was clenching and unclenching her hands, thinking of all that this must mean to the Queen. Edward was asking himself how they could have been so foolish as to have left peaceful England for a country in revolt. Homer could hear the beating of her own heart and was conscious that what was happening in the streets was a part of her own life.

A hammering on the outer door startled them.

Edward strode to the door of the *salon*. 'Do not open it,' he shouted. Then: 'Where the devil are the servants?'

The hammering continued. They heard someone calling: 'Let me in. What's happened to you all?'

256

'It's Richard,' cried Homer; and she ran past Edward and unbarred the door.

Richard strode into the hall.

'Well,' he said, 'you were wise to be cautious. A great deal is happening in the streets today.'

'Oh, Richard . . . Richard,' cried Charlotte. 'What news?'

'They are marching on the Bastille. I do not know what this means.'

'It is a beginning,' said Edward.

'You should have left for Lille a week ago,' declared Richard.

'You are right,' said Edward. 'Yet Charlotte even now . . .'

'Our friends are here,' said Charlotte indignantly. 'Should we run away at the first sign of danger? Should we not at least offer them our help?'

'What can we do to help?' asked Edward.

'That,' retorted Charlotte, 'we may discover. I will ring for wine . . . we need it.'

There was no answer, and Homer said that she would go down to the kitchen and find out why they did not answer the bell.

She left them together; and even at such a moment she was conscious of disappointment in her heart because she imagined that when Richard had shown his concern for their safety, he had seemed to look only at

257

Charlotte. It was some months since she had seen him, and she had told herself that she no longer thought of him as frequently as she once had, nor with the same excitement. Yet he only had to appear and her mind was in a turmoil of emotion — even at a time like this when she supposed the danger in the streets could threaten them.

There was no one in the kitchen.

'Jeannette,' she called. 'Jeannette, where are you?'

There was no answer.

She went into the lower kitchen, and there she found old Berthe who was the oldest of the servants and worked under Jeannette.

Berthe was frightened; there was no doubt of that.

'What is the matter, Berthe, and where are they all?'

'They are out, Mademoiselle. They went out into the streets. And, Mademoiselle, Jeannette left Armand with me . . . but I fear he has slipped out after his mother. He will be crushed in the crowds . . . he will be lost, and Jeannette will kill me.'

'Armand . . . out in the streets! But this is dangerous. We are all supposed to be in today. They cannot have gone out. They were warned . . . '

'When they march Jeannette would be

there. She always said so. She has made the others go with her.'

Homer had a vision of Jeannette, her eyes wild, the revolutionary slogans on her lips, waving her arms, as she called her fellow-patriots to action.

'Young Armand heard them shouting — 'To the Bastille!' ' mumbled Berthe. 'You may depend upon it, that is where he has gone.'

'Then he must be brought back.' She hesitated. Upstairs they would tell her that if Jeannette deserted her child to roam the streets on a day like this, that was her affair. But Armand was not only Jeannette's affair; he was Homer's also. She took a delight in the boy. She jeered at herself sometimes because she felt proud of what she had done in bringing Armand into this house. But for me, she would often tell herself, Armand would still be in that filthy house, and Jeannette an anxious mother. To contemplate her action made her feel powerful, and she liked the feeling.

How vain you are, Homer Trent, she often told herself; yet that had no effect whatsoever on her feelings.

What was the use of her bringing Armand to the house if he was going to be hurt — perhaps killed in the riots? Once more she had to act. Someone must find Armand and bring him back. Who but herself?

She ran out through the back door.

Now she could hear the shouting more clearly, and it set her shivering. The cries were bloodcurdling. This was revolution.

Only once had she seen the Bastille — that grey stone building with its eight towers pointing to the sky, its gateway in the Rue Saint-Antoine, the drawbridges and the dry moat. She had heard stories of the terrible fate which befell prisoners who were incarcerated there. She knew that the crowd was verging on the prison.

So towards the shabby Saint-Antoine district she hurried and, as she neared it she saw the mob, the shrieking terrifying mob, some armed with guns, some with knives and any other implements on which they could lay their hands.

She heard the low chanting voices: 'To the Bastille!' And then she caught sight of Armand. He was running some distance behind the mob, and something told her that, among those shrieking men and women determined on destruction and possible murder, was Armand's mother.

'Armand!' she screamed. 'Armand!'

He hesitated and looked over his shoulder. 'Come here, Armand. Come here!'

She felt her arm seized from behind.

'Ah, Citizeness, you have come to join us, eh.' She was aware of bloodshot eyes leering at her. 'What a pretty citizeness, eh! Such a fine dress, too. Why, I'll swear you are not of the people. Are you an aristocrat, my pretty one?'

'Take your hands off me,' cried Homer.

'We are all equal now, Citizeness, and to prove it, I'll kiss your pretty aristocratic lips now.'

Homer held him off with all her strength. She could smell the wine on his breath. He was very intoxicated and it was clear that he was turning over in his mind why this pretty aristocrat, who had been so foolish as to wander into the streets on such an occasion, should not provide even more amusement than the storming of the Bastille.

He caught at her dress, and she felt the material ripped from her shoulders.

'Mademoiselle Homer.' It was Armand pulling at her skirt. He knew she was in danger and he began beating his little hands against the legs of the man, who was not even aware of his puny blows.

'Run home quickly . . . quickly, Armand,' cried Homer, as she felt her hair caught in those rough hands and was swung off her feet.

She kicked furiously; she struck out blindly. She was aware of hot wine-laden breath, of coarse laughter . . . of the words: 'No good struggling, my little aristocrat! We are the masters now.'

In the distance she could hear the yelling crowds.

She screamed, but what was one scream in all that tumult? She fought savagely yet blindly, but her assailant was stronger than she was.

'Give over,' he cried. 'You'll pay for this, my lady. I'll give you my lady . . . I . . . I'll . . . '

She was half fainting but still she bit and scratched; he cried out in anger as her nails tore his face; and then suddenly she was whisked out of his arms and thrust against a wall. Then . . . she saw Richard.

By that time he had dealt her attacker a blow which had sent him reeling to the ground.

She heard Richard's voice like a whisper in a rushing torrent. 'You fool . . . you little *fool*!' And half fainting she was swung up in his arms.

'Armand . . . ' she began.

'The child is here,' he reassured her.

Then she lost consciousness.

Charlotte had bathed her wounds and she lay in bed, while Armand stood by her beside, watching her. He refused to move, and shook his head solemnly when Victoire told him to go away; he remained, his feet firmly on the floor, looking at Homer.

Victoire scolded her, so did Charlotte; they all scolded.

As for Richard, he was more angry than any.

She rose after an hour. She was not ill, she said; she was not hurt, and needed only a short rest to recover. Charlotte was in the room with her and Armand was standing at the bottom of the bed still watching her.

'Whatever possessed you to go out?'

'I had to bring Armand in,' she said.

'Everyone says you were mad to go out.'

'I had to go,' she said angrily. 'Of course I had to go.'

And Armand, still watching her, silently nodded.

'Richard wants to talk to you,' said Charlotte. 'He wants to impress upon you the need to stay indoors when the mob is abroad.'

'I am tired of being scolded.'

'Well, at least you should thank him for

rescuing you. Oh, Homer, when I think of what might have happened to you but for him . . . They might have killed you. Oh, Homer . . . Homer . . . do not be so foolish again.'

She said: 'I will go to Richard.'

'He is alone in the *salon*, waiting for you.'

Homer slipped on a robe of brown velvet which Charlotte had brought from her own wardrobe for her, and thus she went down to the *salon* where Richard was waiting.

'So!' he said sternly when he saw her.

'I have to thank you,' she said.

He came towards her and put out his hands as though he would catch her by the shoulders; then he remembered her bruises and his hands dropped to his sides.

'How could you have been such an idiot?'

'I told you the boy was out there. He'd gone to the Bastille.'

'To look for his mother! It was her place to look after him.'

'She had left him in Berthe's care. It was the duty of the one who knew he had gone out to bring him back.'

'I don't think you have any conception of what is happening in this city.'

'I have a little more intelligence than you credit me for. Oh, Richard, I'm sorry. You were brave and strong and you saved me from that brute. I ought to go down on my knees and say thank you.'

'If you think I want thanks you're more of an idiot than I took you for.'

'Don't say another word about my idiocy. I . . . I can't stand any more.'

She was astonished, for her voice was shaking and there were tears in her eyes.

His mood changed at once. 'Oh, Homer . . . my dear . . . dear Homer . . . what a brute I am! After that experience you must be shattered, and here I am bullying you. It is only because your welfare is so important to me.'

'Richard . . . I had to go out. You must understand that.'

'Because the boy was lost, yes, Homer. But you should have told me. I should have gone for him.'

'You have never seen him before. How could you have found him? It was for me to go . . . only me. But why do we talk of it? Here I am . . . safe and well. Thank you, Richard, for saving me.'

He took her hands and, holding them firmly, he looked into her eyes.

'Do you know,' he said, 'you need someone to take care of you.'

Always, she thought, it is a matter of

duty. He would look after me because I need someone to do so in these troublous times, because Charlotte would be so happy if he were always there to take charge of me. Never . . . never because *he* needs me.

Her head shot up haughtily. 'In ordinary circumstances I am entirely capable of looking after myself,' she said.

★ ★ ★

Events were moving quickly. The friends of the Royal family were leaving Versailles. Madame de Polignac had left and there was a rumour that only by sheer good luck had she escaped out of the country, for her carriage had been stopped when she was about to cross the border; yet she and her family had by that fantastic stroke of luck managed to keep their identity secret from the mob.

'You see,' said Edward, 'everyone is leaving.'

'Soon,' answered Charlotte, 'the Queen will have no friends left. Surely some should stay with her.'

Often Charlotte made the journey between Paris and Versailles. She would talk to Homer, after those visits, of the courage of the Queen; she was alternately sad and exultant and glowed with some inner purpose which she could scarcely bring herself to discuss even with Homer. It seemed to Homer then that the more impossible these tasks which Charlotte set herself, the more they appealed to her. She might have been a great actress; it was just possible that she might have lived a perfectly happy married life with Edward; but how could she — one frail woman, and an Englishwoman at that — protect Marie Antoinette from the wrath of the people?

So they remained in Paris during that July, August and September; although Edward protested he had come up against the stubborn side of Charlotte's nature which he could not have known existed.

'You should go, if you wish it,' she told him.

But when she spoke like that and he remembered all the misery he had caused her, when he remembered the loss of the child she had so longed to have, and that she would never have another, philanderer though he was, Edward softened towards her; and he said to himself: Charlotte must have her way in this, no matter what the consequences may be.

Jean Pierre and Richard called frequently and brought news of what was happening in official circles. Again and again they urged the family to return to England. Again and again Charlotte refused. Her visits to Versailles, Jean Pierre told her, would not go unnoticed; and friends of the Queen were not popular in Paris.

Still they remained. And there came those terrible October days when the women of Paris marched to Versailles determined on the murder of the Queen.

Marie Antoinette escaped to her husband's apartments just in time, and so lived through that fearful night; and in the morning when the mob had sobered a little and the King — who could still charm his people to some extent — spoke to them, they demanded the return of the Royal family to Paris.

Shut in the house, behind the closed shutters, Charlotte, Homer and Edward heard of that terrible drive from Versailles to Paris, when the shouting, screaming mob hurled insult after insult at the Royal family and their retinue as they slowly lumbered along the road to the Tuileries.

Now that the Royal family were virtually prisoners of the people, it was impossible for Charlotte to visit the Queen.

'You can do no good here in Paris,' insisted Richard, 'and since you will not return to England you should at least leave Paris.'

Jean Pierre said that the town of Lille was comparatively quiet and he could acquire a house for them there.

And at length Charlotte agreed to leave Paris for Lille.

10

It was arranged that they should leave Paris by night, the time when it was safer to do so. So many people were leaving Paris that carriages were liable to be stopped and their occupants questioned. If they could not satisfy their questioners, the mob could become violent, and many would-be *émigrés* were discovered hanging from the *lanternes* — those oil-lamps from the reflectors of which shone a ghastly light on such grisly spectacles.

On the day they prepared to leave, Richard arrived in the late afternoon to announce that he was going to accompany them to Lille.

'I shall feel no peace of mind,' he said, 'until you are safely there. I do not forget that it was my suggestion that you should come to France. If only we were going to Calais instead of Lille! If only you would have the good sense to get back to England!'

But Charlotte was firm. As for Homer herself she also had no wish to leave France. She thought of the alternative: Ketteringham Manor, that mansion which in her mind had become a gloomy place because from the moment she had entered it she had sensed tragedy.

Here perhaps was greater tragedy, but this was the tragedy of a nation; this was living through an important period of history, right at the centre of events. Fear there was, but with it came stimulation. It was very different from the emotions she had experienced in Ketteringham Manor.

Victoire was naturally accompanying them to Lille. Jeannette had hesitated, but Homer persuaded her.

'I belong in Paris,' Jeannette had said.

'What of Armand?' Homer asked.

'He is a child of the people . . . he must serve the people.'

'He is too young to serve anybody. You are his mother, Jeannette. If you are a true mother, the care of your child should come before anything you feel concerning the rights and wrongs of the people.'

And Jeannette's maternal feelings had triumphed over her revolutionary impulses.

'I shall come to Lille,' she said; then Homer smiled and shook her hand.

'I knew it, Jeannette.'

So Jeannette with Victoire and Armand and the bulk of the baggage would travel in one carriage. In another would be Edward, Charlotte, Homer and Richard.

271

And so they waited for the darkness, all on edge as they must be; Charlotte fretting and uncertain, and everyone else reflecting her mood.

It was an hour before they were ready to begin the journey when there was knocking at the front door. They were all startled, all believing that at the last moment something had happened to prevent their leaving.

Richard signed to them all to remain in the room behind the shutters, and he himself went to the door.

'Who is there?' they heard him demand; then they heard the voice of Jean Pierre.

'Quickly . . . let me in . . . '

He came into the *salon*, a heavy cloak wrapped about him; he said: 'Where are the servants?'

'We do not know,' said Charlotte. 'Probably in the streets. They are no longer our concern, although we hope they will continue to look after the house.'

'All except Jeannette and Armand,' added Homer. 'She is preparing to leave with us.'

'That is well.' Jean Pierre threw open his cloak, and as he did so there was a gasp of surprise for underneath it was a girl.

She was small, not more than fifteen years of age; her hair fell in thick blonde curls about her shoulders, her face was white and she seemed a little dazed.

'I have brought Sophie to you,' he said. 'I want you to take her out of Paris with you . . . to look after her . . . It is necessary that she leave at once.'

'What . . . has happened?' asked Edward blankly.

'Her home has been pillaged; her parents are in prison. I managed to rescue Sophie.'

Charlotte went to Sophie and put her arms about her. 'Why, my child,' she said, 'you will be safe with us.'

'Jean Pierre does not tell the truth about my parents,' she said stonily.

Jean Pierre had knelt beside her and Homer felt deeply moved to see the tenderness in his gesture. 'Dear Sophie,' he said, 'they will be taken to the Conciergerie . . . There they will be safe. They will be waiting to have their trial . . . '

But Sophie only shook her head.

Homer looked at the girl's rich gown which was conspicuous among the sober clothes they were all wearing for the journey. 'She cannot go dressed like that. She must change those clothes.'

Charlotte agreed: 'We can find something for her. Homer, could she wear a gown of yours?'

Homer measured the girl with her eyes.

Sophie was about her own height, though more slender, for she had the body of a child; yet she carried her head in the manner of an aristocrat, and that would betray her to the crowd.

'Will you come with me?' asked Homer. 'I will see what I can find.'

Sophie allowed Homer to lead her from the room, and as they mounted the stairs Jeannette appeared in the hall.

'Is anything wrong, Mademoiselle?' asked Jeannette. She was staring at Sophie.

'No . . . nothing is wrong,' Homer answered. She took Sophie's hand and led her upstairs; she was frightened. She realized that because this girl would be with them the journey would be doubly dangerous. Yet it was not that which alarmed her; it was the thought that she could not trust Jeannette.

She dressed Sophie in a grey merino gown which made her look gaunt, slightly older, and like a different girl. Homer plaited the golden hair into severe plaits.

'You could pass for an English girl now,' she said; 'a companion or a governess . . . or some such person. Come, we will show the others what a change I have made in your appearance.'

When she arrived in the salon, they were making plans for the journey, and seeing

274

Sophie in the grey dress they were very impressed.

'An English miss,' said Jean Pierre, striving to be gay. 'Why, I did not recognize you, Sophie.'

'She should travel as an English miss,' said Richard. 'That would be the best plan.'

'Do you speak English?' asked Homer.

'I have learned it, but I do not speak it well.'

'No one would know,' said Homer. 'You must keep as quiet as possible when you are spoken to, and speak little French.'

Sophie nodded; she was beginning to recover from her numbness, and with it came a return of fear, fear of the shrieking mob who had invaded her home, who had carried off her parents.

It was arranged then that she should travel as the English companion of Lady Atkyns; but as such she would be expected to travel in the carriage with Victoire and Jeannette, which was not desirable. Victoire, however, was called in and the situation explained to her; she assured them that she would know how to look after Sophie if the need arose.

It seemed as satisfactory an arrangement as could be made, but Homer was uneasy. It was because she knew the wild nature of Jeannette, who was her friend, but hers alone, and whose zeal for the revolutionary cause went deep — deeper than friendship, almost as deep as the love she felt for her child.

'I will ride with Victoire, Jeannette, Armand and Sophie,' she announced. 'Why should I not? Then I could look after her.'

Her eyes went to Richard's face as she said that. She saw his jaw set in a firm line.

His words made her suddenly ecstatically happy.

'No,' he said firmly. 'It is not necessary. You will ride in the coach with us.'

★ ★ ★

They left Paris after dusk and passed safely through the barriers, riding northwards through the night. At the various towns where they changed horses they encountered suspicious revolutionaries who peered into their carriage and demanded whither they were bound. They were also so clearly an English party travelling with their servants, that they were allowed to go on.

Thus they reached the town of Lille which on account of its proximity to both border and Channel seemed comparatively safe. The house awaiting their occupation was in the Rue Princesse, and here they settled with the help of Victoire and Jeannette.

It was smaller than the one which they had occupied in Paris, and it was agreed that it would be safer to employ no more servants, on account of Sophie's presence, which, Richard reminded them, could put them into real danger.

Before he left for Paris he saw Homer alone.

'I could wish,' he told her, 'that you were in England.'

'Charlotte has no wish, as you know, to return to Ketteringham.'

'I think of that child . . . '

'Sophie?'

He nodded. 'Jean Pierre told us when you took her to your room to dress her in your clothes that her parents had been murdered. The servants of the household know of her escape. It may be that they deplore it.'

'Who could want to murder a child? What good would that do their cause?

'The blood-lust is theirs, Homer; they do not think of the youth or innocence of their victims. They only remember that that girl is an aristocrat, and they long to shed the blood of all her kind.'

'Madness!' said Homer angrily. 'But no harm shall come to her.'

'You know,' said Richard, 'that Jean Pierre is in honour bound to marry her.'

'I know it was arranged between their parents.'

'Perhaps now he will consider it imperative. I wonder.'

Richard was looking at her strangely, and she answered rather sharply: 'That is his affair.'

'It might be . . . others' also.'

She shrugged aside the implication. Then he smiled. 'Oh, Homer,' he said, 'I wish you were safe in England. Yet . . . yet . . . '

'What?' she asked.

'At least you are in Lille,' he said. 'But remember, Paris is not far off. Do not be deceived because this town seems quiet in comparison. Revolution is in the air. It is everywhere in this country — one little spark will make the blaze break out.'

'You concern yourself too much with us. You have your duties.'

'I do not know how much longer they will last,' he said. 'Soon there may be no government of France for mine to deal with. Then I must return to London. I would not wish to do that and leave you here.'

'And why not, pray?'

He drew her to him quickly, fiercely. 'You can ask that?'

'I did.'

'You know the answer,' he said.

She was thinking: Charlotte, always Charlotte. How could you think of marrying anyone else when you love her as you do?

★ ★ ★

How different was the life of Lille from that of Paris. It was difficult to believe that elsewhere in France violent revolution was taking place.

Here the people went about their business, set up stalls in the squares, went marketing, stopping to gossip now and then, talking often of their own affairs rather than what was happening in the capital and other cities of France.

It was true that the citizens did not like the presence of soldiers in the town. There were too many soldiers, they said; they were everywhere, members of the Regiment of the Crown and the Royal-Vaisseaux bringing a dash of colour to the streets in their blue uniforms with sky-blue facings and the Colonel-Generals Regiment in their white tunics with red facings — also they brought something else besides colour: a reminder that all was not well in France.

No sooner had Charlotte and Edward settled in the house with their dependents than they began to receive calls from their

279

neighbours. There were several English people residing in Lille at this time; for the town was prosperous, and popular on account of its position.

The agreeable Sir Edward and his beautiful wife were very soon being sought after, particularly as it quickly became known that they had come from Paris.

Charlotte, to prevent herself brooding on what might be happening in the gloomy Palace of the Tuileries, began to entertain in a style almost as lavish as she had maintained in Paris. Thus the time passed.

Now it seemed to Homer that they were remote from the revolution and there was only the presence of Sophie to remind her of it.

Sophie did not appear at any of the parties given at the house. She became known as the companion of Lady Atkyns — or Milady Charlotte as she was beginning to be called. It was decided that, as there were so many English visitors Sophie, who was supposed to be English, should keep herself in the background and not speak unless she was spoken to and even then say as little as possible.

The poor child seemed still to be slightly dazed; thus one would feel, Homer reasoned, if one had lost home and parents at one hideous blow, and she looked upon it as her particular duty to care for Sophie.

She would sit with her and they would sew together, for Sophie was an excellent needlewoman and seemed to find pleasure in the work. Homer, an indifferent one, talked more than she sewed; but she believed that Sophie enjoyed their companionship.

One late afternoon when they sat sewing, Sophie seemed to throw off her reserve. It was growing too dark to see and the embroidery on which she liked to work had slipped from her hands.

She said suddenly: 'I seem to have been so long in this household in Lille, and it is so different from life at home . . . in the château, I mean. I cannot believe that I shall never see it again . . . never see my father and mother.'

'There will come a time when you will think of it all less and less frequently,' answered Homer.

'I do not think I can ever forget it,' went on Sophie. 'We were all there together, as we had been so many times. The servant came in to tell us that Jean Pierre had arrived. Then there was all the shouting, and they were at the windows . . . I shall never forget their faces. My mother said: 'Run away, Sophie. Do not stay here . . . ' I could not obey her because I was so fascinated by those people. Then I saw part of one of the statues in the garden come through the window and fall at our feet. I saw them in the room. I saw them strike my father. I saw them seize my mother. They were carrying knives, Homer . . . '

'You must not talk of it, Sophie.'

'I *must* talk of it. It is better to talk of it. When I do not, it goes on and on in my mind. They shouted foul things about us, Homer. Then Jean Pierre was there. He was dressed in that long cloak of his and he seized me and dragged me away. We escaped to the back of the château and out into the grounds. I could hear them, shouting all the time . . . '

'He saved your life,' said Homer gently.

'Yes, Jean Pierre saved *my* life, but I think of my parents, Homer, I think of them all the time. Sometimes I wish they had killed me too — or I would if it were not for Jean Pierre. You know, do you not, that he and I are betrothed.'

'He told me.'

'He is wonderful. Do you not think so? When I think of him I do not want to die. We shall be married when I am old enough. I think he is the bravest and most handsome man in the world. And because of him I am glad that I did not die.'

'You have the future to look forward to, Sophie. You must forget the past.'

'I will . . . with Jean Pierre. But all the same I cannot forget their throwing the statue through the window. I cannot forget their faces when they burst into the room — and my mother, staring at them and telling me to run away. Homer, sometimes I dream . . . I dream they are shouting at me: 'We have come for the blood of the Comte and Comtesse'. That was my mother and father. 'Cursed aristocrats', they called us; and they would have killed me too but for Jean Pierre.'

They had not noticed that Jeannette had come into the room.

'I have brought candles,' she said.

Homer started and wondered how long she had been standing there; how much she had heard.

★ ★ ★

In the Rue Princesse life had slipped into a familiar pattern.

There was one woman who came often to the parties. She was a handsome widow, and when Homer noticed her she was reminded of Anthea Frinton. She was a Madame

283

Geneviève Lenglen and it was quite clear that Edward found her very attractive.

Her manner towards him had become proprietary and Charlotte, who had shut her eyes to Edward's minor infidelities, found it difficult to do so in this case.

'I am afraid,' she told Homer; 'that Edward is heading towards scandal in Lille as he did at Ketteringham. With this woman he is quite indiscreet.'

'Charlotte, I believe you no longer have any affection for him.'

'I have tried to revive my love for him,' Charlotte answered. 'I thought I could when we first arrived in Paris. Now I know it is impossible. Nothing will change Edward. He could never be faithful to any woman. I cannot trust him, and it is difficult to love without trust. He is drinking a great deal, too. Have you noticed it is beginning to leave its mark on him? Homer, he has not bothered you?'

'Not while we have been in France. I think he knows that if he did I should tell you at once; and then we should both leave him, should we not, Charlotte?'

'Yes,' answered Charlotte, 'we should have to then.'

'He does not want that. There has been enough scandal.'

'Homer, you share all my secrets. I have heard that Madame Lenglen is to have a child, and that child is Edward's.'

'Oh, Charlotte, you are very unhappy.'

'I did not notice it when we were in Paris. Then there was the excitement, the terror. Now we live this quiet life it is brought home to me what an empty life I live. I have no real husband, no children . . . '

'How I hate him! How I hate myself for not telling you in time!'

'There was nothing you could have done to prevent my marriage. I had to live my life. Do we not all have to make our mistakes and abide by them? You see, I seek excitement. I used to make wild plans for averting the revolution and bringing peace back to Versailles. You see how foolish I am. *I* . . . trying to hold back the wrath of a nation.'

'You are a dreamer, Charlotte. I understand you more than anyone else. Your life is empty now because Edward is not the man you believed him to be and because . . . '

'And because I lost the child I longed to have,' added Charlotte quietly.

'Yet,' insisted Homer, 'it will not always be thus. I am sure of it.'

'And we will always be together until you marry Richard.'

'Richard!'

'You love him, do you not? And he is so fond of you. Homer, why do you refuse to marry him?'

'I have only had to refuse once,' said Homer sharply, 'and I can assure you my refusal was accepted with alacrity. Impulsively Richard asked me because I had to get away, and he thought that was the simplest way of doing it. It is not like Richard to be impulsive twice. The offer has not been renewed.'

'And if it were?'

'So much would depend upon the spirit in which it was renewed. I would not marry a man because it was convenient to do so.'

'I think Jean Pierre is in love with you.'

Homer flushed scarlet. 'He is betrothed to Sophie.'

'Is it for that reason then . . . ?'

'Please, Charlotte,' said Homer quickly, 'I find this conversation a little uncomfortable. I am not eager to marry. What I have seen of yours does not make me long for it.'

'Homer! I am so sorry.'

'There! I have been brutal. How like me! What I knew of my father's marriages and what I imagine that of Jennifer and Mr Eeves . . . No, I prefer to be independent. Please, Charlotte, let us talk of something else.'

★ ★ ★

Change did come to Charlotte's life, as
Homer had predicted, for the Revolution
came to Lille. The familiar sounds were
heard: the shouts, the riots. There was
insubordination among two of the regiments
stationed in the town, and several men
of the Regiment of the Crown and that
of Royal-Vaisseaux declared themselves to
be on the side of the people, while the
officers remained loyal to the King. The
Regiment of the Colonel-Generals, whose
officers were notoriously loyalist, kept order
in their ranks; and they were in command
of the citadel in the city's most dominant
position. However, when the soldiers of the
Crown and Royal-Vaisseaux in conflict with
their officers who had the control of the
cannon, pleaded for refuge in the citadel,
the infantry of the Colonel-Generals revolted
against their officers and threw open the gates
to the mutineers of their fellow regiments.

There was chaos in the town; news was
hastily dispatched to headquarters, and a man
of great military skill and of almost fanatical
devotion to the monarchy was selected to go
to Lille to restore order. The very mention of
the man's name struck awe into the hearts
of the rebellious soldiers; and when Comte

287

Louis de Frotté arrived in Lille he quickly brought about the required result.

Louis de Frotté, a man in his middle twenties, came from Normandy; handsome, charming and of a generous and affectionate nature, he quickly became popular, and his presence in Lille was a matter of great pleasure to its inhabitants. He was invited to the *salons* of the leading citizens and it was not long before he and Charlotte met.

From that first meeting they were attracted. They were two people completely devoted to a single cause, and it did not take them long to discover this. Others might declare their royalist sympathies; but to Louis de Frotté and Charlotte Atkyns the deliverance of the Royal family from its terrible plight was a project which seemed to them both more important than any other.

He discovered that Charlotte had been a friend of the Queen and a frequent visitor at the château and the Petit Trianon.

During that first meeting he said to her: 'I see your feelings match my own. For me there will be no peace until my King and Queen are restored to their rightful place in the country.'

'I share your feelings,' said Charlotte. 'Here I feel so frustrated, so inadequate. I long to do something. But what can I do?'

'We must meet again,' said de Frotté. 'We shall have much to say to each other.'

Homer, who had been at that gathering where the two met, noticed the attraction between them. She thought they made a distinguished pair, and decided that Charlotte had not looked so beautiful since the days when she was in love with Edward. Indeed, she seemed to have come alive again.

Yet Homer was disturbed; if Charlotte was going to fall in love with this man, what could come of their relationship but sorrow? Sir Edward stood between them. Oh, thought Homer, if I could go back to that day in the Green Room, I would act differently. I would do everything in my power to stop that marriage. But what was the use of thinking of that now? It was too late. All she could do was wait on events, and be near Charlotte to comfort her, if need be.

★ ★ ★

That summer had passed and the long winter evenings had now given place to spring. There seemed to be a lull in the affairs of France, as though the revolutionaries did not know their strength; as though, having made the Royal family virtually their prisoners in the Tuileries, they did not know how to proceed.

A year had made a difference to them all. Sophie was leaving childhood behind; she seemed to become a woman and a beautiful one when Jean Pierre was in the house. But Lille was too far from Paris for either Jean Pierre or Richard to come there frequently.

Louis de Frotté was now deeply in love with Charlotte and she with him, but theirs was a strange relationship; Homer felt that they stressed their passion for the return to power of the Royal family so that they might not dwell on that between themselves.

Madame Lenglen was great with child and made no secret of the fact that Edward was the father. There would be scandal in Lille as there had been in Ketteringham. Homer often wondered what the outcome of that would be.

This lull in affairs cannot last, Homer told herself. There is change in the air.

One day when she was helping Charlotte with her toilette, she asked Charlotte what was to happen when Geneviève Lenglen's child was born.

'I cannot say yet,' said Charlotte.

'You will not wish to stay here, with that woman flaunting Edward's child.'

'Calling attention to my barren state,' added Charlotte. 'No, for that reason I would not wish to stay here. Yet I cannot leave France at this time; and as we see it, we could not be more advantageously placed than at Lille.'

'The Comte de Frotté confides secrets to you, Charlotte.'

'He trusts me completely. As you know, Mirabeau has become the friend of the Queen; and we have hopes that he will be able to bring about a happier state of affairs. He is brilliant . . . Mirabeau.'

'And if he does?'

'We shall return to Versailles. For then I think we shall have finished with this wretched revolution.'

'And Monsieur de Frotté . . . and you, Charlotte?'

'What do you mean, Homer?'

'He loves you, and you . . . you have some feeling for him.'

'He is a great man; he is a brave soldier.'

'Oh, Charlotte . . . if only . . . '

'If only!' echoed Charlotte. 'But what is the good of considering that? We cannot go back in time and live our lives again.'

Jeannette was like a ghost of her former self; she was quiet and almost stealthy. Armand had now become a well-nourished little boy, a great friend of Homer's — as was his mother.

But Jeannette's heart was not in Lille. She yearned for her native Paris; her determination to fight for the rights of the people had not diminished one jot and she deplored the fact that she was not playing the part she had allotted herself.

She did not feel that she was betraying the cause by serving these people; they were English and were therefore apart from the conflict. She was buying the well-being of Armand by suppressing her own desires, but there were times when she felt ashamed of herself for doing so.

There was one person in the house whom she could only hate. This was Sophie. They could not hide the truth from *her*. English companion! Had she not heard the girl talking fluent French, had she not overheard her conversations? And did she not know that her parents had been victims of the revolution, as she herself should have been?

It was the presence of Sophie in the house

which caused Jeannette's uneasiness to grow. She, a woman of the people, was aware that an aristocrat was disguised and in hiding in this house. And she, Jeannette, must hold her peace!

However, she soothed her conscience by discovering all she could; and she was not averse to listening at keyholes in the name of the revolution. She longed to expose the girl; yet she must not forget the great debt she owed to Mademoiselle Homer, and it was Mademoiselle Homer who had taken such pains that the girl should be unrecognized; it was Mademoiselle Homer who cared for her, who gave her more sympathy than anyone else.

Sometimes Jean Pierre de la Vaugon came to the house. She knew him for a royalist at heart, although so far he had managed to remain unmolested. He was attached to the foreign office and had continued to be . . . so far.

But she would watch and listen; telling herself that her devotion to Mademoiselle Homer must not make her blind to what she owed the Cause.

There came a day when Jean Pierre called at the house and Homer received him.

Jeannette, making sure that Victoire was not at home, placed herself outside the door of the salon so that she could hear what was said.

It was not easy, for the door was closed, but she could hear enough to understand that Jean Pierre was telling Homer that he loved her.

Jeannette snapped her fingers. Not for her — this French aristocrat whom Mother Guillotine would surely have in the end. For there was the tall Englishman who, although he was attached to some ministry, worked for his own country and played no real part in the revolution.

'It is you I love, Homer. You . . . you alone . . .'

'And what of Sophie, Jean Pierre?'

Jeannette had her ear to the keyhole. They spoke too quietly for her to catch everything. But she heard: 'She adores you . . . You must not think of me . . . Remember what she has suffered. She saw her parents about to be murdered. You were betrothed to her in her childhood. You could never, never desert her . . . You must not think of me, Jean Pierre.'

Jeannette straightened up. She had heard enough.

So she loves him — our aristocrat. Mademoiselle Homer loves him! Perhaps he is not such a villain. Perhaps he works for the people. It is true he saved Sophie . . . but then she was a child and she was a friend. Who can say what any one of us would do when faced with the saving of our friends? Jeannette remembered her own weakness in regard to her son.

What was the use of saying the tall Englishman is for her, if she had set her heart on the other?

Yet Sophie was between them.

★ ★ ★

The spring was over and the uneasy summer was upon them.

Madame Lenglen's child was born — a son — and he was blatantly christened Antoine-Quinton Atkyns and known in their circle as Edward's son. Edward could not control his pride in the boy, and the situation became the main topic among their friends. Poor Charlotte! they said. How does she endure the shame?

Thus Charlotte was reminded of the child she had lost, and Homer wondered how she could bear to stay in Lille.

Louis de Frotté was the answer, and it became apparent to Homer that he and Charlotte shared a secret which was so important that the anguish caused by Edward seemed diminished.

Then Mirabeau died suddenly and mysteriously.

'There,' Charlotte told Homer, 'is the end of our hopes in that direction. No one else will or can seek to bring about an understanding between the King and the revolutionary party.'

Yet Charlotte did not seem disturbed, only excited, on the alert for every caller at the house, as though she expected some important news.

She did not confide in Homer, who guessed that there was something afoot which was of such importance that it was to be a close secret among those involved.

And one hot June day Homer understood, for the news was brought to Lille that the King and Queen, in the company of the Dauphin and their daughter, Madame Royale, the King's sister Madame Elisabeth, and the children's governess Madame de Tourzel, had, in a magnificently equipped berline, slipped out of the Tuileries, escaped their guards, and were on their way to the frontier.

Charlotte was jubilant. Frotté was preparing to leave for Brussels where he would take

296

the standard of his regiment to present to the King.

'Now,' cried Charlotte, 'we are on the road to victory. Once the King is out of France, all his loyal friends will gather about him. The King's armies will march on Paris and that will be the end of the revolution.'

So they waited . . . all France waited . . . for the news of the King's safe arrival on foreign soil.

★ ★ ★

Homer would always remember that hot day at the end of June.

In the square she saw Madame Lenglen with her baby; she saw someone stop to admire the child, and she saw the brazen expression in the woman's face as she became aware of Homer's approach. She heard her voice tinged with malice and with triumph. 'Edward dotes on his Antoine. I tell you this, he will make him his heir, for it is clear that he will never get a son from that woman.'

She heard the high-pitched laugh and, being Homer, she was ready to stride forward and slap the triumph off that silly face.

She might have done so had not her

attention been caught by a rider who came galloping into the square; he was shouting something . . . something about the capture of the King.

The news spread through the town. 'They were stopped at Varennes. They are being taken to Paris. Hurrah for the revolution. Down with King, Queen and all aristocrats!'

★ ★ ★

Now a gloom settled on the house. The Royal family had endured another humiliating experience in the terrible ride from Varennes to Paris; they were installed once more in the Tuileries where they were indeed the prisoners of the people.

Richard came to Lille and argued fiercely with Charlotte.

'I tell you it is folly to stay here. You should leave now . . . while there is time. There can be no recovery now. The King and Queen have lost their last chance. The people will never allow them another like it. Moreover, the mood of the people has changed.'

'They would not harm us,' said Charlotte. 'We are English and safe.'

'No one is safe,' said Richard. 'Moreover, have you forgotten that you are harbouring

Sophic? If this were discovered you would all be declared enemies of the people. And what would happen to that child, do you think, if she fell into the hands of her parents' murderers?'

Homer joined with Richard in urging Charlotte to recognize the folly of remaining. She had not thought, until this moment, of Sophie's danger which must necessarily increase with the change of events; but she was convinced that Charlotte should leave this town where she was forced to suffer the humiliation daily imposed upon her by Madame Lenglen.

It was Sophie's danger which finally decided Charlotte.

★ ★ ★

Homer told Jeannette of their proposed departure.

'Come with us, Jeannette,' she said. 'There will be a home for you in England. There Armand will have everything that a little boy needs. Not only will he receive plenty to eat, but I will arrange that he shall have lessons and learn to read and write. You would be happy in England, Jeannette.'

Jeannette was torn. She could not stop herself picturing Armand, sitting at the table of an English milord and eating good English food, sitting at a desk and writing like a gentleman.

'And if you stay here,' persisted Homer, 'what will become of you? Here there can be nothing but poverty and misery. There you would know peace. Here . . . revolution.'

'Here . . . revolution,' repeated Jeannette. 'Mademoiselle, when I was a little girl I stood begging in the gutters. The mud splashed me from the carriages and I said to myself: 'It shall not always be thus. One day there will be the revolution.' It put heart into me; it made me bear my troubles. And now . . . the revolution is here.'

'That is bitterness, Jeannette, and it never did good to anyone. You will come with us and you will be happy and at peace for the rest of your life.'

Jeannette was silent; and on the day when they were ready to leave she and Armand were missing.

Homer understood. Jeannette had been bred on revolution. To her it meant more than peace and prosperity, and she had made her choice — not only for herself but for Armand.

★ ★ ★

They were jolted on towards Calais. The journey was not long, but it was stiflingly hot in the carriage. Charlotte looked out sadly at the countryside they passed through. Of what was she thinking? wondered Homer. Of the royal prisoners who, so said Richard, had lost their last chance? Of the Comte de Frotté who loved her and whom she loved? Of that love which could not be fulfilled?

Poor Charlotte! This was a sad journey for her.

She would return to Lille or to Paris one day, Homer guessed. She would not stay long away.

Edward, too, must be thinking the same, for he had been loth to part with his little son.

As for Sophie, clearly she was unhappy, for her thoughts were with Jean Pierre.

Thus they reached Calais where their carriage was halted for investigation.

'Your papers, Citizen,' said an official.

Edward produced the evidence of his identity.

'I am an Englishman, as you see,' he said, 'returning to England with my family.'

It was necessary for them to alight from the carriage. The official was apologetic. 'You understood, Monsieur . . . so many émigrés . . . We have orders to use great care.'

'I understand,' said Edward.

'You are Sir Edward Atkyns of Ketteringham in Norfolk, England?'

'Yes,' said Edward. 'And my wife, Lady Atkyns, her cousin Miss Homer Trent, our maid Victoire whom we brought with us from England, and my wife's companion Miss Sophia Brown.'

The official nodded his head.

'Sir Edward, you may return to the carriage . . . and you, Lady Atkyns. Miss Trent?'

'Yes,' said Homer.

'You are the English cousin of Lady Atkyns?'

'Yes,' said Homer.

'You may follow Sir Edward and Lady Atkyns.'

Homer did so as he began to interrogate Victoire.

Homer's throat felt parched. She looked at Charlotte whom she could see was too frightened to meet her eyes in case she betrayed her agitation, while Sir Edward looked nervously out of the window of the carriage.

It was significant that they had detained Victoire for further questions; she was a Frenchwoman and they were suspicious of all their own fellow-countrymen and women who sought to leave France.

Sophie was standing by, anxiously awaiting her turn.

Homer saw that Charlotte was nervously pulling at the folds of her skirt. She moved closer to the window and looked out. The official was nodding at Victoire and Victoire was gesticulating. At length he waved his hand and, scarlet with indignation and fear, Victoire got into the carriage.

The official's voice rang out: 'Miss Sophia Brown of England?'

'Yes . . . ' said Sophie.

'English companion of Lady Atkyns, is that so?'

'It is so,' said Sophie in faltering French which she had practised during her stay with them.

'Not by any chance Sophie, daughter of the so-called Comte de la Marnesse? Not by any chance one who has been wanted by the Tribunal for many months?'

'I . . . I am not she. I am . . . English.'

'Then you will have no objection to answering the questions which will be put to you. You will return to Paris.'

'No! You cannot do this,' cried Sophie, in her agitation speaking fluently in her own language.

Two more officials had come forward. One said to the other: 'Listen to the woman who cannot speak good French!'

Homer leaped out of the carriage; she did not know what she was going to do; she only knew that she could not remain in the carriage and see them take Sophie away.

She ran to the frightened girl, and caught her arm. 'This is a mistake — a great mistake,' she said. 'You are wrong, quite wrong. This is Sophia Brown.'

One of the officials caught Homer roughly by the arm. 'You should not become involved, English miss. We have been informed by one of your servants that you have sheltered this woman in your house for many months. You should take care. We will not long tolerate interference from foreigners in our affairs.'

'You must understand . . . ' began Homer frantically.

'We understand. We have been waiting for you to arrive. We knew you would be coming. We have all details of those whom we are to expect. If you are wise you will return to your carriage. Although we do not wish to quarrel with foreigners while they are on French soil they will be forced to obey French laws.'

Edward and Charlotte had left the carriage.

'Homer,' said Edward sharply, 'get back into the carriage immediately.'

'Sophie . . . ' she began.

'There is nothing we can do for her,' said Edward. 'For God's sake, Homer, you will ruin us all.'

'Come, Homer,' said Charlotte, taking her arm. 'There is nothing we can do . . . *now.*'

That last word held some hope, and wild plans were already forming in Homer's mind as she allowed herself to be led to the carriage.

The official came to the window. 'You are fortunate that we allow you to go on. Understand that we will not tolerate those who come to our country and endeavour to smuggle *émigrés* out of it. Drive on,' he added to the coachman.

Homer did not hear the crack of the whip; she did not feel the jolt as the carriage shot forward. She was looking out of the window at the despairing figure of Sophie.

11

Ketteringham Manor seemed to belong to another world. Day after day they rose to days of calm, so that revolutionary France seemed centuries and worlds away.

Yet Homer, Edward and Charlotte were all fretting to be back there: Charlotte whose heart was with her Louis de Frotté and the Royal family, Edward who had been very loth to leave his son, and Homer who dreamed at night of that dreadful moment when she had realized that Sophie was not to be allowed to leave France.

It was she who had looked after the girl, who had felt maternal towards her, who had rushed to her room at night when she was assailed by nightmares, who had gradually weaned her from the past. And she, Homer, now felt herself responsible for what had happened to her, because it was Jeannette who had betrayed Sophie to the revolution.

It was I who persuaded Jeannette to come with us to Lille, she reminded herself. It was I who told her that we were leaving for England. It was my conversations with Sophie that she overheard. I am responsible for whatever happens to Sophie!

And what would happen?

She had heard the gruesome stories of the trials before the Tribunal, of the rides in the tumbrils through the streets of Paris to the Place de la Révolution where the grim knife was waiting for its victims.

But she is so young, mourned Homer; and there will be no one there to comfort her.

How therefore could she ever know peace again? Never would she be able to rid herself of the thought: But for me it would never have happened!

Days passed, and each was so like the preceding one that she lost count of time. It was a house of shadows, a house of sad memories. Those days, when her fear of Sir Edward had dominated her mind, when she had been concerned with his philanderings with Betsy, Mrs Frinton and Clare, seemed remote and trivial. Whether they were ostracized by their neighbours was a matter of complete indifference to them. Their thoughts were not in this peaceful land.

And as the weeks passed Edward found consolation in a renewed association with Mrs Frinton; Charlotte roused herself from her lethargy and decided to make contact with many of the émigrés who had settled in London. Once a week she was able to read the *Gazette* which gave some account of the state of affairs in France, and she had discovered a paper which was edited by a very eminent *émigré*, Jean Gabriel Peltier. This man had at one time been an ardent revolutionary and had taken a prominent part in the storming of the Bastille; but he had changed sides and become one of the most fervent supporters of the Royalist cause. The paper he brought out in London was called the *Acts of the Apostles*, and this Charlotte read with enthusiasm.

Charlotte also was able to find some anodyne. It was only Homer who must continually wonder as to the fate of Sophie — merely another prisoner of the people, merely another victim of the tumbrils — Homer who could not throw aside her melancholy.

Why did we leave France? Homer asked herself every day and often during the nights. How could we have gone away leaving Sophie in their hands?

Charlotte tried to interest her in the writings of Peltier, but Homer could not see the wide panorama of revolution as Charlotte could; she was overwhelmed by the individual tragedy of Sophie.

Often she wondered what had happened

to Jean Pierre, for there was no news of him. Richard remained in France, for while Louis XVI was still called King of France diplomatic relations continued with other countries; and it was natural that the British government should be eager to keep a watchful eye on events across the water and was anxious to have as many first-hand accounts as possible.

Charlotte asked Homer to come to her bedroom one day, and when they were alone Charlotte said: 'Homer, you are so silent these days. You are grieving for Sophie.'

'I shall never forget her,' said Homer. 'We should never have left her.'

'Had we tried to stay with her, we should almost certainly have been arrested. We could have done nothing for her then.'

Homer's heart leaped. 'What . . . can we do for her now?'

'I do not despair,' said Charlotte. 'Many have escaped, you know.'

'She will be dead by now. It is so long.'

'Who knows? They have so many prisoners. Many are kept languishing in the prisons for months. It is the important ones whom they like to parade before the people.'

'You are seeking to comfort me.'

'Homer, we seek to comfort each other. But I have some news. You have heard of

Jean Gabriel Peltier?'

'I have read his news sheet.'

'I have been writing to him. Homer, we are going to London to meet him. And not only him. There in London are several friends whom I met at Versailles. We have plans, Homer. Do not imagine that I, any more than you, can forget our friends across the water. When these plans are perfected it may be necessary for someone to go to France. My friends . . . they are French and have escaped with great difficulty. If there is work to be done in France, who could do it better than an Englishwoman . . . two Englishwomen?'

New life seemed to come into Homer's eyes. 'Is it possible?' she asked.

'We can hope,' answered Charlotte. 'Could you be ready to leave for London tomorrow?'

★ ★ ★

It was good to be back in London. They put up at the Saracen's Head in Snow Hill and Victoire came with them.

London, with its gay and colourful streets, seemed not to have altered since they had left it; it appeared to be supremely indifferent to events across the water. It was only when they met the little band of *émigrés* that affairs

310

in France were passionately discussed.

Jean Gabriel Peltier had a house in London, and here were gathered together, at all hours of the day and night, those who had escaped the guillotine and were eager to bring about the restoration of the monarchy.

Charlotte found many old friends whom she had known during that period when she had been a frequent member of the Queen's circle. There were tears and sad memories, but the forceful Peltier warned them that this was no time to brood on the past. They had met together for a purpose, and that was to restore the King and Queen to their rightful position and put an end to anarchy in France.

He conducted his guests to a small room in the house, and set guards at the door. Then he addressed them.

'We know of the terrible things which have been happening in France. We have heard of the storming of the Tuileries, the September massacres and the murdering of people such as the Princesse de Lamballe. Only good luck has saved the Queen. The people are crying out for her blood, and unless we can do something, and do it quickly, they will have it.

'We know now that the King and Queen

with the Dauphin and Madame Royale are prisoners in the Temple. We know that our enemies over there have abolished the Monarchy and established a Republic. Our King and Queen, with their children, are in imminent danger. That is why we have made this plan to bring them out of France.'

Monsieur Peltier waved his hand towards Charlotte and Homer. 'We have here two very good friends. I will tell you how good they are. They have offered to be the go-betweens, to go to France and do the most dangerous work of all. They know that if they fall into the hands of our enemies they will face the guillotine. Yet they bravely offer their services. We are grateful.'

Charlotte said: 'The Queen was my friend. I love her dearly. I will face any danger to help her.'

'My dear friends,' went on Peltier, 'we are not going to ask you to go to France, for our agents over there are in touch with Lemonnier and Vicq d'Azyr, the King's physicians, and they are carrying our messages to the King. We have had help from Baron d'Auerweck, a Hungarian nobleman, for he owes much to the favour of Maria Theresa and is therefore eager to serve her daughter. For the time being the revolutionaries are eager to show the people that the King is not living as a prisoner, and thus it is not impossible for our Hungarian friend to visit the Temple. He is preparing a detailed plan which will be of the utmost importance to us should we reach the stage when it is possible to attempt the escape. At the moment, what we need is money for the enterprise; and we who have left our possessions behind us in our unfortunate country find it impossible to supply all that is needed.

'It will be my pleasure to help this enterprise with anything I possess,' said Charlotte.

Jean Gabriel Peltier came to her and kissed her on both cheeks.

'We knew we could rely on your help,' he said.

Homer, who while they were talking could think only of Sophie, broke in impetuously: 'Is it possible for some of your agents to discover what has happened to Sophie de la Marnesse? She was taken from us at the frontier.'

There was silence in the room; then someone said: 'Is that not the daughter of the Comte and Comtesse de la Marnesse?'

'Yes,' said Homer impatiently.

Jean Gabriel lifted his shoulders. 'The prisons are full,' he said. 'Each day men and women leave them for the Place de la

Révolution, but they are replaced by others. It would not be easy . . . '

'But it is not impossible,' cried Homer. 'It is of the utmost importance to me that I should know what has become of her.'

'Rest assured,' Jean Gabriel replied, 'we shall do all in our power to discover.'

★ ★ ★

It was necessary to return to Norfolk to raise the money which Charlotte had promised.

Although Charlotte would not ask favours of Edward for herself, she did so for the sake of the cause to which she was pledged. Edward, whose health was deteriorating rapidly, for his drinking habits had become more marked since his arrival in England, often sank into moods of maudlin sentimentality when he would deplore the sorrow he had caused Charlotte. He longed to see his little Antoine in Lille and he mourned for the son Charlotte might have given him. He would sit in the library, sipping his whisky, and often he would cry weakly.

'My poor, poor Charlotte,' he would murmur. 'I have been a bad husband to you.'

So when Charlotte asked him for money he was ready to give her what she asked.

314

It salved his conscience, he said, to please Charlotte. Thus it was Charlotte's pleasure to supply a large proportion of the money which was to finance the enterprise of freeing the Royal family from the Temple.

Letters came frequently to the Manor House from Peltier in London, and each day there was the excitement of watching for the messengers.

Homer's one thought was for Sophie. Never had they shown with such clarity the difference in their characters. Charlotte dreamed of restoring the Monarchy, altering the course of history. And to Homer the larger issue seemed less important; she could only be concerned with her own personal emotion, which was so great that it obscured everything else.

They were in the library one day, she and Charlotte, and every now and then Charlotte would go to the window and look out. It was several days since they had had news, and they were expecting it hourly.

'Something must have gone wrong,' said Charlotte. 'We have been so long without news.'

'It would be difficult, I suppose, to get news of her,' murmured Homer. 'One young girl . . . when there have been so many. How can these people send a girl like that to her death, Charlotte?' Homer beat her fist on the table. 'How can they!'

'They are capable of anything,' said Charlotte.

'I can understand their anger against the King and Queen. We must face the truth. There is great misery in France and the Queen has been extravagant. Oh yes . . . I can understand that. But to take a young girl who has done nothing . . . nothing . . . to harm them . . . and because of her birth to murder her! I cannot bear to think of it.'

'You must be calm, Homer. You must realize that this is revolution . . . the most hideous revolution that has ever occurred. If we can save the King and Queen . . . if we can gather together an army, the revolution can be fought and we can bring law and order back to France. Then young girls like Sophie will be safe.'

'If . . . if!' cried Homer. 'But when? And what is happening to Sophie in the meantime?'

'Someone is coming along the drive. Yes . . . it is . . . it is Peltier's man. Come, Homer, we will go and meet him.'

'Do not be too eager,' said Homer. 'Perhaps even here in England we should be cautious. How do we know who is watching us, waiting to spy?'

Charlotte smiled sadly. Homer could not forget that Jeannette, whom she had befriended, was the one who had betrayed Sophie.

'You go then,' said Charlotte. 'Quickly, Homer. I am sure he has important news.'

Homer brought the messenger into the library, and as soon as he was there Charlotte took the letters he carried.

She read them and turned pale. Homer went to her and read them with her.

Contact had been made with the King in the Temple, but he had refused to consider escape. The flight to Varennes had been disastrous, he said, and another failure would worsen matters. For himself, to escape might be a comparatively easy matter; but he would not think of escaping alone and leaving the Queen and his children in the hands of their enemies. Thus the attempt had failed, not through the revolutionaries but through the King himself.

There was a further letter. This contained the terrible news. The King had been sent for trial.

Charlotte held the letter limply in her hand. Homer led her to a chair and made her sit down; and all the time one fact was beating in her brain. There was no news of Sophie.

* * *

On a gloomy January day a letter arrived by post at Ketteringham Manor. It was addressed to Charlotte and was from Jean Gabriel Peltier.

Charlotte read it and handed it to Homer who, hopeful as ever that it might contain some news of Sophie, read:

> 'My dear honoured friend,
> All that we can do now is weep. The crime is to be carried out. Judgement of death has been pronounced. Orléans voted for it, and he is to be Protector. There is nothing for us to look forward to but revenge. And revenge there shall be!
> Jean Gabriel Peltier.'

Charlotte covered her face with her hands; and after a while she went to her room to mourn in private.

A week later the whole country was ringing with the news.

Louis XVI of France was no more. He had been brave and calm right up to the moment when the hideous guillotine had severed his head from his body.

Charlotte came down from her room, purpose shining in her eyes.

'Homer,' she said, 'this strengthens my purpose. This shall not be the end. There is still the Queen; there is still the Dauphin. And Homer, next time . . . we will not leave it to others. I shall go myself. I shall find some means of seeing the Queen. I am determined that this time I shall succeed.'

'You mean to go to France, Charlotte?'

'They will try to dissuade me, but I mean to go.'

'I shall come with you,' said Homer; and still she thought of Sophie.

12

Homer was out when Richard arrived at Ketteringham Manor, and Charlotte received him with great pleasure.

'It is wonderful to see you in these terrible times,' she said. 'You have just come from France. You will have news for us.'

'What can I tell you,' said Richard, 'but what you already know? There is no longer a Monarchy in France, only a Republic, and affairs are at this time in a most unsettled state. I expect I shall be going back later, but first I am having a few weeks' holiday. So I came with all speed to see you here. How are you all?'

'Saddened by the tragedy,' said Charlotte. 'Edward is in a sorry state.'

'What ails Edward?'

'He takes too much whisky and it is beginning to have its effect. There are times when he drinks himself insensible . . . Dr Sharman has warned him, but he takes no heed. He says that one day Edward will die of apoplexy if he does not desist.'

'And . . . Homer?'

'Homer grieves a great deal, Richard. She

thinks constantly of Sophie. She blames herself for what happened. You see, she says that if she had not brought Jeannette with us to Lille, Sophie would be with us now. I tell her she is not to blame, but she will not see it.'

'I heard news of Sophie.'

'Richard!'

'Yes, I have heard that the poor girl had been transferred to the Conciergerie.'

'That means . . . ?'

'That her next step will be to the guillotine.'

'This is terrible news.'

Richard nodded.

'Homer will be frantic with anxiety.'

'What has happened?' Homer had come into the library wearing a tailored riding habit which was very becoming. 'Richard!' she cried.

He strode towards her, took her hands, and imprinted a brotherly kiss on her cheek.

'It is good to see you,' she said. 'But, tell me . . . what is going to make me frantic? You have news of Sophie?'

'I was telling Charlotte she is in the Conciergerie.'

'Then she is alive!'

'Yes . . . she was alive when I left Paris.'

'She is alive!' cried Homer, her eyes

flashing. 'Then there is some hope.'

Charlotte came to her and put her arm about her. 'She has been taken to the Conciergerie. It is that prison to which those are taken who are said to be destined for death. Even now . . . '

'No,' cried Homer. 'It is not so! I know it is not so. She is still alive, and we must find some means of saving her.'

'My dear Homer,' said Richard, 'you must be brave. This is revolution . . . thousands have died and are dying. Sophie has lost her parents . . . She is doomed, I fear.'

Homer stamped her foot in rage. 'It is merely a young girl whose parents have been murdered and she is of no importance to you. But there are some to whom she is of importance. They will not shrug aside her death.'

She looked at Richard whose face showed the strain of living in France through the last months; he seemed five years older than when they had last met and, feeling suddenly tender towards him, she thought: Why do I always talk as though I am angry with him?

Richard said almost coldly: 'You do not know the temper of the people. It is changing . . . rapidly for the worse. You and Charlotte and Edward would not now escape as easily as you did, if you attempted to smuggle an aristocrat out of France.'

Charlotte intervened. 'Richard, I am planning to go to France.'

'You must be mad!'

'We would have brought the King out of the Temple if he would have come. He is dead now but the Queen is not, nor are her son and daughter.'

'Charlotte, you do not understand what is happening in France.'

'I fancy I do, Richard,' Charlotte answered gently. 'I was there, you know, for a long time. I have friends in London who are French. We correspond and we meet. I am very conversant with what is going on in France.'

'If you were you would not talk of going there. You might as well talk of committing suicide.'

'Is that so?' said Charlotte. 'You must tell us what you have seen over there.'

Homer cried: 'Are you going to let him dissuade you from going?'

'I think,' answered Charlotte, 'that we should listen to what he has to say.'

'Your plans to rescue the Queen — they are too ambitious,' said Homer. 'Surely a plot to rescue a comparatively insignificant girl would be more likely to succeed.'

'It is clear to me,' interrupted Richard, 'that you are both utterly ignorant of what can be done.'

'We must listen to Richard,' said Charlotte. 'He has returned from France, you know.'

'I cannot forget Sophie . . . ' began Homer.

Charlotte put her arm about her. 'We are forgetting our guest,' she said. 'Richard has just arrived. We must make him welcome. I will have a fire lighted in the walnut room, Richard. When Edward wakes he will be so pleased that you have come.'

Charlotte was looking at Homer as though imploring her to say no more; and Homer fell silent.

* * *

It was an hour later when Homer went to her bedroom. As she entered, Charlotte rose from a chair.

'I have been waiting for you,' she said. 'I guessed you would come soon.'

'Charlotte,' cried Homer passionately, 'we shall be prevented from going to France.'

Charlotte shook her head. 'No! That is what I must tell you. Do not say much before Richard. Listen to what he has to say and appear to be impressed. I tell you this:

324

we are going to France. We are going to save the Queen and her family as well as Sophie, but we must be careful. If we are not, you can see that great efforts will be made to stop us, and however determined we are that these shall not succeed, they will hamper us.'

'I see.' Homer's eyes glinted.

'Now listen. We are leaving for London at the end of the week. It is a visit we have long decided we must pay. We shall say nothing about going to France. I was stupid to have mentioned this in Richard's presence. We shall tell no lies. We are going to London. All that we shall remain secret about is the fact that we are also going to Paris. But we want no opposition. So therefore we will listen quietly to all Richard has to say. We will let him talk, let him believe that he has persuaded us to drop what he thinks are our childish schemes ... Then we will slip away.'

Homer smiled slowly.

* * *

The following days seemed strangely unreal to Homer. She rode sometimes with Charlotte and Richard, sometimes with Richard alone.

On one occasion he said to her: 'How is life for Charlotte now?'

'You mean with Edward?' she answered.

'Yes.'

'Edward, as you have seen, has gone from bad to worse. He still visits Mrs Frinton, and I believe there are others. He drinks a great deal.'

'It does not seem possible,' said Richard slowly, 'that he can go on like this.'

What thoughts were in his head? she wondered. When Edward is dead, Charlotte will be free. Homer wondered about Louis de Frotté who wrote regularly to Charlotte, and she remembered Charlotte's happiness when she received one of those letters. If Charlotte were free would she marry Louis de Frotté?

Poor Richard! It seemed incredible that the woman he loved could not love him as he wished to be loved. Louis de Frotté was handsome, romantic perhaps; yet Richard . . . well, he was himself, and unique. But perhaps, thought Homer sadly, I am the only one who sees him like that.

She said gently: 'He has been warned again and again by the doctor; and each week we can see the change in him. Unless he gives up drinking I do not think he can live much longer.'

'It is sad,' he said, 'to throw away a life.'

'When so many people are being taken,' she added bitterly.

'You think of Sophie . . . and Jean Pierre.'

'It is so long since we have heard of him.'

'I know where he is. I saw him before I left.'

'You saw Jean Pierre! And he knows Sophie is alive, yet he is doing nothing to save her!'

'Homer,' said Richard seriously, 'I told you, did I not, that affairs have worsened over there. Jean Pierre is being hunted now. If he is found he will doubtless precede Sophie to the guillotine.'

'Where is he?' she asked, and her voice was a whisper.

'He is in Lille . . . with an English family there. He is disguised as their coachman. You know he speaks good English . . . good enough to fool his fellow-countrymen that he is a compatriot of ours.'

'And he knows . . . of Sophie's plight?'

'He knows. That is why he will not leave France. He cannot, he says, while she lives, while there is any hope.'

Homer felt the tears on her cheeks, and tried to dash them away before Richard saw them, but she was too late.

'It's the tragedy of it all,' she said. 'The tragedy of it!'

Then she touched the flanks of her mare

and turned her homewards.

The mare broke into a gallop. She could hear Richard's horse pounding along behind her; but he only caught her up as they reached the Manor, and by then she had recovered her composure.

★ ★ ★

Richard rode with them to London, and when they arrived he went to his lodging while they put up at the Saracen's Head. This time they had not brought Victoire with them.

The day after their arrival Charlotte, with Homer, called on Jean Gabriel.

He was excited. He had news for them. An attempt to bring the Queen out of the Temple was being made this very day. It had all been carefully arranged. One of the Guards of the Temple, Francois Toulan, once an ardent revolutionary, had become so touched by the Queen's plight that he longed to help her. A certain General Jarjayes, who had been in constant touch with the *émigrés* in London and was working with them to bring about the Queen's escape, had, in collusion with Toulan, actually entered the Queen's cell in the disguise of the lamplighter and had had a word with her.

His plan was to have her jailers drugged by means of snuff, to which they were very partial; then Jarjayes, in the guise of the lamplighter (whom it was possible to bribe) would enter the cell, presumably to attend to the lamps. He would bring with him the cloaks of municipal councillors, which the Queen and Madame Elisabeth would put on; the children would be disguised as the lamplighter's children, for fortunately the man often brought them with him when he came to see to the lamps.

There was only one man who had the power to lead them out of the prison; this was Lepitre, a member of the Commune who was now in charge of the Temple prison. He was an ex-schoolmaster and, although he had taken an active part in the revolution, he hated violence and longed for an opportunity to escape to the peace of the countryside. This had been discovered by the observant Toulan; also that Lepitre was susceptible to bribes.

Jean Gabriel spread his hands.

'So you see our plan has every chance of success. Lepitre has provided the forged passports. As soon as our party leaves the prison they will find carriages waiting for them; they will be driven with all speed to the coast, where a boat will be ready. Lepitre will be with them to help them through any difficulty on the road. It is costing a fortune to bribe this man, but he has accepted the bribes and will do the work. Oh, my dear friend, we failed to save the King, but we shall save the Queen. Long live Louis XVII of France!'

Charlotte listened, enraptured, to this account, but Homer stood looking blankly into the future.

Then she turned to Charlotte. 'And . . . Sophie?' she asked.

Charlotte said: 'Homer, what could we do . . . what *could* we do!'

Jean Gabriel noticed Homer's blank expression.

He said suddenly: 'Ah, I had forgotten the news I had for you. It is in the excitement of what is happening. Our agents have discovered that Sophie de la Marnesse will come formally before the Tribunal tomorrow week.'

'Before the Tribunal . . . What does this mean?'

'It's a trial . . . a farce of a trial . . . but it will take place, and they will condemn her to the guillotine.'

'They shall not,' said Homer, clenching her hands tightly. 'It shall not be!' she murmured.

＊ ＊ ＊

The next day it was a sorrowful group who gathered in Jean Gabriel's apartment.

He addressed them solemnly.

'The attempt has failed,' he said. 'Madame Tison, the wife of the Queen's jailer, had grown suspicious of Lepitre; moreover, she managed to convey these suspicions to him. The timid Lepitre lost his remnants of courage. He declared he could not go on with this enterprise; he dared not. Instead of the peaceful life in some distant countryside, he visualized the fearful knife. So,' Jean Gabriel finished, 'we are now where we were before this plan started. The Queen is to be transferred to the Conciergerie.'

Charlotte cried: 'We have trusted people who have not enough heart for the work. If one of us had been in the position of Lepitre, do you think we should have lost heart? We are using people who take bribes — rather than those who work for love.'

Homer's heart had begun to beat wildly. She knew what Charlotte was going to say.

And immediately Charlotte said it. 'I will go to France. I will find some means of speaking to the Queen.'

'My dear Lady Atkyns,' said Jean Gabriel, 'you might find a way into the Conciergerie.

You have money with which to make that possible. But when you came face to face with the Queen, when you spoke to her . . . what good would that do?'

Charlotte smiled at them — her beautiful serene smile. 'Do not imagine that while you have been forming your plans I have been idle. I have made a plan of my own. It is a simple one. My friends, some years ago I was an actress, and for one of my most successful roles I wore the uniform of a soldier. You were not in London then, and did not see me in *The Camp*. It was said that I made a tolerable young soldier and went through my paces like a trooper. I intend to find some means of acquiring a uniform, and in this guise I will speak to the Queen.'

'But you would speak to her . . . words are of no use.'

'My plan went farther than that. I would suggest that the Queen put on my uniform, and I her gown, and that she march out of the prison to a waiting carriage while I stay behind.'

'It *is* possible,' said Jean Gabriel, and every pair of eyes in that room were fixed on Charlotte's glowing face. 'But you know that it is also suicide?'

'I am English. They would not dare send me to the guillotine.'

'They would tear you to pieces when they knew what you had done.'

'I am the Queen's friend,' said Charlotte. 'I have sworn that I will give everything I have to save her. Even if it is my life, I am prepared to do so.'

There were tears in Jean Gabriel's eyes. 'This is noble indeed. My dearest lady, we revere you for making this suggestion. But you could not do it. It is out of the question. We thank you, every one of us. But your scheme is madness . . . madness.'

Charlotte was silent; and all in that room believed that she accepted their verdict — all except Homer.

★ ★ ★

The salt breezes caught at Homer's hair and she pulled her cloak closer about her. She had made Charlotte lie down and had covered her with a blanket. The sky was clear and the stars brilliant.

She sat beside Charlotte's sleeping figure and the boat gently rocked her. She was surprised that Charlotte could sleep, but supposed that she was worn out with exhaustion.

A strange mission — two helpless women crossing that strip of water because they had determined to save the lives of two women.

A hopeless task. That was what they would have been told by anyone to whom they confided their mission. Yet both felt compelled — at the risk of their lives — to attempt that hopeless task, for neither of them believed it to be hopeless, each was determined on success.

The stillness of the night, the sight of sleeping people, the rocking of the boat, sent Homer's thoughts back into the past — which was strange when the immediate future loomed so terrifyingly before her. Perhaps, she thought, it is because I am afraid to contemplate what lies before us that I think now of the parsonage far back in the past. She remembered clearly the day she had first heard Charlotte's name, and then again the day she had determined to go to her.

She had always known that her life and Charlotte's were inextricably bound together. Thus it was not strange that they should be here on this boat which was taking them to a country of revolution, each with a single thought in her mind: Rescue.

'Good evening, Homer.'

A figure had loomed up beside her; it was a man, wrapped in a long cloak and, as he lifted his hat, she recognized him.

'Richard! What are you doing here?'

'First may I ask the same question of you?'

'We are going to France.'

'That would seem obvious! But how could you be so *foolish*!'

'And you?'

'I suspected something of this. I asked for you at the Saracen's Head and heard that you had left on the Dover coach. Then I knew. I followed you with all speed and arrived in time to catch the boat.'

'So you have come to watch over us.'

'I could not let you go alone.'

'Why not?'

'Why not indeed! Homer, what is your purpose? Is it Jean Pierre?'

'What could I do for Jean Pierre?'

'You have heard romantic stories of how people, who were living under the threat of the knife, have been smuggled out of the country. You were always wild. You always thought yourself capable of achieving the impossible.'

'How could one turn the impossible into the possible if one did not believe it possible to do so?'

'This is no time for argument. Tell me what you intend to do.'

She hesitated; he had gripped her wrist

and repeated: 'Tell me! Tell me!'

She could not betray Charlotte's plan, for Charlotte had said that its success depended upon no one's sharing her secret. Yet Richard was demanding, and she would have to tell him something.

'We cannot desert Sophie.'

'What can you do?'

'We do not know; but we can see her.'

'At the Tribunal!'

'There is nowhere else.'

'And what will you do? Demand her release? Push aside all the officials of the trial, take her arm, and calmly walk out to a waiting carriage?'

'Do not laugh at me, Richard. This is a serious matter.'

'I never felt less like laughing in my life. What do you imagine will happen to you if you call attention to yourself at the Tribunal? That is not an English court of justice. Try to imagine the scene: the prisoners condemned in advance because they are aristocrats; their judges determined to extract payment for everything they believe they have suffered under the old régime; and the mob . . . some of whom find their way into the court room; others waiting outside to torment the prisoners, to fall on them and murder them if they are not well protected by their guards ... How can I make you understand? This is a country steeped in a bloody revolution — and you think that you can calmly walk into the court room and demand the release of a prisoner, for no other reason than that she is a friend of yours. Homer, you are behaving like a child.'

She lifted her head and her hood fell back; her face was stern in the starlight. 'This is Sophie,' she said. 'She is betrothed to Jean Pierre. She is a young girl who has done harm to no one. But for an action of mine she would be at peace in England.'

'Are you doing this for Sophie's sake?' he asked.

'I do not understand your meaning.'

'Or for some other reason?'

'What other reason?'

He was silent for a while. Then he said: 'Could it be your pride ... your damnable pride?'

And then in the rocking boat she experienced a moment of self-revelation.

She wanted to lean against Richard, to feel his arms about her, for she knew that she loved him ... that she would rather quarrel with him than be friends with anyone else; that this excitement and stimulation which he aroused in her was all part of her love for him.

How wonderful it would be if this tangle of emotions could be straightened out and woven into a conventional pattern! And how childish of her to hope that this could be so when, looking ahead, she could already see the lights of Calais and knew that she and Charlotte were coming into close contact with death itself.

And if they came out of this adventure alive that would not be the end.

For Charlotte had made a disastrous marriage and, even if she were free of it — as surely she must soon be — she would not turn to Richard but to Louis de Frotté.

Richard and I are the outcasts, she thought, for I love him and he loves Charlotte.

Even now she guessed that his presence here was not for her sake but for Charlotte's.

The sound of their voices had awakened Charlotte from her doze. She sprang to her feet.

'Richard!' she cried in dismay.

Homer fancied he flinched a little.

He said: 'You did not imagine I should let you come alone.'

He was smiling at Charlotte and in the dim light his face looked inexpressibly tender.

Poor Richard! thought Homer. And then: Poor Homer!

338

13

Richard had, as he said, resigned himself to their folly.

They had reached Paris without mishap and Charlotte and Homer had put up at an inn not far from the Conciergerie, while Richard went to his usual lodging.

Richard knew nothing of Charlotte's plan for Charlotte had said that if he had an inkling she was sure he would do all in his power to prevent her carrying it out. This was obvious, thought Homer, for if Charlotte were successful she would be placing herself in a position even more dangerous than that in which Sophie stood today.

Watching Charlotte during those days Homer thought: She has a dedicated look. Thus must the saints have looked, the martyrs on the way to the stake to die for their faith.

Charlotte was going to give herself to the mob that the Queen might be saved.

It was well that Richard knew nothing of her plans.

He had argued with Homer again and again to try to persuade her to abandon her scheme. What was she going to do? She was going to Sophie's trial; she was going to swear that Sophie was not Sophie de la Marnesse, that she was an English girl, Sophia Brown, who had spent a great deal of time in France. Charlotte would be with her, thought Richard, to add her testimony to that of Homer.

It was a crazy scheme, said Richard. Who did they think would listen to them? He would have a conveyance waiting to take them with all speed out of Paris, for he feared they might be roughly handled by the mob.

Then, in case they should succeed in bringing about the release of Sophie, he had arranged for a boat to be waiting for them. It would be necessary to leave French soil with all speed.

★ ★ ★

All through the night Homer lay awake, nor did Charlotte sleep.

The Tribunal was to take place in two days' time. By then Charlotte would have made her attempt.

Perhaps, thought Homer, this is the last night I shall ever be with Charlotte.

When she paused to think of what lay

before Charlotte her own task seemed slight. Charlotte was going to offer her life; she was going with outstretched arms towards a hideous death. But Charlotte was an idealist; her whole life proclaimed her to be that. Charlotte made dreams and tried to live them.

And now she was coming close to death.

She had made her plans; she had long been in correspondence with her friends in Paris. They would be waiting for the Queen when she walked out of the Conciergerie in Charlotte's uniform. Charlotte's great plan was to deceive them for as long as possible. There would be a whole night, she reckoned, before anyone would know that the woman in the cell was not Marie Antoinette but Charlotte Atkyns.

The morning came, and Charlotte went to see her friends to make the last-minute arrangements.

Richard called at the inn to see Homer, but she asked the maid to say that she was not there. She hated lying to Richard, but she could not face him. She was terribly afraid for Charlotte, and she feared that if he questioned her she might betray her friend.

So she remained in that room, and she thought of all that Charlotte had meant in her life and how, if this succeeded, Charlotte would have played a part in the history of France. And for that, Charlotte was bartering her life. If only she could stop her even now! The excitement of the journey, her own plans for the rescue of Sophie — they had temporarily overshadowed the enormity of this thing which Charlotte was going to do.

At dusk, she told herself, I shall help Charlotte to dress in the uniform of one of the guards; and then she will say good-bye to me and, if she succeeds, she will die.

And Charlotte could succeed; she was aware of that. Her own plan for Sophie's deliverance might be foolish. But Charlotte was backed up by powerful men. Bribes had already been passed from hand to hand, and Charlotte had every chance of succeeding.

* * *

She helped Charlotte dress in the uniform of a guard, which a large sum of money, delivered in the right quarter, had secured for her.

Charlotte, standing at attention there, might have been a soldier. She was a good actress if not a great one, and it was not beyond her powers to play the part of a soldier.

342

'How do I look, Homer?' she asked.

'You look the part.'

Homer wrapped the cloak about Charlotte and adjusted the hood.

'Now,' she said, 'you look like yourself.'

'Then we are ready . . . Homer, what is the matter?'

'Charlotte, if you are successful . . . '

'I shall be successful,' said Charlotte.

'Then . . . this is good-bye.'

'Do not forget I am English. They will not dare to harm me.'

Homer shook her head. 'This is not the time to deceive ourselves,' she said. 'Consider the significance of what you are about to do. For myself . . . I am going to try to save a girl who is of little importance to them. You . . . will make possible the escape of the Queen.'

Homer felt dizzy with emotion and faint with apprehension, for in Charlotte's eyes shone the light of martyrdom.

'Charlotte . . . I cannot bear this. You must not do this. I love you, Charlotte, and I have just realized that I may have to live the rest of my life without you.'

'Hush, Homer. It is time we left,' said Charlotte. 'Do not say good-bye. Come, play your part. Come with me to the waiting carriage. And when I leave it, drive back to the inn, taking my cloak with you.'

Together they went out to the carriage.

★ ★ ★

Homer had returned; she had hung the cloak in a cupboard. What could she do now but wait!

Where was Charlotte now? Had she reached the prison? Had something gone wrong, as it had at every attempt to bring about the escape of the Royal family? How could Charlotte succeed when others had failed? Yet Charlotte's was a simple plan, one which had been carried out with success on more than one occasion.

I do not think I want her to succeed, thought Homer. I love Charlotte more than I could ever love a cause. I want Charlotte to come back to me, and then I should not care what happened. How slowly the time passed. Where was she now? She would be in the cell if all had gone according to plan. She would be talking with the Queen. They would be changing their clothes now. Would Marie Antoinette make the soldier that Charlotte had? The Queen also was an actress. Had she not performed at her own theatre at the Petit Trianon?

This moment . . . the cell door will be

closing on Charlotte. Homer could picture her slumped on a chair by the table, her head in her hands. Thus she would remain . . . waiting . . . waiting . . . counting the minutes . . . while the Queen walked out in Charlotte's uniform . . . right out into the streets, to the alley where the carriage would be waiting.

Now! Now!

* * *

An hour had passed, and steps were ascending the stairs. The door opened, and Homer could not help it if a flood of relief swept over her. Her emotions were released and she flung herself, sobbing, into Charlotte's arms.

Charlotte's face was tense and white. She had failed; Homer knew that. Yet she had returned in safety.

'Oh, Charlotte . . . Charlotte,' sobbed Homer. 'I thought I should never see you again.'

'I failed,' whispered Charlotte.

'Come, let me help you out of these things.'

'I see now that there could be nothing but failure,' said Charlotte.

'You did your best. Did anyone see you come up here?'

'I do not think so.'

'Let me help you out of these clothes.'

'Homer . . . Homer . . . I have *failed*!'

'You did nobly. Others have failed before you.'

'I failed,' went on Charlotte, 'because she would not have it otherwise.'

'You saw her . . . ?'

'I saw her. It all went according to our plan. Oh, Homer, it could have been so easy. She might have been speeding away to the frontier now. I might have been there in the cell.'

'I cannot help but thank God you are here with me, Charlotte.'

Charlotte did not appear to hear those words. She said: 'It all happened so simply. I saw her . . . Oh God, how she has changed! She . . . so dainty, so beautiful as she once was . . . now to be living in that cold damp cell. She has grown so serious. She mourns the King. She is concerned for her children. It was not the Marie Antoinette I knew, with whom I came face to face in the Conciergerie.'

'Charlotte, you spoke to her then!'

'I begged her to change clothes with me. I told her that I would remain in her place; that I had friends who had arranged that she, as a member of the guard, would be safely conducted out of the Conciergerie, to a carriage awaiting her.

'Her answer was to thank me with tears in her eyes. Then she said: 'But I could not go, and leave my children behind. The Dauphin and my daughter are in *their* hands. I could not escape and leave them.' And she was firm. I could not persuade her. She kissed me and thanked me for my love and loyalty, and then . . . she sent me away.'

Homer could not answer her; her emotions choked her; she could only cling to Charlotte's hands as though she feared some evil power would snatch her from her.

★ ★ ★

It was stifling in the Hall of the Tribunal, and outside the crowd was dense. They had arrived early, but they would never have forced their way in if Richard had not been with them, making a passage for them, brandishing his stick as he went. Strangely enough, such was his personality that the crowd parted for him.

Homer, with Charlotte beside her, stared about her. The air was full of the sickly smell of sweating people and the faces of the crowd alarmed her, for she sensed that there could be few in this hall who did not long to shed the blood of all aristocrats.

Richard had been against the project until the last moment when, seeing that he could not persuade them to give up the idea of coming, he announced his intention of accompanying them.

The President called for order, and one by one the prisoners were brought before him, to be condemned to death, their crimes being that, as aristocrats, they were the enemies of the people.

When Homer saw Sophie she did not at first recognize in this unkempt creature the young girl whom Jean Pierre had brought to them at Lille. Sophie's once beautiful hair was dank about her shoulders; the flesh had fallen from her face and form; her gown — the one she had been wearing when she had been arrested — was hanging about her in rags.

All Homer's fear vanished at the sight of her. There was only indignation left, an indignation so fiery that Homer felt capable of doing battle with every bloodthirsty revolutionary in this court.

Richard had tightened his grip on her arm. 'Wait,' he cautioned. Then he whispered: 'I will speak for you.'

'No,' she said fiercely. 'I will speak. And you and Charlotte shall be my witnesses. But

I shall be the one to speak. I shall be the one . . . if they should turn against us . . . whom they will punish.'

'Be calm, Homer,' he murmured, and he would not slacken his grip on her arm.

At length — and it seemed that they had waited hours — it was Sophie's turn to stand before the President.

'Sophie de la Marnesse, aristocrat and enemy of the people!'

Homer's voice rang out clearly: 'I protest. That is Sophia Brown, who served in the house of Lady Atkyns with me.'

All eyes were on Homer. Her cheeks were flaming, her eyes blazing.

Sophie had seen her and her face changed, for despair was replaced miraculously by hope.

'Who is this?' asked the President.

'My name is Homer Trent. I am companion and cousin to Lady Atkyns. I lived with her in Lille, and Sophia Brown was with us at the same time.'

'And you say this woman is an English-woman named Sophia Brown?'

'I do,' said Homer firmly, for, she told herself, I have said it.

'We have witnesses to assure us that this woman is Sophie de la Marnesse, daughter of Alphonse and Emilie de la Marnesse, once styled Comte and Comtesse, and enemies of the people, who were justly dealt with some time since.'

'I say this woman is Sophia Brown, an Englishwoman and outside the jurisdiction of this court.'

Richard and Charlotte had stepped up to stand beside Homer.

'Who are you?' demanded the President.

'I am Richard Danver, diplomat in the service of the British government,' said Richard.

'I am Lady Atkyns, the employer of Sophia Brown.'

The President was looking at Richard, whose words had implied that he was acting on the part of his government. There was an uneasy silence while the President consulted a paper on his table. He turned to the man on his right. 'Is the chief witness against this woman in the court?'

The man rose. 'Citizeness Moulins,' he called.

A woman was coming forward. Homer caught her breath, for Citizeness Moulins was Jeannette.

'Citizeness Moulins, you lived in the house of Lady Atkyns for some months, and while you were there you discovered that a woman masquerading as Sophia Brown

350

was in actuality Sophie de la Marnesse.'

Jeannette had turned and was looking full at Homer. Homer met her gaze steadily, and Jeannette could not read what she saw in her face. Was it reproach? Was it scorn? Whatever it was Jeannette could not face it. She lowered her eyes.

There was a sudden disturbance at the back of the room and a young voice piped up: '*Maman*, it is Mademoiselle Homer!' It was the voice of Armand, and it touched Homer strangely; it was not without its effect on Jeannette.

Homer said: 'Jeannette, why did you do this?'

Jeannette still could not meet her eyes. The voice of her son had unnerved her, had brought back the memory of Homer, walking into the house with him on that day when she lay unable to move, suffering the most terrible anxiety she had ever known.

She was a good servant of the Republic. She believed that all aristocrats must die, and she knew full well that the girl, whom Homer spoke of as Sophia Brown, was in truth Sophie de la Marnesse, an aristocrat who, because of her origin, deserved to be a victim of the knife.

Jeannette heard herself say: 'I . . . I believed her to be Sophie de la Marnesse,

Mademoiselle Homer.'

'But she is Sophia Brown. Was it the similarity of the first name which misled you? Oh, Jeannette, you were so zealous in the cause of the Republic that you let yourself believe Sophia Brown was this woman you speak of.'

Now Jeannette lifted her eyes. She was a woman; she was a mother; and what was the use of trying to serve a cause with all her heart and soul when her emotions got in the way of her loyalty?

She had sworn to herself on that day when Homer had brought Armand into the house that one day she would repay her — even as she had sworn to repay the aristocrats for the poverty and suffering of her youth.

What were Homer's eyes saying now: I brought Armand into the house. I did not ask payment then. But I do now. I ask . . . no, I demand, the life of this young girl for what I did for you and Armand.

Jeannette then spoke clearly. 'The Englishwoman is right. I was too eager to serve the Republic. Because this woman is named Sophia I deluded myself with the belief that she was Sophie de la Marnesse, who is an enemy of the people. I informed the Tribunal that she was escaping to England

and she was arrested because of this. But now I must own that my zeal to serve the Republic overcame my judgement. I ask pardon of the Tribunal. This woman is she whom the Englishwoman says she is.'

Again there was that heavy silence, followed by whispering among the President and his henchmen. A delicate situation — a possible Englishwoman, a protégée of Lady Atkyns, who had clearly interested the British government in the girl's case.

Was the case proved? Never mind. It was a delicate one. The knife was hungry, but the prisons were full of those who would shortly satisfy its rapacious appetite.

'The woman may step down and join her friends,' said the President. 'We are satisfied that there has been a regrettable mistake in this case.'

Sophie came to them. Richard acted promptly. He asked for a written pardon, which was given. Then with an imperious gesture, he seized Sophie's arm and, waving his stick, made a path for his party through the crowd.

A few seconds later they were in the carriage rattling through the streets of Paris.

★ ★ ★

353

Homer felt the sea breezes in her face. She was exultant. Sophie was safe and Charlotte was still with her. She herself was in love, and to love without a shadow of doubt was a great adventure.

Her mind was filled with images of the court-room; and against that background of sweating faces made ugly by the blood lust apparent on so many of them, she saw Richard — strong, dominant, serene and protective. She believed that without him they could so easily have failed.

In that dangerous moment she had felt as she had so often in his presence — safe.

They had eaten in the inn parlour. Sophie had taken a bath; she was now wrapped in one of Charlotte's cloaks; and they were about to join the passengers who were going aboard the boat.

Homer turned to Richard, suddenly remembering. 'But you said you had arranged for a boat . . . '

'You will not need it now. All is well. Sophie's case has been dismissed by the Tribunal. She is no longer escaping.'

'But where is this boat?'

'Do not give it another thought. I will see you in Norfolk.'

'But Richard . . . '

Three pairs of eyes were regarding him

with surprise. He stepped back a pace and, taking off his hat, bowed to them.

'We shall meet again soon,' he said. 'In Norfolk.'

'But you did not tell us . . . ' began Charlotte.

'There was no time,' answered Richard. '*Au revoir*. I shall be with you soon.'

So the boat began its journey to safety, leaving Richard behind in France.

14

Messages awaited them at the Saracen's Head.

Sir Edward had had a stroke and was very ill. They must return at once.

The messages were several days old.

They left London by the first coach, and, when they arrived at the Manor, it was to find that Sir Edward was dead.

★ ★ ★

It was a week after their return. Sir Edward had been buried in the nearby church and his vast fortune now belonged to his widow. Charlotte found that the passing of Edward filled her with sorrow. She did not love the man he had become but she could not forget the bridegroom whom she had idealized. So she wept for those early days of hope and ignorance.

One day, a week after their return, when Homer and Charlotte had been walking in the grounds enjoying the September sunshine, Victoire came running out to tell them that visitors had arrived.

Homer's heart began to beat with hope and apprehension. Constantly she had thought of Richard in France and longed for his return.

She wanted to ask Victoire who had come, yet she was afraid to; and she ran ahead of Charlotte into the house.

'Richard!' she cried, and it seemed to her that she betrayed all the emotion she had been feeling, by the manner in which she spoke his name.

He stood smiling at her; and for a few seconds she saw only him.

But Sophie came running into the hall. Homer heard her laugh and there was a note of sheer happiness in that laughter.

'Jean Pierre!' cried Sophie.

Then Homer saw that it was indeed Jean Pierre who stood beside Richard.

Sophie was hugging him and he was returning her embrace, when over her head his eyes met Homer's.

'Richard brought me here,' he said. 'It was a risky thing to do, but he did it.'

Richard had taken a step towards Homer, and she felt her hand caught in his firm grip.

'I brought him back,' he said. 'I was not going to let you do all the rescuing.'

'So that was why you went back.'

'It very nearly did not happen,' said Jean Pierre. He looked at Richard and smiled. 'If you hadn't had the boat waiting for us ... I should not be here now ... nor would you.'

Richard shrugged his shoulders. 'What matters that now?' he said. 'It is what *is* that is important — not what might have been.'

* * *

Homer rode out from the Manor. She wanted to feel the wind in her hair. She wanted to escape to solitude, to be alone to discover herself.

The winter was near. There were red berries in the hedges, and the leaves of the black bryony were turning bronze. She reined in her horse to a walk beside the river, and then she heard the sound of another horse's hoofs.

She turned and saw Richard.

'Well, Homer,' he said, as he pulled up beside her, 'I brought him home for you, you know.'

'For me?'

'Because I knew you were in love with him.'

'You are so certain that you are always

right. Has it ever occurred to you that you might be wrong?'

'Not in this case.'

'Then I will disillusion you. You are absolutely wrong. I am glad you brought him home. It was a brave thing to do. But you brought him for Sophie . . . not for me.'

'And you brought her for him . . . did you not? You brought her because you love him and you believe that he loves her.'

She began to feel very happy. 'One of your duties is to interpret the actions of foreign governments, is it not?'

He raised his eyebrows.

Then she went on: 'I hope you are more successful in understanding their secrets than those of your acquaintances. If you are not, you will never succeed in your diplomatic career.'

He laughed and brought his horse close to hers. 'It's good to be with you,' he said. 'No one else taunts me as you do. And do you know, I have discovered that I like being taunted — by you.'

'You were always arrogant. I remember you in the coach . . . I wondered, who is that arrogant young man?'

'You thought I possessed other characteristics than my arrogance. Otherwise why should you lock your door against me? Homer, do you think I do not know you? You had to risk your life to bring her home. Why? Because she was betrothed to Jean Pierre. You pretend to be as sour as vinegar and you are as sweet as honey; as hard as iron, and you are soft as silk. You brought her home because you thought he loved her and you love him enough to do that.'

'I am surprised that you should endow me with such nobility of character. And you . . . why did you risk your life to bring him home?'

'Because he is a friend.' Then he said: 'Let's have done with this banter. Why should I wish to hide my feelings? I will tell you the truth. I brought him home for you, Homer, because I thought it was the only way to make you happy. You were on the boat. You were safe and going home to England. I wanted to be with you. Do I have to explain how much? I wanted to say: Let him stay there. She will forget him in time. And then . . . '

'And then?' she prompted.

'I said to myself, Homer is a young woman of sense. She nearly married me once before. If he were not there she might consider it again. Then . . . I went back for him.'

'No, Richard,' she said. 'No!'

'Yes,' he said, 'it's true. I will tell you now. Of course I'm in love with you. How could it be otherwise! Who else makes me laugh? Who else makes me glad I'm alive? If that is not being in love — it's something even more desirable.'

'How odd,' she said, 'that you should feel like that about me! That is exactly how I feel about you.'

He took her hand and kissed it.

'There's no help for it, Homer,' he said. 'We have to admit it. We are in love.'

Happiness such as this was too much to endure, coming so soon after all her anxieties and fears.

She turned suddenly and dug her heel into her horse's flank.

She heard him thudding along behind her.

★ ★ ★

They were married when the October mists were rising from the Yare. 'Not a big wedding,' said Charlotte, because she had so recently become a widow.

'Not a big wedding,' echoed Richard. 'It is our wedding, and we do not wish to share it with a crowd.'

And after the ceremony, when the few

guests had departed, Charlotte showed them a letter she had received from Jean Gabriel.

'I did not show it to you before,' she said. 'I would not have any sadness *before* the ceremony. Her trial took place on the fourteenth. On the sixteenth she rode in her tumbril through the streets of Paris and laid her noble head beneath the knife. She was regal to the end; and she gave no sign of fear. It was what we would have expected of her.'

'Oh, Charlotte!' cried Homer. 'How sorry I am! You tried to save her . . . you tried so hard.'

What will she do now? wondered Homer. Will Louis de Frotté be able to comfort her?

Richard was looking at Charlotte with that tenderness which had caused Homer so much misgiving in the past, and which she now understood was the same sort of emotion Charlotte aroused in herself.

Let her be happy, as I am! thought Homer.

'They have murdered her,' said Charlotte, 'as they murdered her husband. But they are wrong if they think this is to be the end. The Dauphin still lives.'

As she turned to them they saw the purpose shining through her tears.